CALLING THE BALL

CL Mustafic

A NineStar Press Publication

Published by NineStar Press
P.O. Box 91792,
Albuquerque, New Mexico, 87199 USA.
www.ninestarpress.com

Calling the Ball

Printed in the USA
First Edition
September, 2018

Print ISBN: 978-1-949340-81-5

Also available in eBook, ISBN: 978-1-949340-78-5

Warning: This book contains sexually explicit content, which may only be suitable for mature readers.

A vacation to the sunny, seaside, resort city of Durres, Albania puts some space between Henrick Kohler and his closeted ex, Klaus, giving him time to get his life back together. While there a chance run-in with superstar footballer, Valentino 'Tino' Alessi, sends Henrick running in the other direction. With no intention of being either another notch in someone's bedpost or their secret lover, he offers friendship but nothing more. He doesn't want to risk his heart with what he sees as just another Klaus, but with the added ability to ruin his life on a much more spectacular level.

Tino can't catch a break, even doing a nice thing for a fan lands him in hot water. When he's suspended until his latest mess is straightened out, Tino does the only thing he can think of—he goes holiday home hunting in his favorite resort town. Tino falls hard and fast for the blond Austrian who wants nothing to do with him romantically, but he accepts the offer of friendship when his efforts to woo Henrick get him nowhere.

Friendship is what they agree to, but both men realize there's just something there neither of them can deny. What will it take for them to overcome everything and realize there's no time like the present to grab on to what they want?

To Ashley Fae, my knewest sanish friend. Thank you for all the support you've given me in the short time we've known each other.

Chapter One

STRONG HANDS GRIPPED Henrick's slim hips and lifted him, effectively breaking the connection between him and the man beneath. Henrick slumped forward to land on the broad chest of his current lover, Klaus, who easily rolled them to the side before completely disengaging and getting out of bed. Henrick sighed and rolled onto his stomach.

"Going to shower." The way Klaus said it made clear there wasn't an invitation for Henrick to join him hidden in the words—not that he'd expected Klaus to ask him to share the shower, but a change in routine wouldn't hurt.

Henrick grunted in acknowledgment and folded his arms under his head as the shower started in the adjoining room. He was beginning to drift off just a little by the time Klaus emerged from the bathroom, vigorously rubbing his short brown hair with a towel. Klaus threw the used linen onto the bedroom floor before bending to retrieve his boxers. Henrick watched as the muscular man pulled them up over long, well-toned legs, but then to Henrick's surprise, Klaus sat on the bed, stretched out, and leaned against the headboard near Henrick's feet. He reached for the remote and turned on the television.

"Are you going to shower?" he asked, as he settled on a sports channel.

"Mmmm, probably, but don't want to move yet." Henrick almost purred when Klaus started stroking his thigh absentmindedly as he watched the sports news.

"Wore you out, did I?" Klaus couldn't hide the hint of pride in his voice. Henrick snorted but nodded—never hurt to stroke a man's ego a little. "Rest a bit then."

Henrick was once again half-asleep when Klaus's softly muttered "What's the jackass done this time?" startled him awake.

"Who?" Henrick knew Klaus was passionate about his football and followed several of the players on his favorite teams.

"Alessi. That ass is in trouble again."

Henrick studied his bed partner's profile as the sports news anchor's voice announced in the tone – of what Henrick thought was barely disguised glee—they reserved for bad news.

"Valentino Alessi, the bad boy of the Bundesliga, is at it again. This morning, headlines across Europe were accompanied by pictures of the league's number-one striker entering a hotel room in Rome with two girls who, upon further investigation, turned out to be underaged. Articles in both the Sun Times of London and the Morning Press of Rome detailed the entire event from when Alessi met the girls in the hotel restaurant until he exited their hotel room over two hours later. The girls' names haven't been released, since they are minors, but so far the children's parents have not responded to repeated requests from the media as to their awareness of the incident. Roman police chief, Antonio Scalari, said in a statement to press that the situation is being looked into, and if it is deemed necessary, the appropriate charges will be filed. This isn't the first time Alessi's come under fire for his indiscretions in the bedroom. It's only been a year and a half since Paulo Gianotti stepped..."

"I hope that bastard gets what's coming to him," Klaus growled, drowning out the news anchor.

"I'm sure they need to wait until all the facts are in before they can hang the man." Henrick pushed himself up and got out of bed. He was no fan of Valentino Alessi, but he wasn't ready to pronounce guilt on the say-so of the media. "I'm going to shower now." Klaus waved him away and turned his attention back to the TV after only one quick glance at Henrick's ass.

After showering, Henrick was prepared to dress and leave since that was how his hookups with Klaus usually went, but he was surprised to find Klaus still lying on the bed in his underwear when he'd finished in the bathroom. Henrick stepped up to the side of the bed next to Klaus and looked down at him. "Aren't we leaving?"

Klaus put a finger inside the towel cinched around Henrick's waist and pulled him closer. "I thought maybe we could order some dinner from room service. We need to talk." One hand wandered across Henrick's hip and then back to squeeze one of his ass cheeks.

Henrick didn't like the sound of that. Neither the getting a meal together after sex nor the "we need to talk" was anything Henrick wanted to hear out of Klaus's mouth. They never spent any time out of the bed together after sex unless it was on the rare business trip they took together where they ended up sharing a room. The last time they'd needed to talk, Klaus told Henrick he was dating Lydia in accounting. So needing to talk never meant anything good. The two things combined caused a deep sense of foreboding to creep into Henrick's body.

"You don't have to buy me dinner to tell me it's over." Henrick tried not to sound upset at the prospect.

Klaus released Henrick's ass and grabbed his hand instead as he tried to turn away. "Who said it was over?"

"Did you rent the room for the whole night?" Henrick asked as his breath quickened.

Klaus frowned. "I did because I thought it being Friday and all that we could make a night of it." He made it sound as if it was something they did all the time.

Henrick shook his head. "No, the last time we spent an entire night together was when you convinced me that you dating Lydia was just for your public image so it wasn't really cheating when we were together." The sour taste in his mouth proved just how dirty it still made him feel to be fucking a man who was in a relationship—fake or not. If Henrick had been in Lydia's place, he wouldn't see it as any less than cheating on Klaus's part.

Releasing Henrick's hand, Klaus turned to sit on the side of the bed. "It's not cheating. I'm not in love with her, and you know that. But I can't get anywhere with the company if I'm not on track socially. Do you think I want to be stuck in this position forever? If I want to move up, I need to do something that will make it easier for me to do so."

Henrick turned away from Klaus because he knew what they needed to talk about now, and he didn't want Klaus to see the tears he knew would come after Klaus said the words. "Okay, so tell me what it is exactly you need to do to get that promotion you want so badly."

Klaus cleared his throat, a nervous habit that meant bad news was on its way. It was one Henrick knew all too well. "I've asked Lydia to marry me."

Henrick deflated, and his shoulders sagged under the weight of rejection. It was what he'd expected but had hoped wouldn't happen. "So that's it then. This was supposed to be some kind of last hurrah before you went off to find wedded bliss in the arms of a woman you claim to have no feelings for." He couldn't pretend that he didn't care because he did—a lot.

Suddenly Klaus was behind him. Henrick tried to step away, but he was no match for the powerful arms holding him against a sturdy body almost twice his size. "Henrick, there's no need to be so dramatic. Nothing has to change between us. I still want you, and I can always get away to meet up with you." As if that was the answer to all the problems Henrick had with him marrying Lydia. Henrick realized Klaus just didn't get it.

He struggled, but Klaus wouldn't let him go free. "Klaus, let me go. If you marry Lydia, this is the last time you'll *be with me*. I won't fuck a married man. You know I had issues even when you were just dating her, but once you take vows I can't in good conscience help you cheat on her." Klaus finally released him with a little shove that made him stumble before he caught his balance.

"You can't blackmail me into not marrying her. If it's you or her, then I'll choose her," Klaus spat bitterly.

"I'm not trying to blackmail you. I knew this thing we had was just sex. You were never in it for anything other than getting off as often and as quickly as possible. You made that abundantly clear, but I'm still not going to be your something on the side when you're a married man." Each word that came out of his mouth stabbed him a little deeper because he'd hoped one day Klaus would change his mind and actually want a real relationship.

"You're being unreasonable, Henrick. What difference do a few words and a couple of rings make?" Klaus rubbed at his stubbled jaw in obvious frustration.

Turning to look Klaus in the eyes, Henrick wanted to make sure his words were heard clearly and understood fully. "They make a world of difference to me." They meant his dream of one day being the one Klaus chose to have a life with was over. He'd have to stop kidding himself about there being anything behind those occasional soft looks Klaus gave him. He needed to move on because now that Klaus had actually said he'd choose Lydia when push came to shove, he knew he would never come in first in Klaus's life, and surely he deserved to be number one in someone's life.

"You're making this all about you. What about what I need? Do you ever think about how difficult this is for me?" Klaus sounded like a petulant child.

The anger rose hard and fast in Henrick's chest. "Are you kidding me? All I ever do is think about what you want. You wanted to keep this on the down low, so I haven't told a single soul about who I'm always sneaking out to see. For over two years now, I've kept your secret. You wanted to keep this thing between us just physical, no emotions, just meaningless sex, and I went along with that too. But you've crossed the line now by asking me to do something against my morals, so what—so that you can have the best of both worlds?" Henrick wanted to throw the question back in Klaus's face and ask, *What about me?* What about what he wanted? But he didn't because he knew Klaus didn't care about anyone except himself.

He'd kept his voice low to avoid sounding shrill and hysterical, but he could feel himself balancing on the edge of a cliff. Bending to pick up his discarded clothes, he knew he needed to get out of the room before he said something that would reveal his feelings to Klaus. It didn't matter how hard he'd tried to keep his emotions out of the bedroom, somewhere along the way he'd fallen in love with the big clueless oaf. If Henrick were being honest, Klaus's obliviousness to his feelings hurt more than his finally choosing Lydia.

Klaus grabbed ahold of Henrick's shirt as he tried to pull it over his head, making him scowl at the other man, but Klaus didn't let go as he started talking. "Just stay for a bit. We can talk this through, and you'll see that I'm not asking you to do anything more than what you have been doing. I like you, Henrick. I enjoy the time we've spent together. I realize I should have given you more to keep you happy with our arrangement. I've been selfish. I see that now, and I'm prepared to give you more of what you need. We can spend more time together, not just fucking; maybe we can catch a movie or a game, sort of like a date."

Klaus's voice had taken on a wheedling quality, which Henrick hated because he almost always gave in to it. Not this time, he told himself, as he ripped his shirt out of Klaus's grasp. He wanted to scream that it was too little too late in Klaus's face, but he held back. "I don't think that's such a good idea. What if someone starts questioning you hanging out with the gay guy from the office? What will your *wife* think of that?" Henrick sneered instead as he pulled the shirt on. After jamming his legs into his jeans, he buttoned them with trembling hands as he waited for Klaus to say something more.

"Maybe you should just think about my offer and get back to me." Klaus crossed his beefy arms over his chest and leaned against the wall as if it was no big deal that he was breaking Henrick's heart.

"Oh, I'll think about it all right." Henrick's anger boiled over into rage, and he needed to get out of there, away from Klaus to somewhere he could let his emotions out. "I'll think about it while I'm out cruising for a new cock." He stuffed his socks into his jeans pockets and his bare feet into his shoes before turning on his heel and opening the door.

"You'll regret leaving like this, Henrick. I know you have feelings for me—"

Stepping into the hallway, Henrick slammed the door on whatever else Klaus had been about to say. He was done hiding in the closet with someone who didn't even love him enough to make it worth the hassle of keeping it a secret. After exiting the hotel, he flagged down a taxi, gave his address to the driver, and sat back in the seat to avoid conversation with the cabbie so he could think. He needed to fix his life. He had plenty of friends and friends-with-benefits all over Europe, but that wasn't enough anymore. Henrick wanted someone who would put him first for once—someone who loved him more than everything else in their life. Was that asking too much, just to be the most important thing to one person? Henrick didn't think it was and made a vow right there in the back of that cab. Henrick Kohler wasn't going to settle for second best any longer.

VALENTINO ALESSI SLUMPED into the soft leather of the big chair. He knew why he'd been summoned to his agent's office and also why the team manager was there, looking constipated while he waited for Tino to get comfortable. His agent leaned forward, elbows on the desk and hands clasped beneath his chin. Tino braced himself.

"Okay, Tino, let's hear it. Why are there pictures of you going into and then, after a time long enough that it suggests you were not just signing a couple of autographs, coming out of a hotel room with two underaged girls on the cover of every tabloid from here to Sweden?" Bernardo Calivari asked the question even though he'd already heard the story from Tino earlier.

Bernardo was naturally Tino's first call after being awakened at seven the previous morning by the ringing of his phone to find it was a reporter wanting an exclusive on the next chapter in Tino's scandal-prone career. Bernardo was only having Tino repeat the story for the benefit of the team's manager, Martin Trumm, who'd flown into Rome just to meet with them so he could hear Tino's excuses in person. It was a show and Tino knew he had to play along.

"They came up to me in the hotel's restaurant and asked me if I'd go back to their room to meet their little brother who's terminally ill. I went. The parents were in the room with the kid. All you have to do is call them and ask." Tino was concise and to the point as he watched Martin's face for a reaction, but the guy was unreadable as always.

"You know who that family was, right?" Martin asked.

"I do now." And Tino knew why there was such an uproar because Herr Friedberg was the owner of one of the most successful snack food companies in Germany, but he was also a very private man. When he met the man, Tino had no idea he was in the presence of such power and wealth. The family had been polite, and the young boy was just as starstruck by a famous footballer as any other eleven-year-old boy Tino had met.

"Then you know that if this turns sour you'll be in a very bad position," Martin said.

"Like I said, all you have to do is call Herr Friedberg, and he should be able to tell you he was there along with his family when I went into that room." Tino had no idea why making a phone call to clear his name seemed to be such a hardship for the two men.

Bernardo cleared his throat to get everyone's attention. "I've already tried contacting Herr Friedberg's office in Berlin but was informed that he's handed operations over to his partner for the time being. I asked if there was a way to get in touch with him, but I was informed that Herr Friedberg and his family have taken a vacation to their private island. The only way to contact them there is to send a message along on the ferry that goes out to the island carrying supplies every other day, but the man himself left instructions that they are not to be disturbed for any reason." Bernardo pulled a couple of papers out of a stack and looked at them before he shook his head and lay them back down. "Apparently his sickly son has taken a turn for the worse, and the family has gone there to grant his final wish to visit his favorite place one last time. I'm not sure how reliable my source is on this last bit, but I've been told that the boy is not expected to live much longer, and I don't think it would be wise to try to contact—"

"But just a quick call couldn't hurt," Tino interrupted. He knew it was selfish, but he was only thinking of all the crap about to come his way over the press's allegations if something wasn't done quickly.

Bernardo's lips turned down in a frown as he looked at Tino. "The man's son is dying, Tino. I realize this will be harmful to your reputation, but I believe we must wait until Herr Friedberg returns. Though a phone call will save you from this"—waving his hand over his tabloid-covered desk, Bernardo made clear what he was talking about—"interrupting a family granting their child's last wish will make you seem cruel and heartless, and that may do more damage to your reputation than you can reasonably recover from."

Tino sighed and let his head drop back on the chair. Bernardo was right, but it just added to the big mess the situation was bound to become. No, not a mess—a complete catastrophe—if his name wasn't cleared right away. Tino had only been trying to do something nice for a sick kid, and now he was looking like the world's biggest slimeball who fancied a bit of underaged flesh. "Fine, then what should I do?" Tino asked without looking at either man to indicate to whom the question had been directed.

"Well, the GFA has already convened and decided that a suspension is the appropriate course of action on their part until you can prove these allegations are false," Martin said. Tino sat up and sent a glare in his direction. He couldn't decide if Martin was happy about the news, or if the slight lift of the corner of his mouth was just his disgust showing.

"So I'm out, then, until we can clear my name." Tino had figured as much when Martin hightailed it to Rome on the redeye, but he'd still held out hope.

Martin nodded. "It's best if you lie low for a bit."

"And what exactly should I do to accomplish that? No matter where I go people know who I am, and add to that the reporters have already started following me around, so how do you propose I *lie low*?" Tino was agitated, but he had to keep his cool. Clenching his fists so his fingernails bit into his palms helped a little.

"Take a vacation; go see your family. Just stay away from the reporters and keep your nose clean," Bernardo said as Martin nodded in agreement.

They'd obviously discussed Tino's fate before he'd joined them and decided he should hide out instead of facing the press. It pissed Tino off because he believed it only made him look guilty, but handling these sorts of things was what he paid his agent to do. It was Bernardo's job to determine what was best for Tino's career, and even if Tino detested the advice, he usually took it and came out better for it.

"Fine, I guess you have it figured out. I don't even know why I needed to drive all the way in here. You could have just emailed me my directives," Tino said with a small amount of animosity.

"Tino, you know I'm only looking out for your best interests, and a scandal like this could carry over even after your name has been cleared. You were already under the microscope after the Paulo fiasco. One would think you'd have learned your lesson and made sure nothing you do can be misconstrued by the press. Remember our little talk about looking over your shoulder at all times?" Bernardo asked.

"Yeah I remember. I also remember how that one ended."

"Me too. You came out of that one looking like a saint, but it put your love life on their radar. You should have known that you, plus a hotel, plus a couple of nice-looking young women would draw them to you like flies to shit. Now, you need to just give this some time to blow over. When we hear anything about Herr Friedberg's situation, we'll make sure we waste no time in getting a statement from him. Until then, Tino, son, take my advice and try to stay out of the spotlight." Bernardo stood and rounded the desk to stand in front of Tino.

"What your agent is really trying to say is, keep it in your pants for once, and everything will eventually work out. They always do for guys like you," Martin said snidely.

Tino nodded and bit his tongue. Getting into a pissing contest with the manager of his team was not going to get him anywhere. "Fine, I'll go." Tino stood and shook Martin's hand quickly and then turned to Bernardo. "Please let me know as soon as there's any news." He shook Bernardo's hand, but the big burly agent pulled him into a surprise hug.

"You're a good boy, Tino. I know you're telling me the truth and you know why I do, but to clear your name in that way would only do more damage than good," Bernardo said into Tino's ear low enough so Martin couldn't eavesdrop.

Pulling out of Bernardo's arms, Tino inclined his head to acknowledge he understood. "I know. Don't worry. It never even crossed my mind." He assured his agent with a smooth lie, but he had thought about coming out and ending the speculation on the matter and clearing his name at the same time—that being gay was at least better than being thought to be a pedophile, but apparently he'd been wrong.

Bernardo looked relieved as he smiled. "Okay, well then, I guess we're done here for today. Tino, let me know where you decide to go, so I know how to get ahold of you." Bernardo made meaningful eye contact with Tino before turning to Martin. "You and I still have a bit of business to attend to." Martin nodded and took the seat Tino had vacated.

Tino knew when he was being dismissed, so he went to the door but hesitated before opening it. "I think I'll take that vacation you mentioned."

"That's good, Tino. Go get some rest and try to relax a bit," Bernardo said, but his tone was dismissive, telling Tino he'd already moved on to the next order of business.

Tino left the office building and waited for the valet to bring his car around to the front. The smile on the guy's face as he pulled up in Tino's Lamborghini made Tino grin in return. The guy jumped out and held out the keys. "This is the greatest car ever, signor Alessi," the young man said enthusiastically.

Tino took the keys, dug in his pocket for a tip, and handed over the bill he'd fished out. "Thanks for taking care of her for me." Tino slid into the driver's seat of the low-riding car.

"No problem, signor Alessi." The kid put his hand on the door as if to shut it but then leaned down to make eye contact. "You know I don't believe what they're saying about you on the Internet."

Tino tried to make the wan smile on his face look a bit more believable before he said, "Thanks, that means a lot coming from a fan."

The kid chuckled. "Oh I'm not a fan. I'm a Real Madrid guy all the way, but I still think it's crap. Have a nice day, signor Alessi." He slammed the door before Tino could respond to his little dig.

Tino pulled onto the crowded narrow street and headed out toward the interstate. He decided to drop by his family's vineyard, but it was only a short stop on his way to his final destination. He was going to take a vacation as soon as he could get it set up, but he figured he may as well see his family.

He had plenty of time to think on the drive across the country to his parents' vineyard outside of Bari. Tino was too young to be thinking about retirement. At twenty-nine, he was at the peak of his career, with at least another five years of playing to look forward to, but the thought of being able to live his life free of public scrutiny was getting more and more appealing with every passing kilometer. He came to one decision he believed would make his life feel more real to him and decided there was no time like the present to start making some changes.

He hit the button to turn on his Bluetooth and another to call his parents' house. The ringing on the other end of the line filled the small interior of the car with sound. After four rings, Tino was about to give up hope that his call would be answered, but the ringing ended abruptly and a laugh came down the line.

"Hello, Tino, is that you?" his mother's voice asked after the laughing stopped.

"Yeah, Mama, it's me. What's going on?"

"Oh, nothing. I was just cooking dinner and your niece decided to help. The flour canister is still a bit bigger than she is though." Another chortle, and then after a short pause, the mirth was gone when she asked, "So what's new with you?"

"Mama, I know you've seen the papers." He hated the way she worried about him over the things they said in the papers, but it was something he'd learned long ago he had no control over.

"I have seen the papers, but you know we never believe what they write about you."

"I know, Mama, and I'm happy you don't. Listen, I'm heading your way right now. I'm about an hour away, but I was wondering if it would be possible to get the whole family over tonight." Tino's palms were sweaty on the wheel as he waited for her answer. He was really going to do it if she could gather everyone on short notice.

"Oh I'm so happy you're coming for a visit, and of course, I can get everyone over, but I need to go so I can make some more tortellini or there won't be enough. See you soon, honey," she said before abruptly hanging up.

Tino smiled a real smile for the first time that day. It was just like his mama to forget her phone manners when there was about to be a food shortage. Tino turned on the radio and switched the station from the sports news channel to one that played rock-and-roll music. He hummed along, feeling at peace with his decision to finally tell his family he was gay. He needed their support in case things took a turn for the worse and the situation got ugly. How was he to expect them to stand behind him if they didn't know what they were up against?

Chapter Two

HENRICK SAT ON his sofa wrapped in a blanket and eating a tub of ice cream—his second of the day—while watching sappy romantic movies on his computer. He'd gone to sleep the previous night with all kinds of thoughts running through his head on how he could improve his life. Unfortunately, morning brought with it a deep unsettling feeling that he'd screwed up badly, even if he knew he'd done the right thing, because there was no way he could date a married man even if the marriage was for appearances only.

Henrick couldn't shake the thought all through breakfast, and by the time he'd returned from his shopping trip—where the urge to buy ice cream, cookies, and cakes overtook him—he was sure he'd just ruined his only chance at a relationship. No matter how screwed up the thing he had with Klaus was, it was the only stable, lasting relationship he'd ever had. Even if neither of them had been monogamous, he'd always thought of Klaus as his primary lover, the one he'd always come back to.

Instead of doing his normal Saturday chores around his small apartment after shopping, he shoved his purchases into the cupboards and settled on the sofa for a movie marathon where everyone got their happily ever after. Henrick pulled a tissue out of the box next to him and wiped his eyes and nose before leaning forward to start another movie, but his cell phone rang, interrupting the movement. He bent over almost double as he reached for the phone and forgot the half-melted tub of ice cream still clutched to his chest. The creamy fluid poured out onto his blanket before he could correct his mistake, making Henrick dissolve into tears at the sight of the mess.

His phone stopped ringing and beeped to let him know the caller had left a voice message. Before he could get up to put his blanket in the dirty clothes hamper, the phone started ringing again. This time Henrick set his snack on the table before leaning over to snatch his phone up.

"What?" he asked as sharply as he could through another wet sob.

"Henrick? Henrick, is that you?" the voice on the other end of the line asked.

"You called my number; who else would it be?" He was irritated at the caller for no reason other than the fact that he was in a bad mood.

"Hey, what's wrong?" Oskar asked.

"Nothing's wrong, Oskar. What do you want?"

"I was wondering if I could borrow that little vacuum cleaner you have because I need to get in behind—"

"It's fine. You can borrow it. I don't need the whole story. Just come up and get it." Henrick hung up. Oskar had lived in the apartment under his for the past two years, and they had become friends of a sort, but he'd learned quickly to not let the man get started on a story unless he had an hour or so he wanted to waste.

Getting off the couch, Henrick balled up his blanket and carried it to the bedroom where he threw it in the clothes hamper before digging the little hand vac out of his closet. Oskar knocked on the door just as Henrick returned to the living room, and he answered without a thought as to what he looked like after a day of sniveling on the couch.

The door swung open to reveal his neighbor who stood there with a ready smile on his handsome young face, but Oskar's jaw dropped, and his eyes widened as he took in Henrick's appearance. He ignored the vacuum Henrick was holding out for him to take, and pushed past into the apartment. He watched Oskar take in the trash-strewn sofa and coffee table and then tried to rush past him to start gathering cookie wrappers, used tissues, and the almost empty ice cream container, but Oskar grabbed his arm to stop him.

"What's going on, Henrick? Did someone die?"

Henrick shook his head. "No one died. I'm just feeling like a slob today and didn't clean up my mess."

Oskar squinted his hazel eyes and frowned. "Don't lie to me. I can tell there's something wrong. I may not be as sensitive as all your gay friends, but I'm not completely clueless." He crossed his arms over his broad chest and waited.

"I didn't say you were, and for your information, some of my gay friends are much more clueless than you, even if you are a big sweaty heterosexual."

Oskar was younger by a few years but less worldly by a couple of decades. The fact that Henrick was the first gay man Oskar had ever had any contact with astounded Henrick as much as it fascinated the younger man. Oskar never failed to point their differences out. It left Henrick to wonder if Oskar was uncomfortable with his sexuality, hence the constant reminders that Oskar himself wasn't gay, or if Oskar was really just that naïve in social situations and didn't know it wasn't polite to always bring it up.

Oskar ran a hand through his messy sun-bleached brown hair and then looked at it. "Not too sweaty," he said. Henrick couldn't help the snort that slipped out. Oskar was just too cute for his own good sometimes. "So, tell me what's wrong." Oskar pushed again for an answer.

"It's nothing you can help with, Oskar. I'm fine, really I am." Henrick tried to usher Oskar to the door, but he didn't let Henrick move him more than a step before he shook his head. He put his hands on his hips, drawing Henrick's attention down his torso to settle on the man's narrow waist. He admired how shapely his neighbor's young body was for a moment before his attention was brought back to Oskar's face when he coughed.

"I don't like the thought of leaving you alone like this."

"Like what? I told you I'm fine, and I meant it." Though he was touched by Oskar's concern, he was sure Oskar didn't want to hear about his relationship problems.

Oskar's lower lip punched out in a pout that made him look like an adorable but petulant five-year-old. "You just look like you could use a friend, and I was just trying to be a good friend. We are friends, aren't we, Henrick?" Oskar asked as a thoughtful frown drew his eyebrows together.

Henrick turned to put the vacuum he was still holding on the side table, rolling his eyes before turning back to Oskar. "We are friends, but I'm sure you don't want to spend your Saturday listening to me whine about the one that got away." He was trying to give Oskar an easy out so he wouldn't have to make up his own excuse to run away when he found out what Henrick had been crying about.

Oskar nodded and Henrick thought he was off the hook, but then he grabbed Henrick's arm and dragged him to the couch. After sitting, he pulled Henrick down next to him. "Okay, I know it's not fun to listen to me go on and on about the stuff I find interesting or even just about daily stuff but you always do. I know you think I'm just a kid, and I don't know anything, but really I want to help you. If getting it off your chest will help, then I'm here. I'll spend all day listening to you talk about some guy that obviously didn't know what he had and was stupid enough to let a great guy like you get away—"

Henrick covered Oskar's mouth to stop his babbling, but what Oskar had said about him being a great guy made him smile as he did it. "He didn't so much let me go as he made me want to go."

Oskar smiled at his victory and settled back onto the sofa. "What did he do?"

For some reason, Oskar's simple question opened the floodgates, and Henrick couldn't stop the words from coming once he let the first one pass his lips. He told Oskar the whole sordid story. From the first fumbling drunken attempt at frotting in Klaus's office after the Christmas party that ended in them both sprawled in a heap on the floor, laughing until tears rolled down their cheeks, to the previous night in the hotel where his heart was broken and tears of a different sort were shed.

"Klaus is going to ask Lydia to marry him so he can advance in the company. I can't in good conscience help him cheat on her, so I broke up with him. He chose his fake girlfriend over me, and it hurts so much. That's why I've been sitting here crying all day."

Oskar listened to the whole story, only adding an occasional "What a jerk" or "How could he do that to you?" By the time he was finished, Henrick felt like a brick the size of a Volkswagen had been lifted off his chest. He didn't realize how much stress had built up while being forced to keep it a secret. He hadn't even told Hedy and Gerta, his closest friends, about his relationship with Klaus. Melting back into the sofa, he took the tissue Oskar offered him. He blew his nose in what was probably not a very attractive manner, but since Oskar wasn't someone he was trying to impress, he didn't care.

"You feel better now, right?" Oskar asked.

"Yeah, strangely I kind of do, but what do I do now?" Pulling at the tissue clenched in his fist, he wasn't expecting much in the way of advice from Oskar.

"Has he tried to call you?"

"He texted a couple of times," Henrick answered, surprised by Oskar's question.

"Well, then maybe you need to get away. You said you work with him, and he probably knows where you live, so there's going to be no way you can avoid talking to him at some point. If it were me, I'd go somewhere with sand and palm trees." Oskar stared off over Henrick's shoulder with a wistful look.

Henrick had to admit Oskar had a good point. He wouldn't be able to avoid Klaus at work—well, at least not for long. The prospect of having not only to see Klaus but having to see him with his new fiancée, Lydia, made him want to just up and quit his job. Knowing that wasn't an option, he started to think about the holiday Oskar had mentioned. He hadn't had a proper holiday in over a year; surely he deserved one and, like they say, no time like the present.

"Henrick?" Oskar asked, breaking into his thoughts.

"Huh?"

"Are you okay? You looked like you checked out there for a minute."

"Uh, yeah, I'm fine. Just thinking about what you said. I think it's a good idea; going on holiday, that is. I may know just the place." Henrick was already thinking about where he could go.

Oskar smiled proudly at Henrick's acceptance of his idea. "I wish I could afford to go somewhere, but photography doesn't pay as much as I thought it was going to. Wish I could get a gig shooting for some big magazine or something but, oh well, maybe someday." Oskar shrugged before pushing himself to the edge of the sofa in preparation to stand, but Henrick put his hand on Oskar's thigh to stop him.

"Thanks, Oskar, I really needed someone to talk to today, and you were there for me. I appreciate it. I couldn't have told all of that to any of my other friends, so really you did me a big favor, and if there's anything I can do for you..." He let his offer trail off when Oskar's eyes darted down to where Henrick's hand lay on his thigh. Oskar flushed a bright red, and although he tore his eyes off Henrick's hand, he wouldn't make eye contact. Henrick jerked his hand away as if the denim underneath was made of lava. "I didn't mean it like that!"

"Oh...umm... I guess... I didn't... I'm... Vacuum? I mean..." Oskar was clearly flustered.

Henrick laughed at the ludicrousness of the situation. "Oh, Oskar, you really are just too sweet sometimes. Of course, you can borrow the vacuum, and the offer of another favor—nothing sexual—still stands."

Reddening even more, Oskar nodded and even tried a small smile of his own in response. "I'm sorry. I don't know why I'd think you'd be interested in me anyway."

Henrick stood and Oskar followed. He handed the vacuum cleaner over. "If you were gay, I'd be all over that." Henrick made a gesture to indicate Oskar's body, then giggled because he was sure if Oskar's face got any hotter it would burst into flames. "I'm sorry again. I'm just saying you're a good-looking guy, but I'm not a total masochist. Falling for a gay guy who's in the closet is bad enough, but I'm not about to fall for a straight guy. That would just be stupid."

"Oh well, yeah I guess so." Oskar didn't sound convinced that Henrick wasn't hitting on him.

He led Oskar to the door and opened it. "Thanks again for the shoulder to cry on. Keep the vacuum as long as you want."

"I'm glad I could help, and I'll have the vacuum back to you by tomorrow," Oskar said as he walked through the door. He turned around before Henrick could close it. "Let me know when you plan to take that holiday. I'll keep an eye on your apartment for you if you want."

"Sure, thanks."

Nodding, Oskar turned to leave, and Henrick watched him walk down the hall before going back inside. He had plans to make, phone calls to place, and an acquaintance to beg, if he seriously wanted to get the hell out of Salzburg and onto a warm sunny beach.

FIFTY-THREE MINUTES after he'd talked to his mother, Tino pulled into the long drive that led to the main house. The gravel on the driveway crunched under his tires as he drove slowly down the winding tree-lined lane. There were enough familiar cars parked in the large circle in front of the house that Tino knew his mother had been able to wrangle most, if not all, of the family into one place for the evening. He barely had time to switch off the ignition before his door was thrown open, and he was being hauled out of the seat and into the arms of his older brother, Costantino.

"Little brother, it's been a while," Costantino said as he hugged Tino.

"Life's been busy, Costa." Tino squeezed his brother hard before Costa let him go, only to be dragged into another hug by his older sister, Maria. He hugged and greeted each of his two older sisters, their husbands, and his two younger brothers before he made it to the front steps where his parents stood waiting to greet him with big smiles.

His father pulled him into a bone-crushing hug and kissed both his cheeks. He let him go with a pat on the back that pushed him a couple of steps to his mama. Her eyes glistened with tears as she held out her arms to him. Tino wrapped his arms around her and lifted her off the ground. "Mama, it's so good to be home," he said into her neck, where he'd pressed his face to stop himself from crying at the warm welcome he always received from his family.

"My bambino, it's so good to have you home. I don't know why you don't visit more often," she said through tears she didn't try to hide.

Tino smiled and felt the need to cry recede. Only in his family would returning after six months away be treated like a reunion between long-lost relatives. "I'm sorry, Mama. I've been busy."

"I know you have, but you still need to make time for family; it's important. Now put me down so I can feed you properly. I'm sure you haven't eaten a decent meal since Christmas."

Tino laughed as he set her back on her feet and followed her into the house along with the rest of the family. Tino looked around his childhood home for signs of guests, but the usually busy parlor was vacant. "Where are the guests?" he asked as they passed into the formal dining room.

"We sent them on an excursion for the evening. They won't be back until late tonight," his father answered.

"You didn't have to do that for me." Tino felt guilty about making extra work for his family so he could visit in peace.

"It wasn't just for you," his other older sister, Patrice, said. "It was planned for tomorrow anyway. We just moved it up a little."

Tino took his seat at the table in-between his mother and his youngest brother, Quentino. He waited until everyone was seated and his father said grace before asking, "So how has business been this year?"

"It's been good. Last year's yield was better than we projected, and we bottled almost a thousand more than we had expected." His father looked proud of the accomplishment.

"The tours are almost completely booked through the summer, and the fall's looking pretty good also," Costa added, since he and his wife ran that aspect of the business.

Tino nodded. "I'm glad to hear that." It meant the money he'd given his father three years before to save the family business had been a good investment—not that he would have thought twice about it anyway. Tino hadn't even felt a dent in his savings after giving his father a million euros. The vineyard could have survived losing one season's harvest when the vines had been devastated by insects, but the subsequent year's drought had wiped out all hopes of the bumper crop they had needed to rebound from the bugs. His father had laid it all out for Tino and left it up to him to decide if he wanted to help or not. Tino hadn't hesitated, and his family was doing well once again.

Costa reached across the table and poured Tino a glass of wine. "This is last year's bottling. It's good—got good flavor and just the right amount of acidity. It's bound to be even better with a couple of years' age on it."

Tino lifted the glass and sniffed the deep-red wine—it had a nice fruity bouquet. Swirling it in his glass before he took a sip, he let the flavorful liquid roll around his mouth for a few seconds before he swallowed. "That's really nice. You're right. I can see this one being one of the best vintages in a couple of years," Tino said, agreeing with his brother.

"You need to eat. You're too thin." His mother plopped a ladle full of tortellini onto his plate and covered it in white sauce, scolding him as she dished out more plates around the table.

"I'm not thin, Mama." His mother was the typical Italian mother and grandmother—well, if you didn't picture them all as round elderly women, always trying to feed someone.

"So, did you come home to hide out?" Selena asked. Selena, Costa's wife, wasn't known for her subtlety, but the question was blunt even for her.

Tino choked on his second sip of wine, and his younger brother, Agustino, pounded his back as he returned to his seat at the other end of the table. When Tino finally got enough air to reply, all eyes were on him. "I'm actually only here until I can catch the ferry to Durres. I've decided it's time to look for a holiday home."

"Do you think this is really the right time for that?" his father asked, worry creasing his brow.

"I need to get away. The media has never bothered me in Albania, and the hotel staff knows me well enough that I'm no longer a curiosity to them. I always planned on buying something there, and now is as good a time as any since I have some free time on my hands." Trying to pass it off as nothing, Tino took a bite of the tortellini.

"You could stay here. No one will bother you when you're at home with your family." His mother looked from him to his father, who nodded.

"I know, Mama, but there are still the guests, and I just need some time to myself."

"So, we're just a pitstop on your way?" Costa asked, sounding slightly irritated.

"No, there's something else that I wanted to talk about before I leave. Something I want to tell you all, something I should have told you years ago," Tino said, trying to psyche himself up for a conversation that was long overdue.

Once again, all eyes were trained on Tino, but it was his father who voiced the question on everyone's mind. "What is it, son?"

"Well, you remember the thing with that guy Paulo—"

"That son of a bitch who tried to extort money from you—"

"Papa, he's not a son of a bitch. Well, maybe he is sort of, but he wasn't trying to blackmail me. He was telling the truth, and although I don't approve of his methods, he was right to do what he did." Tino waited for the truth to dawn in the eyes of his family, but when it didn't come quickly, he added, "We were together. He was upset when the media outed him, and I didn't step up beside him and declare my sexuality because I'm gay too."

The gasps came first and then the grumbling began, but it was Costa's reaction that caught everyone's attention. He stood up and leaned over the table to get into Tino's face. "Bullshit, you're gay! You've been dating that supermodel, and now you've been caught with two young girls. You're just trying to find a way out of this new mess you've made, but no one's going to believe it's true. It's too convenient an excuse this time, Tino," he bellowed. Tino sat there and listened to his brother's tirade without saying a word, feeling he deserved his brother's anger.

"Tino...is this...? Are you sure?" his mother asked while clutching at her chest.

"Of course, he's not sure! He's just trying to weasel his way out of trouble, just like all the other spoiled celebrities do!" Costa renewed his assault on Tino's character.

The scraping of chair legs across the marble tiled floor drew everyone's attention to the head of the table. The patriarch of the family stood with his hands braced on the table in front of him, head hanging down between his shoulders. Holding his breath, Tino waited for his father to tell him what a disappointment he was and to get out of the house and never return. But Bettino Alessi, Tino's beloved father, didn't say those hateful words to his second son. Instead, he directed his dark stare at his eldest.

"You sit down," he said before turning a searching gaze toward Tino. "Is this true, Valentino? Are you a homosexual?"

Tino looked down at the table and took a deep breath before looking back up to meet his father's eyes. "Yes, Papa, it's true. I wouldn't make something like this up. I'm sorry it's taken me so long to tell you all the truth, but I have always been afraid you wouldn't want me to come home anymore if you knew."

"Oh, Tino," his mother sobbed before throwing her arms around him the best she could as they both were still seated at the table. "My bambino, how could you ever question our love for you?"

"But how can you believe him, and if you do, don't you care about the family's reputation? What are people going to say when they find out he's...that he's...like he is?" Costa asked their father.

Bettino straightened his posture while heaving out a heavy sigh. "Without Tino, this family would have no reputation to protect."

"Papa, you don't—"

Bettino held up his hand to stop Tino. "I want them to know what you did, Tino." He looked around the table at his children and grandchildren before beginning once again. "He doesn't want me to tell you this because he doesn't want you to feel indebted to him, but Tino is the one who put up the money to save the vineyard and winery. Without his financial help, we would have gone under. Tino is my son just as sure as you are Costa, and I will not have anyone questioning his right to be what he is in my home. Anyone who has a problem with that is welcome to leave." Again, Bettino looked each of his children in the eye, only to have them look quickly away from the challenge they found there.

The murmurs around the table started again, but this time they were about Tino saving the family business and not taking credit for it. Tino chanced a look across the table at his brother, who sat back in his chair, but still seemed to be angry enough to avoid eye contact with everyone else at the table.

"Tino, is it true? Did you really give Papa all that money and not tell us?" Maria asked as she held her little son in her arms.

Tino nodded. He still didn't want the recognition from his family. He liked just being another one of the kids when they all got together, equal footing and all that, despite his fame and fortune out in the rest of the world. This little revelation would cause an imbalance that would make Tino stand out in a way he didn't want to when he was with his family.

Standing, Maria rounded the table and put her son in Tino's lap to free up her arms, which she wrapped tightly around Tino's neck. "Thank you so much. If it means anything, you are still my snot-nosed little brother who wouldn't leave me alone until I pounded you hard enough to go running to Mama or Papa to tattle. I love you, and that will never change no matter who you choose to be with." She kissed his cheeks before gathering her child and stepping away.

Tino wasn't paying attention to what was going on around him. All his siblings lined up behind Maria and each took a turn hugging and kissing Tino and accepting him for who he was. Costa stood behind his wife, and Tino studied his older brother over his wife's shoulder as he hugged her. Tino could tell Costa wasn't happy, but he'd play along under their father's watchful gaze for the sake of family harmony.

Costa shook Tino's hand and gave him a half hug. "If you are what you say you are, I have no problem with it. But if it's just a story to get out of trouble and I find that out, I don't care what Papa says, you'll no longer be my brother."

Tino took a minute to think over what his brother had just said, and then he smiled, pulling Costa into a real hug and pounding his back. "You just said you accepted me if I'm gay but not a liar! I knew you weren't the hardass you were pretending to be," Tino said as he stepped out of the hug. "I promise you, I'm not a liar. You know better, Costa."

Costa nodded and turned back to take his seat. Dinner was still a lively occasion even after Tino's big confession. He loved his big loud family and promised himself that once he was able, he'd find himself a good man and start one of his own.

Chapter Three

HENRICK'S PLANE LANDED a few minutes late, so it was almost midnight when he stepped onto the gangway at the Tirana airport. Pulling his small carry-on behind him, he followed his fellow passengers out into the airport to find his luggage. He spotted his bright-red bag almost immediately and sighed in relief. He made his way through passport control and customs easily before hitting the main terminal to look for the sign with his name on it. It was a familiar process, and Henrick felt at ease as he walked up to the man holding a sign bearing his name, pointed at it, and then himself.

The dark-skinned man smiled and asked, "*Ju flas shqip?*" Henrick shook his head because he didn't even recognize what language the man was speaking. The smile stayed in place as he asked, "*Govorite li bosanski?*" Though Henrick did recognize that language, he still shook his head. The man squinted. "*Parli italiano?*"

Henrick shook his head. "*Sprichst du deutsch?*"

The man laughed, and it was his turn to shake his head. "I have not gotten around to learning the Deutsch yet, so I guess we will have to speak English."

Henrick snorted. "Gage told you I spoke English didn't he?" Henrick asked because it sounded like the sort of prank Gage would play and get a kick out of.

"Yes, he and Nikola told me you spoke English but thought it would be funny if you thought I could not. I guess you are more unflappable than they thought because you did not seem worried."

"Yeah well, I figured you knew how to get me to the apartment, and from there, I was going to be on my own anyway." Henrick shrugged. It wouldn't be the first time he'd had to go it alone in a country where he didn't speak the language.

"I am Esad. Please forgive me my little joke," he said as he held out his hand for Henrick to shake.

"It's no problem, Esad. I'll put the blame squarely on Gage's head, where it belongs." Henrick shook the offered hand.

"Ah yes, easier to blame him. Now let me help you with those bags." He reached for both, but Henrick only let him take the bigger of the two suitcases and Esad shrugged. "This way to the car. We have about an hour drive, depending on traffic, which should not be that bad at this time of night."

After following Esad out to the car, Henrick waited while the other man stowed his bags in the trunk. Esad opened the front door for him and then shut it after his passenger was settled in. He rounded the car and got in the driver's seat. Henrick wished it was light out so he could see the scenery as they drove, but the countryside was poorly lit, even where it was more populated, leaving him to stare into the dark.

"So, may I ask how you know Nikola and Gage?" Esad asked after a period of silence.

"I met both of them while on a business trip to Sarajevo. We keep in touch. Can I ask you the same?"

"Yes, of course you can. I have known Nikola for some time, worked for his uncle on some business deals here in Tirana. He asked me to oversee the renting of the apartment along with picking up guests from the airport and making sure they get settled. It is just one of my many jobs," Esad said with a wave of his hand.

"So, you do other things besides—" Henrick's phone ringing from his pocket interrupted his next question. "Excuse me while I see who's calling." Henrick fished his phone out and looked at the screen. "Sorry, I have to answer this." He swiped the screen to accept the call. "Hello, Papa, why are you up so late?"

"You were supposed to call when your flight landed. Your mother and sister are worried," his father said, sounding both tired and cranky.

Henrick slapped his forehead. "I'm sorry. I forgot. My flight got in a bit late, but everything's fine. The driver picked me up, and we are on our way to Durres as we speak."

"I'm still not so sure you should have gone off to Albania by yourself. It may not be safe." His father had been saying the same thing over and over for the past week, but both Gage and Nikola assured him he would be perfectly safe in Durres as long as he stuck to the touristy area, which he fully planned on doing.

"I'll be fine. Now go tell Momma and Lena I'm okay and go to bed. I'll call you in a couple of days and let you know how everything is."

"Okay, son, I'll tell them. Good talking to you. Good night."

Henrick put his phone back and looked at Esad. "I'm sorry. I know that was rude, but it was my papa. I forgot to call when my plane got in."

"It is not a problem, and we are almost there." Esad smiled and turned his attention back to driving as they entered the city.

Henrick turned to take in the city of Durres—as much as he could see while going one hundred and twenty kph from the highway, at least. Then before he could blink, it seemed they had left the outskirts of the city behind, and Henrick couldn't see the sea anywhere near where they were heading. Esad took an exit off the highway that turned into a little winding road. Finally, they hit a more populated area, which took on the look all tourist destinations had. There were hotels, bars, and restaurants lining the road on both sides, but Henrick wondered what sort of resort area closed down, because there were only a handful of people out on the street. "Where are all the holiday makers?"

"You are early. The season does not officially start here until next week. You will have a bit of peace and quiet for a few days, but after that you will not." Esad pulled into a near-empty parking lot and shut off the car.

Henrick got out and looked around. He was surprised by all the trees surrounding the back of what he assumed was the building in which Gage and Nikola had bought their apartment. Esad handed him his laptop bag and carry-on before leading him to the building. They climbed three flights of stairs to a landing that had four doors. Esad opened the first one on the left and turned on the light before letting Henrick enter behind him.

"Well, here we are." Esad set the keys on the counter in the little kitchenette just off the entry before walking through into the living room and then through a door. Henrick followed but stopped to look at the living room which was three times the size of the kitchen. It was furnished nicely with a sectional sofa and a couple of chairs. "This is the bigger of the two bedrooms, so I put your suitcase in there, plus the other room is pink." Esad raised an eyebrow.

Henrick smiled because, of course, Gage would paint a room pink for his little princess. "That's great, thanks Esad." Henrick stepped past him and went into the bedroom to put his carry-on next to his other bag.

"I know it's late, but Gage said I must go through his list with you before I leave, but do not worry, it is a pretty short list." Esad looked apologetically at Henrick who inclined his head in a go-on gesture. "Okay, first he says to tell you that it is most important that you do not drink the tap water. I have made sure you have a couple of day's supply of bottled water in the fridge. Then he said next is that everything else you will need is in this folder." Opening a desk drawer, Esad pulled out a green folder.

Henrick laughed as he took the folder from Esad's hand. "Is there anything else the big man wanted me to know?"

Esad blushed. "No, but Nikola had one thing he wanted me to tell you. He said you should make sure that you do not hit on Esad because he does not want to have to find another person to look after his apartment." His flush deepened as he looked away.

Henrick laughed harder than he had since his breakup with Klaus. He just couldn't stop himself because the image of Nikola with his hands on his hips and a stern expression on his face as he told Esad to relay that last message was one of the funniest Henrick's mind had ever conjured. His fit finally petered out after a few minutes, but when he looked up at Esad, his mirth returned at the puzzled expression on the other man's face. He giggled a bit more before choking out, "I'm sorry; it's not you."

Esad huffed and crossed his arms. "I do not know why that is so funny. He said to me to not take it bad if you did because you hit on everyone. Yet you did not. Am I not attractive enough for someone who hits on everyone?" Esad asked, looking genuinely hurt.

Henrick wasn't sure if something was getting lost in translation, but he hoped he hadn't actually offended Esad by not hitting on him, because that would be truly funny, yet not so funny at the same time. Henrick schooled his expression. "I've turned over a new leaf as they say. I am no longer the flirty man Nikola knew from Sarajevo." It had just occurred to him that he *had* been trying to be more serious because he needed to change the type of men he attracted, didn't he?

Esad's posture relaxed and he smiled. "I was not really upset, but Nikola said to guard myself against you. So far you have not done anything that I find offensive."

Henrick put his hand on Esad's arm. "I would normally flirt with you. You're a handsome man, but I'm tired. I'm also just coming off a bad breakup, so maybe if you come back sometime after I've had time to relax..." Henrick said, leaving the rest unsaid so Esad could fill in the blank on his own. His words made the other man grin.

"There, at least now I can tell Nikola you tried a little," Esad said, his crooked grin widening. "Now, I will leave you if there is nothing else you need."

"I think I'm good, just going to take a quick shower and then probably go to bed." He walked with Esad to the door but then stopped him before he could leave. "I thought Gage said this apartment was right on the beach, but it didn't look like it could possibly be."

Esad looked surprised. "Just go out on your balcony. Now I must go. My number is in those papers Gage left, so if you need anything please call. Have a good night."

"Thanks again, Esad. Good night," Henrick said before he closed and locked the door behind him.

Henrick hurried over to the sliding glass door, pulled the blinds back, and unlocked the door so he could open it.

He could hear the waves gently lapping at the beach before he even stepped out into the warm night air. The balcony was large with a table and chairs already set up in the middle. The space ran the entire length of the apartment, and he noticed there was another door that he figured must lead to the bedroom. Henrick walked to the railing and peered out at the moonlit sea only meters from his doorstep. He felt a sense of calm wash over him and knew he'd made the right decision in taking a holiday. Getting out of Salzburg and away from Klaus would do him a world of good.

TINO WOKE UP when the call over the loudspeaker went out that they were an hour from port. He stretched as best as he could in the tiny little berth of his cabin. He didn't care what anyone said, paying for a first-class passage was well worth it to not have to sit in a chair all night while crossing the Adriatic. After dressing, he went to have a small breakfast in one of the top-floor restaurants and then made his way to the deck so he could watch their approach into the Durres seaport. He'd have to make his way below deck to get his car soon, but the fresh morning sea air helped to revive him in a way coffee couldn't.

Tino presented his passport at the gate to the exit of the port when he pulled up to it. He got his entrance stamp and a "Have a nice stay" from the man who handed it back. Tino navigated the streets with ease, enjoying the fresh morning air that rushed in through his open windows. Durres wasn't a huge international destination—yet—but the Italians had gotten a jump on the rest of the world. Once the borders had been opened for travel, they'd found a paradise full of flat sandy beaches that had been hidden away during the Cold

War. The people were welcoming and more accommodating than their neighbors to the south. Many Italians had opened successful businesses in Albania, and the export trade with the country meant Tino felt at home surrounded by familiar brands of everything from his favorite cookies to the same toilet paper he used at home.

The main road was wide, and Tino followed the signs leading to the Plazh but went farther out to Golem where the resort he frequented was located. He liked the privacy being out of the city provided, plus the Mali Robit district had, in his opinion, the best beaches and fewer people. In a little under half an hour, he pulled into the parking lot and got out of his car, a security guard watching him closely from his post by the building.

"*Buongiorno!*" Tino called out to the man. He got a smile and a wave in return before the man went back to just standing there like a statue. Tino entered the lobby of the hotel, and the front desk clerk smiled broadly at him as he approached.

"*Buongiorno*, signor Alessi. It's so good to have you back with us," the woman greeted in Italian.

"*Buongiorno*, Signora. It's always nice to be back," Tino said warmly.

"We have your usual apartment ready, stocked especially for you as always." She punched keys on the computer in front of her before handing Tino his key. "Is there anything else I can do for you, signor Alessi?"

"Yes. Could you have someone bring my bags from my car to my room, please?" Tino asked as he handed over his car keys.

"Of course. I will get Dardan to do that immediately."

"No need to hurry, just whenever he has time. Thanks." She nodded but picked up the phone and started talking rapidly to the person on the other end. The only words Tino understood were "signor Alessi," so he figured he'd have his luggage before he got the chance to take off his shoes.

Turning away, Tino crossed the lobby and took the only elevator to the top floor where his apartment was one of only two occupying the space. He entered the large, one-hundred-and-forty-square-meter apartment. On the island that separated the kitchen from the living room, there was a basket filled with fruit, cookies, nuts, and a bottle of one of Durres's finest wines. Tino pulled the little card off the cellophane covering the assortment of treats and read: *Welcome back, signor Alessi. It is always a pleasure having you in our establishment. Should you need anything at all, feel free to call me—355.52.511.876. Enjoy your stay. Luan Kastrati*. Tino snorted; the owner of the resort certainly knew how to add a personal touch.

Tino dropped the card on the counter when a sharp rap sounded on his door. He opened it to find Dardan standing there holding his bags. "Ah, Dar, I see you are looking as well as ever," Tino said to the strapping young man.

"Thank you, signor Alessi, and you also. Where would you like your bags?" Dardan got straight to the point, never one for too much small talk.

"In the bedroom is fine." Stepping back, Tino let him into the apartment. Dardan carried the bags through to the master bedroom and laid them on the bed. Tino followed the broad tanned back, shiny with the sunscreen the man used for his work on the beach. He took a deep breath through his nose, and the smell of coconuts, sand, and salt wafted off Dardan's skin and hit him full force. Tino closed his eyes against the sudden rush of need that hit him.

"Oof, crap," Dardan muttered as he collided with Tino. Tino opened his eyes to find Dardan's face only inches from his own. "Sorry, signor Alessi, I didn't know you'd followed me in here."

Tino stepped back and patted Dardan's shoulder. "It's fine, Dar, no harm done."

Dardan smiled nervously as he nodded. "Do you need anything else before I go?"

Tino's mind supplied him with the image of Dar on his knees, wide eyes looking worshipfully up at Tino as he opened those full lips to take the head of Tino's cock into his mouth. Tino knew then he needed to get laid and fast before he ended up getting himself into trouble—again. "Nope, nothing I can think of. Thanks for getting my bags so quickly," Tino said as he turned away from temptation. He fished out a bill and handed it to Dardan in exchange for his car keys as he opened the door for him.

"Thank you, signor Alessi." Dardan pocketed the money. "If you need anything else, you know where to find me."

"Sure do." Tino closed the door after the young man and turned back to the little note on the counter. He knew of something he needed that Mr. Kastrati could help him procure. He grabbed his cell phone and dialed the number before he could give it any more thought. He just needed a little something to take the edge off, and if he had to pay for it, oh well, he'd spent money on far more frivolous things before.

"COME IN, COME in, Mr. Alessi," the real estate agent, Marco Barton, said as he stood from his office chair.

Tino had stopped at the open office door the secretary had pointed him to when he'd asked for Mr. Barton. The man behind the desk was a study in contradictions. He had the dark coloring of the natives but was dressed as most of the Italian tourists in a light linen shirt, khaki shorts, and flip-flops, and to add to the confusion, his speech had a heavy British accent.

"I was delighted to get your call yesterday. I have quite the list of properties to show you since you didn't give me much in the way of what you were looking for other than on the beach." Marco walked across the office as he spoke and shook Tino's hand with vigor.

"A friend of mine recommended you, said you helped him buy both his house and the property he runs his restaurant out of."

"Ah yes, you mentioned Mr. Collins on the phone. You played together for a time, didn't you?"

Tino nodded. "Yes, for a short time at the beginning of my career but at the end of his. He was a sort of mentor to me."

"Mr. Collins is a very nice man, and his restaurant has food that is simply to die for, if you can manage to get a reservation, that is," Marco said with a wink. "But I suppose we should get down to business, yes?"

"Yes, let's. As I said on the phone, I'd like something move-in ready. I realize there are a lot of new construction projects, but I'd rather not wait for something to be built. I'd also prefer a villa, not a flat; other than that, I'm pretty open to seeing almost anything you have to show me." Tino was eager for the distraction of looking at property.

Marco grabbed a briefcase and a set of keys from his desk. "Well then, like I said, I have a very big list. I'm sure we'll find the perfect place for you to enjoy your holidays. We'll take my car if you don't mind," he said before closing and locking his office.

"That sounds fine. Do you have many properties in the Golem district?"

Marco waited until they were in the car and pulling out of the parking garage before he answered. "I have a few. Is it your preference to be south of Durres?"

"I like the area and I know it, but I'm willing to look at whatever you have."

"I'm sure there will be many you will find appealing and at a price you'll not find anywhere else on the sea," Marco assured him.

"If you say so." Tino turned to watch the city pass by as the real estate agent babbled on about the various places they'd see.

TINO NEEDED A drink and a swim by the time his day house hunting had come to an end. He'd looked at a tiny bungalow and a huge mansion and then everything in-between the two but, nothing jumped out at him and said 'Me! I'm the one! Pick me!' He'd thanked Marco and left him with the promise to call to schedule the next round of showings soon.

After changing into a pair of dark-purple speedos, Tino pulled his chin-length black hair into a small ponytail on the back of his head, grabbed his little bag with his wallet and room key, and headed down to the pool. It was only four o'clock but he was on holiday, so a drink in the afternoon wasn't out of the question.

The pool area wasn't too busy, not like it would be soon when all the European schools let out for summer and the families started to arrive. Tino took advantage of the fact that there were enough empty chaise lounges that he could have a small cluster to himself and claimed two by spreading the folded towels out over them, ensuring that no one would sit next to him.

He settled into one and waved one of the pool bar waiters over so he could order a drink. The waiter smiled politely while handing Tino a frosty glass and being instructed to put it on the bill for his room. Tino sipped his fruity drink while watching a little girl jump from the side of the pool into the waiting arms of her young father. Her high-pitched giggle as she hit the water made him smile every time.

When his beverage was gone, he got up to take a quick swim to cool off. He lowered himself into the water and swam a few laps before getting out and ordering another drink. The little girl's mother walked over and chatted with her family before walking off into the resort, leaving the child to have her fun with her indulgent father.

Tino finished his second cocktail and thought about ordering another when *he* walked into the pool area from the beach. The slight blond man surveyed the seating area and then picked a chair at the opposite end of the pool. He spread out a towel, adjusted his tight little swim trunks, and sat down. Tino watched with interest as the guy produced a bottle of sunscreen and started to slowly smooth it over long pale limbs and then over his slim but nicely defined chest and stomach.

Tino shifted because the other man's little show, whether he knew what he was doing or not, was making Tino's speedo a little too tight. Tino continued to watch while trying to talk his arousal down from the ledge. After looking around him, the blond lay back on his chair and stretched out in the sun. Tino wished the guy hadn't been wearing those dark sunglasses because he had a thing for blonds with blue eyes, and finding out if the guy across the pool fit that description was quickly becoming a priority for Tino. He sat there obsessing about it until he couldn't take it any longer.

Tino stood and walked to the edge of the pool. Standing there a moment just looking at the other man, Tino wondered if maybe he was staring back behind those mirrored lenses. He had to know what color his eyes were so without any further hesitation, he dove into the pool and swam the length below the surface.

Chapter Four

HENRICK WOKE TO the sounds of the sea from his open balcony door. After running across the street to the little bakery and buying himself some Nutella-filled croissants, he'd set the coffeepot to brewing. He ate his breakfast on the balcony while watching the sea ebb and flow, then read through the papers Gage had put together for him. They contained everything he'd ever need to know to survive during his stay, plus much more.

Henrick quickly cleaned up and got ready to go to the beach. Carrying a small bag he'd packed with water, snacks, sunscreen, and a towel, he slipped on his sunglasses and flip-flops. The beach was almost empty, so Henrick had his choice of chairs. He picked one in the front row, and when a handsome young man came up to him, he gave him a bright smile.

Again that strange language that Henrick figured must be the native tongue was what the man used when he addressed Henrick. Henrick shook his head and decided to go with English since Deutsch wasn't as common. "I'm sorry. I don't understand. Do you speak English?"

The young man nodded, and his brilliant smile widened. "Yes, I'm sorry, but are you a guest at the hotel?" He pointed to the hotel next to the apartment building.

"No, I'm staying in that building there." Henrick pointed to his building. "The owner told me I could use these chairs. They have some sort of agreement to use the hotel's amenities?" Henrick said with a slight uptick at the end to make it sound like a question.

"Oh, yes, okay then that's fine. I'm sorry to have bothered you." He adjusted the wide-brimmed hat he was wearing as he spoke.

"No problem. Is it okay if I use these then?" Henrick asked, indicating the two lounge chairs and umbrella he'd picked.

"Yes, go ahead." Before turning to leave, the man watched as he spread his towel out.

Henrick let his eyes wander over the man's smooth, tanned skin and the cute butt under the tight board shorts made him think he may like the local scenery for more than just the natural wonders. He stowed his things and walked out into the water, surprised at how gradual the slope was, and it took him a good hundred meters of wading before the water was even waist-deep. He dove under before coming back up to float on his back, letting the salty water aid his natural buoyancy. Henrick felt at peace for the first time in weeks.

He spent most of the day enjoying the water and then the sun and the water again before he went to the hotel's pool to sunbathe a bit before heading in for dinner. Making sure to cover his entire body with sunscreen for what felt like the tenth time that day, because he didn't want to look like a lobster if he dozed off in the afternoon sun, he'd just lain back on the chaise lounge when he noticed a man at the other end of the pool looking in his direction. Henrick still had his sunglasses on, so he watched—knowing that no one could tell where he was looking—as the man dove into the pool. He almost jumped in surprise when the same man surfaced right in front of his chair moments later.

Henrick lay still and kept watching while the man pulled himself smoothly out of the water and walked over to the chair next to his. The man picked up the courtesy hotel towel lying at the end of the chaise lounge and started to rub his lightly haired chest before he reached back and pulled out the band that held his hair. It was that action that caused a spatter of cold water to land on Henrick's own sun-warmed skin, making him start with the unexpected chill.

"*Mi scusi, mi dispiace bello,*" the man said, but his grin betrayed his apology. Henrick was sure the man had meant to splatter him with water to get his attention.

Henrick didn't speak Italian, but he certainly could recognize the language when he heard it. "*Schon in Ordnung, halb so wild,*" Henrick answered; a little water never hurt anyone. He dipped his finger into the puddle between his nipples and ran his moistened fingertip down to his belly button before he looked up over the top of his sunglasses at the man standing over him.

"*Ah una presa in giro carino Tedesco.*" His lip twitched at the corner of his full lips before his grin turned to a genuine smile. He sat down on the lounge chair next to Henrick.

Henrick studied the man's face, and when recognition hit, he hid his surprise. The man on the chaise lounge, flirting with him, was none other than Valentino Alessi. The Bundesliga bad boy himself, in the flesh, leering openly at him in public made Henrick's pulse quicken. His mind fought for control of his body. No matter how hot the man in front of him was, there was no way Henrick was going to even entertain the idea of doing anything other than sending him on his way.

"Sorry, *aber ich verstehe Sie nicht. Ich spreche kein italienisch,*" Henrick said, hoping to cut off any further discussion between them. He watched as Valentino cocked his head as if considering something before he turned and lay back in the chair, staring out at the pool.

"I bet you speak English just fine though, am I wrong?" he asked without looking in Henrick's direction.

Henrick considered his options. He could pretend ignorance and hope Valentino would leave him alone, or he could admit he did speak English and have to make up an excuse as to why he didn't want to continue a conversation with the man. Just when Henrick decided on feigning ignorance, the young man he'd been referring to in his mind as the beach chair boy walked into the pool area. When he saw Henrick, his eyes lit up with recognition. Henrick looked away quickly, but it was too late because he realized the man had the small cooler bag he'd taken to the beach with bottled water in it. Resigned to his fate, he pushed his sunglasses onto the top of his head and made eye contact with him.

"Sir, you left this under your chair. I figured since you took all your other belongings you must have forgotten it, and I saw that you'd come in here to the pool, so, here." He held out the bag for Henrick to take.

"Thank you for returning it to me." Henrick glanced at Valentino, who was grinning, as he proved the man's assumption right.

"It's not a problem." The man's smile never wavered until he noticed Henrick wasn't sitting alone, and then a small frown appeared on his handsome face as he addressed Valentino. "Signor Alessi, nice to see you again. Are you enjoying your stay so far?"

"Yes, Dar, I'm enjoying it very much, and things seem to be looking to get better as we speak," Valentino said with a sideways glance at Henrick.

Henrick noticed when the beach chair boy, Dar, flinched at the other man's words before he looked over at Henrick with what seemed to be something like concern on his face. "I'm glad to hear it. I have to go now. Just wanted to make sure you got your bag, sir." Dar bowed his head in Henrick's direction.

"Thank you again and please call me Henrick," he said before he remembered that Valentino freaking Alessi was listening with avid attention, and now he'd supplied him with a name.

"Dardan, but people call me Dar," the man said as he held out his hand for Henrick to shake. Henrick took it, and the extra little bit of pressure Dardan used to squeeze his hand made him glance up. The look in the other man's eyes held the kind of interest that surprised Henrick, but he supposed it shouldn't have; the guy did chase him down to return a three-euro bag.

"Nice to meet you, Dar." A small flirty smile briefly touched Henrick's lips as a little bit of encouragement for the guy before he could remind himself he was taking a vacation from hookups on his vacation from life. He got a megawatt smile in return as Dar let go of his hand and tipped his head at both Henrick and Valentino, before turning on one heel and striding off.

"So, *Henrick,* are you on holiday by yourself?" Valentino asked after Dardan made his exit.

"No, I'm here with someone." The statement popped out of Henrick's mouth before he could stop himself from grabbing the lifeline the other man had inadvertently thrown him. He pulled his glasses back down to cover his eyes so they wouldn't give him away. He wasn't a good liar and had a feeling Valentino Alessi would spot his fib from a mile away.

"Really? Is he here at the pool?" Henrick didn't miss how Valentino's question made it clear he'd already decided which way Henrick swung.

"Maybe he is." Henrick hoped Valentino would get the hint and stop trying to engage him in conversation, but his vague answer backfired.

"Oh this could be fun. Let me see..." Valentino said as he looked at the few people around the pool. His eyes landed on a man with a belly big enough it left one wondering if the guy was even wearing a pair of shorts until he picked the precise moment when Henrick's eyes were on him to turn around and prove that he was indeed wearing a speedo about ten sizes too small if the amount of hairy butt crack showing was any indication. Henrick shuddered involuntarily.

Valentino chuckled. "No, I suppose not that one then." He pointed at another man who was a bit slimmer, but the shine off the top of his head was almost blinding. "You like them older?" he asked with a little twinkle in his eye.

Henrick had just about enough of the teasing smirk on Valentino's too handsome face. "How do you know it's not that guy?" He pointed to the handsome young father playing with his adorable little girl.

"Ah yes, he's very attractive, so you have a child then?" Valentino's skeptical look told Henrick he wasn't buying it.

Henrick shrugged, but then as par for the course on this occasion, a woman walked up to the man, and the child's squeal of "Momma" ruined any chance Henrick had of convincing Valentino that was his family.

"Oh, so not that one either then." Valentino chuckled and continued to survey the prospects around the pool.

"He's actually back at the apartment waiting for me," Henrick lied easily.

"Oh well, I guess he's a lucky man then." Valentino stood, the smile finally disappearing from his lips as he did. "It was nice to meet you anyway, Henrick. I hope you have a pleasant holiday."

Henrick felt a little bad at the obvious disappointment in the other man's words, but there was no way he was going to change his story to make him feel better. He smiled politely up at Valentino. "It was nice to meet you too and the same to you." Only then did Henrick realize that Valentino hadn't actually introduced himself but figured he probably relied on people knowing who he was anyway.

He watched Valentino walk around the pool, pick up his things, and leave without a backward glance in his direction. A little pang of regret hit Henrick in the chest, but he shook it off. One hot night in the bed of someone like Valentino would do nothing to help him get his life back on track. He didn't want to end up like that one guy did, left to the mercy of the press after being accused of slandering a big football star. Henrick didn't know the whole story but he'd bet that guy had been telling the truth, and Valentino Alessi had left him to fend for himself against the gossip-hungry wolves to save his own reputation as a heterosexual stud.

Henrick stretched out on his chair once again and wondered if a brief fling with a guy who worked on a beach would be a setback in his plan to bring order to his life. Dardan was cute—young and cute. He smiled to himself as he thought about the look on Valentino's face when he told him he was there with someone. The guy probably thought he could have any man or woman he wanted, but Henrick had given him a reason to think twice on that one. Damn it, why did his mind wander back to Valentino when there was a perfectly good, safe, nonfamous man who might be interested in him to think about? No, not even going to entertain another thought about you-know-who because he was turning over a new leaf just like he'd said he was, and that man was not what he was going to find under that particular leaf.

TINO COULDN'T GET the blond, blue-eyed man, Henrick, out of his head. He'd fled the pool area much sooner than he'd planned because the thought of watching Henrick with his boyfriend—if the man decided to join him at the pool—had just proven to be too much for him. He was left with nothing to do but pace his apartment in solitude. He'd never had someone be so dismissive of him, like he was just a pest to be ignored, and might have been able to let it go if he hadn't witnessed the exchange between Henrick and Dardan.

What had made Henrick's blue eyes soften and then his lips curl up invitingly at a lowly hotel worker when he had Europe's premier striker sitting next to him practically begging for his attention? Tino rolled the question around in his mind on an endless loop, and the only two possible conclusions Tino could come up with were that either Henrick was really on holiday with someone, or he was playing hard to get because he knew who Tino was, hence the flirting with Dardan to make him...jealous? If that was his plan, well, he'd been successful because Tino was obsessing about the whole encounter, and damn it if he hadn't felt a flare of envy toward Dardan when he got the look Tino had been hoping he'd receive from the little blond man.

Tino couldn't resist the pull of his balcony. He walked out to lean on the railing, from which he could see the pool area, and his eyes were drawn to the spot where he'd left

Henrick over an hour earlier. He was still lying there basking in the late-afternoon sun, oblivious to the man six floors above him who was hungrily eyeing his prone form. Tino stood there mesmerized by the sight of all the skin Henrick had on display.

He didn't know how long he'd been standing there creeping on the other man like some sick pervert, but he was startled when Henrick sat up suddenly and looked around him. He stretched and pulled his sunglasses off to rub his eyes like a sleepy child. Tino smiled softly to himself when it occurred to him that Henrick had probably dozed off while relaxing by the water; good thing he'd slathered all that sunscreen on.

Tino kept watching as Henrick got up, stretched again, and walked around to the stairs that led into the pool. He walked in gingerly—the water was probably cold on his sun-heated skin—but once the water was past his shorts, he went under completely. He slowly paddled around the pool before getting out, drying off and picking up his things. Tino watched as he walked out of the pool area and back to the beach.

Tino wondered where Henrick was going, but he wasn't left in the dark for long. He only had to walk to the other side of his balcony to follow Henrick's progress, but it was worth it when he watched him walk into the apartment building next to the hotel. He now knew where the other man was staying, which may or may not come in handy if Tino decided to accidentally run into Henrick and his boyfriend to scope out the situation.

Tino stood there for a few more minutes, and just when he decided there was nothing else to see and turned to go back in, Henrick appeared on the balcony next door a couple of floors down. Tino's heart skipped a beat. He stood there frozen as he waited to see if anyone would join Henrick on the balcony, but Henrick only hung his swim trunks up on the little drying rack before disappearing back inside. Tino wasn't sure if he was relieved or not at not having seen the mysterious boyfriend, but he wasn't going to spend any more time staring at the empty balcony when his stomach told him it was time to eat.

Tino showered and dressed casually before he made his way down to the beach where he took his flip-flops off and walked barefooted at the edge of the water. The restaurant he was heading to was only about five hundred meters down the beach and was known for having the best scampi pizza in Durres. The thought of eating an entire pizza while enjoying a nice bottle of wine lifted Tino's spirits as he watched the sun start it's decent into the sea.

He hadn't been paying much attention to his surroundings, caught up in the vibrant colors of the sunset, but the familiar cadence of the Deutsch language drew his attention to a couple of men standing a few meters down the beach from him. Henrick was smiling up at another man as they spoke animatedly to each other. Tino almost stopped to watch them but decided it wouldn't do him any good to torture himself now that he knew Henrick really did have someone. He passed by silently as Henrick put his hand on the other man's arm as he laughed; the sound pierced Tino's gut as he went by them without notice.

The host at the restaurant seated Tino on the patio a little out of the way as he requested. The table afforded Tino a nice view of the beach but also a clear line of sight to the entrance of the restaurant. The waiter who came to serve him was one Tino knew well from previous visits. "Ah, Alan, it's good to see you're still around. How are the knees these days?" Tino asked the older gentleman.

"Signor Alessi, so good to see you back with us. Of course I'm still here. You know I won't let a little arthritis keep me from my work. Now what can I get for you tonight?"

"I'll have a bottle of your house wine and the antipasto with focaccia to start with, Alan." Tino ordered without looking at the menu.

"Of course, I will be right out with your wine," Alan said before he turned to leave.

Tino sat at his table and watched the four other diners, who were, of course, split into couples. They leaned close as they talked, making it seem as if everything they had to say to each other was a secret. The women's laughter was high and tinkling while the men smiled silently at the beauties they clearly treasured. Tino never had time to think about how lonely he really was. With training, traveling, and his endorsement deals, his schedule was always jam-packed, and he was starting to think it was better that way, less time for introspection.

Alan appeared at his table with an uncorked bottle of wine and made a show of pouring a small amount into one of the two wineglasses that were already on the table so Tino could taste it. Tino had just lifted the glass to his nose when a flash of blond hair caught his eye. After swirling the wine, he took a sip, while not taking his eyes off Henrick. He put his glass on the table and smiled up at Alan briefly. "This will do nicely, thanks," he said as his eyes went back to the entrance.

Henrick seemed to be alone as he stood there waiting for the host to seat him, and Tino had a flash of inspiration. "Alan, do you see that young man at the door?" Alan looked behind him and then back at Tino as he nodded. "Can you do me a favor?"

"Sure, signor Alessi, if it is in my power to do so, I will be happy to help."

"If that man asks for a table for one, would you seat him here with me?"

Alan smiled mischievously. "Of course, signor Alessi, I will see what I can do to make that happen." Alan walked over to the host and bent in close before pointing at Henrick and then at Tino while whispering into the host's ear. The host looked over at Tino and nodded.

Tino sat waiting with some apprehension as the host approached Henrick. He half hoped Henrick would be asking for a table for two, his boyfriend joining him later for whatever reason, but the other half hoped exactly what was happening would happen. The host was walking straight toward Tino's table with Henrick following him. Henrick's face went from relaxed to confused to slightly—okay, more than slightly—annoyed.

Tino plastered a big welcoming smile on his face as the waiter pulled out the chair for Henrick. Henrick looked from the chair to the waiter and then scowled at Tino before taking his seat. Tino released a breath he hadn't realized he was holding when Henrick didn't tell him to fuck himself and walk away. He really wanted to find out what was up with the other man—where was his boyfriend and why all the hostility toward Tino?

Tino gestured to the bottle of wine. Henrick squinted at Tino and then the wine, and finally, after what felt like a lifetime, he gave a slight nod. The host poured a glass of wine for Henrick and topped off Tino's almost-full glass. As soon as the host left, Alan showed up with the antipasto and focaccia bread and placed it in the center of the table.

"Would you like to place your dinner order now or later?"

Alan waited patiently while Henrick finished sipping his wine and set his glass down. "Do they speak English here or only Italian?" Henrick looked a little nervous as he waited for Tino's answer.

Tino bit his lip because the thought of Henrick having to place his order through him made Tino want to smirk, which would have been bad. "Only Italian, unless you know Albanian of course. He wants to know if we'd like to place our dinner order now or later."

Henrick sighed. "Okay I came here because I heard that they have the best—"

"Scampi pizza?" Tino interrupted him to ask.

"Yes, that's what I was told."

Tino turned to Alan. "We'll have a large scampi pizza and when this bottle of wine is empty, I would like another brought out right away."

"Of course, signor Alessi."

After the waiter had gone, Tino waited for Henrick to say something, but the man sat there studying his wineglass. Tino picked up a piece of prosciutto and a chunk of mozzarella and put them on his plate. "Try some of the antipasto; everything on the plate is very good."

Finally, Henrick glanced up from his glass at Tino. "Why am I sitting here, with you? What do you hope to gain out of hijacking my dinner?"

Tino fidgeted and then lied. "I don't hope to gain anything. I just saw you come in alone and thought if you weren't eating with your boyfriend, we both could use some company. Where is he?"

"Where's who?" Henrick asked before he picked up his wineglass again.

"Your boyfriend. I saw you both on the beach just before I came in here. I figured you were discussing where to eat."

He figured he may as well tell the truth about having seen them together; it made his question about where the boyfriend was seem less out of left field.

Henrick's brow scrunched up in a way Tino found completely endearing before it smoothed back out when the man smiled. "Oh yes, well you see, he's allergic to shellfish, and I really wanted to try the scampi pizza, so we decided to go our separate ways for dinner and meet back at the apartment afterward for dessert." Henrick lifted his eyebrow as if the intended innuendo in his words wasn't enough to make what he was hinting at clear.

Tino nodded, though something about what Henrick said didn't ring true, but he decided to play along anyway. "That sounds like fun. I'm sure he'll have a delicious dessert waiting for you." Henrick gulped his wine, and Tino quickly refilled his glass. "Have some food before that wine hits you."

Henrick picked a few bits off the plate and transferred them to his own. It amused Tino to watch the other man as he fastidiously made little bite-sized portions with an even amount of meat, cheese, olives or pickles, and bread. When he had five of the perfect little mini sandwiches constructed on his plate, he stopped building, dipped one in the seasoned olive oil, and popped it in his mouth. He chewed slowly, and his eyes fluttered shut for a moment, obviously enjoying the flavor combination he'd made. Never having felt the need to lean across a table and kiss someone the way he did at that moment, Tino was transfixed by Henrick.

Henrick's eyes popped back open, and Tino tried to pull his away from the long column of Henrick's neck as it convulsed while he swallowed. "You want one?" Henrick asked, startling Tino into grunting an unintelligible sound.

"Huh?" Tino finally managed to ask.

"Do you want to try one?" He pointed to his plate, and Tino could only nod because he really did want to try the thing that made Henrick look like he'd just tasted heaven. Henrick picked one up, dipped it in the oil, and reached across the table with it pinched between two fingers. Tino knew Henrick expected him to take it from him, but as Tino's lips closed over Henrick's fingers, he realized he probably should have used his hand.

Henrick pulled his fingers free and jerked his hand back to his side of the table. He picked up his wine and drained it for the second time, then put the glass down a little hard before looking up to meet Tino's eyes. "I know who you are, Valentino," he said as if making an accusation Tino couldn't refute. "I'll be up front with you and tell you right now that I'm not interested."

Well, that had been a bit blunt for Tino's taste, but at least he knew where he stood at the moment. Of course, hearing his name roll so easily off Henrick's tongue only made Tino want him to say it more and more and maybe even scream it a time or two.

Chapter Five

HENRICK SAW DISAPPOINTMENT in Valentino's expression after he told him he wasn't interested, but he shored up his resolve to not give into the man sitting across from him. He didn't want to be sitting there with him in the first place, so if Valentino couldn't handle the truth, too bad for him since he'd been the one to press the issue. Henrick took another sip of his wine but then put it back on the table. He was going to get drunk if he wasn't careful. He picked up a bit of his food, dipped it, and tasted it. It wasn't until he was licking the oil from his fingers that he remembered they'd just been inside Valentino's mouth. He pulled his fingers away from his lips and wiped them on the napkin instead.

"So can I ask why?" Valentino fidgeted nervously when Henrick didn't answer right away and then added, "Other than that you have a boyfriend, that is."

Henrick took a moment to ponder which one of the many reasons he should give Valentino for his disinterest in jumping into bed with him, finally settling on the one that hit closest to home for him. "I don't want to end up another Paulo Gio-whatever his name was." Referring to the last man the media had linked romantically to Valentino Alessi made the man grimace.

"I see, and what makes you think I'm interested in you in a way that would end up with you in his place?" The muscle in Valentino's clenched jaw twitched.

Henrick had to think about his response because maybe he had been assuming too much when it came to Valentino. Maybe he was just on holiday alone and wanted someone to hang out with, but why pick an obviously gay man to be that someone? Henrick was no fool. He knew people could tell he was gay without having to work at it. He didn't hide what he was and made no apologies for the fact that he was a bit swishy. Also, the looks Valentino had been giving him at the pool were anything but I-want-to-be-your-friend.

"Are you saying you weren't hitting on me at the pool?"

Valentino picked up another bite of food, put it in his mouth, and slowly chewed it. Henrick waited him out. He knew a stalling tactic when he saw it, and Valentino extended it to include a sip of wine before finally sitting forward with his elbows on the table and looking Henrick straight in the eyes. Henrick had to stop himself from falling into the light-amber pools because Valentino's eyes were beautiful up close in a way the magazine covers just couldn't capture.

"I will be totally honest with you. Yes, I was testing the waters to see if you might be interested." When Henrick opened his mouth to say something, the other man held up a finger to stop him. "But it doesn't mean you would have wound up like Paulo because you don't know the whole story behind how Paulo ended up where he did."

"You mean fired from his job and disowned by his family, or as the scapegoat for the media to pick apart until he tried to commit suicide that they then tried to cover up as an accidental overdose?" Henrick may have pushed it a little too far if the pained look on Valentino's face was any measure. He let his words hang between them for a few seconds before the guilty feeling got the better of him. "I'm sorry. You're right. I don't know the whole story, only what the media wants the public to know, but I'm sure you have people who helped decide what should be heard and what should be kept quiet."

Valentino nodded and looked like he was finally going to say something, but the old waiter chose that moment to come out with their food. Henrick sat back and waited while Valentino talked to the waiter as he removed the half-eaten appetizer. He replaced it with the pizza Henrick had wanted to try so badly, but all of a sudden, the sight of it turned his stomach a little. The waiter put a slice of pizza on his plate and then one on Valentino's before leaving them once again. Henrick stared at the food in front of him, which looked delicious, but he couldn't bring himself to touch it.

"I should have stepped in before it got to the point it did, but I was following the advice of people I trusted, and I regret that decision to this very day," Valentino said quietly.

"Did you love him?" Henrick blurted the question before he could think it through, so he tried to take it back. "You don't have to answer. It's none of my business."

Valentino's eyes softened into limpid pools, and a small smile pulled his lips up, transforming him into the most handsome man Henrick had ever seen. "I did, or at least I like to think that's what it was."

Henrick had to drink half a glass of wine to try to get enough moisture back in his mouth to reply. "Then it must have been hard for you to go through what you did with him." Henrick finally gave in and admitted that maybe Valentino had suffered over the situation too.

"Eat your pizza, Henrick, before it gets cold," Valentino said, putting an end to the conversation that obviously made him uncomfortable.

A shiver ran down Henrick's spine, but he'd be damned if he'd admit it was because of the way Valentino Alessi said his name. After taking a moment to gather himself back together, he rearranged the toppings on his slice of pizza so he'd get a taste of each of the ingredients on each precise bite he'd take. The first bite tickled his taste buds in a way that made him let out a little moan he was sure Valentino shouldn't have been able to hear, but the responding chuckle told him otherwise. He tried not to blush—he usually never got embarrassed enough to blush—as he looked shyly up at the man across the table, immediately hating the way he liked how Valentino was looking at him.

"It's good, right?" Valentino's eyes sparkled in the low light of the restaurant.

"Mmm hmmm." Henrick hummed his answer while he chewed.

"You really enjoy your food." It was a statement, not a question, so Henrick didn't feel the need to say anything in response. Valentino took a bite of his pizza, and Henrick wished he could reach over and rearrange his toppings so he'd taste what he had in his perfect bite but he resisted the urge.

"So this obviously isn't your first time in Durres. What do you do when you're here?" Henrick tried for a normal conversation once he'd swallowed the food in his mouth.

Valentino finished his slice in two bites and grabbed another before he answered. "Well, normally I just do the usual holiday things. Swimming, sunbathing, boating occasionally, but this time I'm actually looking for some property." Valentino refilled their glasses with the new bottle of wine the waiter had stealthily dropped off.

"What sort of property are you looking at?" Henrick asked before he took another amazing bite.

"A holiday home."

"Have you seen anything you like yet?" Henrick liked that they had found a safe topic of conversation and would gladly talk about vacation homes for the rest of the evening if it meant the end of the awkwardness between them.

Valentino peered at him over the rim of his wineglass. There was that little twinkle in his eyes again like he was also enjoying the topic. "Not really, but I've only been out one day. I'm not sure what I'm looking for exactly," he admitted.

"I know what I'd want if I were looking for a house here." Henrick finished his pizza and smiled at Valentino when he put another on his plate.

"Tell me then, what would you want if you were looking for a house, and money wasn't an object?"

Henrick smiled at the thought of having the kind of money the man sitting across from him did and going to buy a house on the beach. Sipping his wine, he wondered when his light buzz had turned into something a little more like tipsy.

"I would want a house with a huge portico and a pool that looked out onto the sea. A big outdoor kitchen with a firepit and outdoor seating for at least twenty so I could throw parties." Henrick stared over Valentino's shoulder, imagining his dream home.

"What about the inside, or do you plan on living outside?" Valentino asked with a chuckle.

Henrick found himself laughing along before he answered. "No, don't be silly. Of course, the inside would be spectacular too. There would be a huge gourmet kitchen, maybe with patio doors that opened completely to the outside, so when you have a party it's all open space. Then, in the living room, there'd be stone floors with plush rugs, a big fireplace, and high ceilings with exposed beams, sort of like a ski lodge to remind me of home a bit. Upstairs, there would be a huge master suite. The bathroom would have one of those showers that has like ten heads and a tub big enough for two with ten jets. The bedroom would have a huge bed with down comforters and ten pillows. There would, of course, be a balcony, where you could drink your morning coffee, and right next to the doors would be another fireplace with two chairs where you could curl up with a blanket and read a book." Henrick finally stopped when he realized he'd been talking for an awfully long time. He was drunker than he thought.

Valentino was laughing at him, and this time Henrick did feel the heat of a blush creep onto his cheeks. "Sorry. I guess I was on a roll there," Henrick apologized.

"Don't, there's nothing to be sorry for. I liked listening to you describe the house of your dreams." Valentino paused and stared at Henrick for a bit before he cocked his head and smiled. "But I do need to know a couple of things now."

"Oh and what are those things?" Taking another drink of wine he surely didn't need, Henrick waited for Valentino's questions.

"One, what's with needing ten of everything? Two, I noticed you liked to eat, so do you also cook, because you seemed to be pretty focused on having not one but two big kitchens? Three, would the chairs in the master bedroom be negotiable?" His crooked grin lent him a boyish charm that Henrick would need to be on guard against.

Henrick heaved an exaggerated sigh for Valentino's benefit before he answered. "When I like something, I tend to go overboard, and ten seems to be a good number. I can't cook anything except noodles, but I fully intend to find a man who can cook for me—that in fact *is* the number one thing I look for in a man. And why would the chairs be up for negotiation, Valentino?"

"Call me Tino, Henrick, please." Henrick nodded. "So you don't cook? At all?"

Henrick sat up a little straighter. "Why? Because I'm small? Because the short skinny guy is always supposed to do the woman's work like cooking and cleaning while the big strong manly men go out and make all the money?" It irritated Henrick that people always assumed because some of his mannerisms were effeminate he naturally would tend to do traditionally feminine things.

"No, I just thought you liked to cook, but if your boyfriend cooks for you, then who am I to say anything?"

He could tell Valentino was trying to placate him, but his hackles were still up.

Henrick snorted into his wineglass. "Yeah, right." Henrick downed the rest of his wine.

"Are you saying he doesn't cook for you?"

Once again, Henrick's mouth betrayed him, but at least this time he could blame it on the alcohol. "He never even took me out to eat, let alone cooked a meal for me." Henrick was thinking of Klaus instead of his fake boyfriend. His eyes started to burn with unshed tears at the thought of what he'd never had and couldn't see himself getting if he kept going the way he was.

A hand on his cheek startled him into looking up. Valentino was still the most attractive man Henrick had ever seen, even through the wavy haze of his tear-filled eyes, but his mind wasn't so far gone as to forget the danger that lay ahead if he allowed anything to happen between them. Just as Valentino's thumb wiped away the first drop of moisture that managed to escape and run down his cheek, Henrick jolted back in his chair.

"Henrick," Valentino said softly.

"I'm sorry. I had too much to drink. I need to go." Henrick got shakily to his feet, pulled out his wallet, and threw some lek on the table. He had no idea how much the meal cost, but he wasn't going to hang around to find out. "Thank you for the company."

"Henrick, you don't have to go." Henrick shook his head while turning away to hide the rest of the tears that threatened to fall. "Please, at least let me pay the check and walk you back. I want to make sure you get home safely." Valentino stood and grabbed Henrick's arm to stop him.

"That's not a good idea. I need to go. I'll be fine." Henrick shook free of the other man's grip and walked as steadily as he could manage to the door.

Once Henrick was outside on the beach, he ran. The cooler night air helped to clear his head just a bit, and the blood pumping hard through his veins sobered him some by the time he reached his building. Taking the stairs two at a time to his floor, he unlocked the door with a shaky hand. He felt much better when the door was locked behind him—providing him at least some measure of comfort in knowing there was a firm barrier between him and Valentino freaking Alessi.

TINO CALLED ALAN over so he could pay the bill. Henrick was drunk, and Tino wanted to get out of the restaurant as quickly as possible to make sure he made it back to his apartment in one piece. Something about the sad, vulnerable look on Henrick's sweet face made Tino want to protect him—even if it was just from himself. Alan caught on to Tino's urgency and quickly ran his credit card and returned with the slip for him to sign. Tino grabbed the cash Henrick had thrown on the table and realized there was almost five times what the meal cost in the pile. Henrick would wake up thinking he'd been robbed.

Tino looked for Henrick the minute his foot hit the sand, but there were only a few people out strolling in the moonlight and none of them were the little blond he was looking for. Jogging down the beach, Tino kept his eyes on the sand, looking for fresh footprints leading into the water. He hoped fervently that Henrick, in his inebriated state, hadn't decided going for a swim was a good idea, but there wasn't anyone flailing about in the water to fuel that fear, so Tino put it out of his mind. He made it to the apartment building he'd spied Henrick in earlier. There was no way Henrick could have made it all that way in the few minutes it had taken Tino to pay the bill, unless he'd run at a full sprint, which Tino found highly improbable since he'd been quite unsteady on his feet when he left the restaurant.

Tino stood there in indecision. Should he try to figure out which apartment Henrich occupied, based on his knowledge of where the balcony was, and charge in there to make sure Henrick was safe, or should he back off, figuring the man could look after himself? Knowing if he barged in on Henrick and his boyfriend he'd lose whatever small inroads to friendship he'd made that evening, he stepped back and looked up to Henrick's balcony. There were lights on behind the blinds, but Tino stood there until he saw a definite shadow pass by one of the windows that was Henrick sized, giving him confirmation that Henrick was indeed safely inside.

Tino sighed in relief and let out a shaky chuckle before chiding himself for being stupid enough to think Henrick needed his help. He was a grown man. He didn't need Tino to walk him home like a child. After Henrick's outburst about the smaller man being looked at as the one who filled the woman's role in a relationship, Tino knew Henrick most likely wouldn't appreciate his concern. Tino fingered the wad of bills in his pocket and smiled. He had a legitimate reason to see Henrick again right at his fingertips. With that thought in mind, Tino headed into the hotel's bar for a quick nightcap to further calm his nerves.

IT TOOK TINO exactly thirty seconds to figure out that the sound of the shower running was what had interrupted the best dream he'd ever had. He'd been dreaming of Henrick, of course. They were in Henrick's dream home, and somehow Tino had managed to prepare a perfect dinner for them, even though he couldn't cook more than eggs and toast on a good day. He'd made after-dinner coffees, and they'd taken them up to the master suite to sit in front of the fire because in his dream there was a chill in the air, causing Henrick to cuddle into his side as they watched the logs crackle, and in the distance, the sun set over a dark choppy sea that could only mean winter was upon them.

The shower stopped abruptly, and Tino tensed because he had no idea who was about to come through the door. He pretended to be asleep but on his side with one eye cracked enough to catch a glimpse of the hairy legs that stuck out from beneath one of the hotel's immaculately white towels as they walked across the bedroom. The hair on the legs was dark, telling Tino he hadn't by some miracle ended the booze-filled night in the bar with Henrick in his bed.

To Tino's surprise, the man didn't try to wake him but instead quickly and quietly dressed. Tino rolled onto his back, still feigning sleep, so he could see exactly whom he'd spent the night with. The man didn't look back at the bed as he walked to the door. Tino was startled when he looked into the mirrored closet door, and his eyes met those of the young father he'd watched at the pool the previous day. The emotions on the man's face changed quickly from surprise to fear, but ultimately, a truly regretful, guilty look won out as he turned to break the indirect eye contact. He didn't say anything as he left, and Tino didn't think he had any right to try to soothe the man's guilty conscience, so he let him take his silent leave.

Closing his eyes, the night came rushing back to Tino. The shots, the young man so enamored of the big football star who had struck up a conversation with him that he forgave the occasional roaming hand lingering too long on his arm or his thigh. More shots, then to the bathroom where Tino pushed the young man up against the wall and rubbed his hardness against the shorter man's taut stomach and promised unimaginable pleasures if he'd just follow Tino to his apartment. The hesitant look on the guy's face, as he got into the elevator with Tino, turned to pure need as Tino pinned him face-first into the wall of the elevator and reached around to shove his hand into the man's shorts so he could fondle the other's arousal. The whispered, *I've never done this before. I don't know how*, sent shivers down Tino's spine as he sank to his knees in the very room where he was now lying and took the swollen length to the back of his throat, silencing the young man except for the soft moans escaping his full parted lips.

Tino shut the memory down then because, after the look the young man had given him while trying to sneak out, the guilt lay heavily on his chest. He'd used his fame to make a starstruck fan bend to his wishes, something he tried very hard never to do. It was one of the first lessons Nigel Collins, his mentor, had taught him—do not abuse the power you have because of your position. The only consolation Tino had was he hadn't done anything more than blow the guy before rubbing greedily against the young man to attain his own orgasm.

After climbing out of bed, Tino called down to order breakfast before getting in the shower. He timed it almost perfectly so his meal was being set up on his balcony soon after he'd gotten dressed. He tipped the guy and sat down to eat, but before he could dig into his ham and eggs, a familiar voice pulled him to the railing. Looking down, he found Henrick on his own balcony with a cell phone pressed to his ear. He was pacing as he talked—rather loudly at times. Tino wished he knew more than a few words in Deutsch because whatever Henrick was saying seemed to be upsetting him more and more as the conversation dragged on.

Finally, Henrick ended the call, slammed his phone down on the table, and sank into one of the chairs, putting his face in his hands. Henrick's shoulders shook, but he cried silently or at least too quietly for the sound to reach Tino, who stood above him helpless to provide the comfort he could tell Henrick so desperately needed. He briefly thought about calling out to the other man but stopped when Henrick stood abruptly and wiped angrily at his eyes before turning and disappearing into the apartment.

Tino returned to his cold breakfast and wondered if Henrick had been talking to the man who never cooked for him. He shouldn't be happy, but if Henrick broke up with his current boyfriend, it meant Tino might get a shot at proving he wasn't just after a quick fuck. Then he would have to figure out a way to get Henrick to see beyond the public persona to the real Tino so he could convince him that no matter what happened in the future, there would never be another Paulo because the next time Tino was in that situation, he was going to step up for the man he loved.

TINO WASN'T PROUD that he'd taken to stalking Henrick from his balcony. On the first day, while Tino had been finishing his coffee, he watched as Henrick exited his building and walked out onto the beach. He talked to Dardan—making the hair on the back of Tino's neck stand up—and after some laughing and arm touching, Henrick made his way to the front row of chairs and spread out his things. He lay there in the sun, looking totally relaxed despite his earlier phone conversation.

Tino got up after about twenty minutes and placed a call to his real estate agent to set up a time to look at some more properties later in the day. He couldn't sit there and stare down at Henrick for hours no matter how much he wanted to. Then he called Rijeka, the supermodel who also happened to be Tino's girlfriend, and left a message with her personal assistant because she was still sleeping and would be until at least early afternoon. Tino knew her schedule, which was why he'd opted to call when he did. He loved Rijeka as a friend but she was like a protective mama bear when the press was after him, and he just couldn't deal with her yet.

Marco was waiting in the parking lot for him when he arrived, so Tino got in the other man's car after greeting him with a wave. "Did you have any success in finding what I described?"

Marco cleared his throat. "Well, I'm not sure we'll be able to find everything you wanted. There are a few that have many of the options you listed. I'm very pleased you've given this more thought. It'll be much easier to at least weed out the ones that are completely wrong for you."

"I guess you can say I had my eyes opened to the possibilities, and now I know better what I'm looking for." Tino was thinking of the way Henrick's face had gone all dreamy as he described the perfect holiday home. Not that Tino had any expectations of Henrick ever seeing the home he decided on, but Tino realized all the things Henrick had wanted would please him too. At least it was a start.

"I'm willing to do the footwork now that you've a clearer picture of a home that you'll love," Marco said after giving Tino his best park-bench-picture smile.

They looked at many homes that day, but every one of them was lacking at least one crucial ingredient. By the end of the six-hour tour, Marco had started telling Tino that if it was just something cosmetic, he could always have it changed to suit him. Tino was starting to think it might be his only option if he wanted the perfect house.

On the second and third days, Henrick followed the same routine, going to the beach and managing to get the same two chairs in the front row even though there were beachgoers who arrived earlier than him. He always spoke to Dardan for a few minutes before making himself comfortable, and Tino watched him every morning until he had to meet with Marco to view more properties. Tino noticed when Henrick's skin started to take on a golden glow that gave him a healthier look than the pale creaminess of his skin presunbathing.

With an envelope in hand, Tino made his way down to the beach. He'd waited until Henrick waded out into the sea so he wouldn't *accidentally* run into him. Waving Dardan down, he waited while the smiling young man jogged over to him.

"Hey there, signor Alessi, what can I do for you today?" Dardan asked cheerfully.

"I was wondering if you would give this to the young German man I was sitting by the pool with the other day." Tino held out the envelope containing Henrick's money.

Dardan's eyebrows furrowed, and Tino waited for the unspoken question that didn't come; instead, Dardan took the envelope from Tino's hand. "Sure, signor Alessi, I'll make sure he gets it." Dardan looked over his shoulder to the sea where the recipient of Tino's letter was obliviously floating some three hundred meters out.

"Thank you, Dar, I appreciate it." With his mission accomplished, Tino turned on his heel and left.

He'd tried and failed to convince himself the money was his way to start up a conversation with Henrick. A way to get the man to agree to have lunch with him or dinner which would lead to more talking and eventually maybe a tender good-night kiss when Henrick let Tino walk him to his door, but Tino didn't want a contrived meeting. He wanted this thing with Henrick to happen naturally, if it was going to happen at all, so he removed the temptation the only way he knew he could without Henrick finding out Tino knew where he was staying. He didn't want to just slip the envelope under Henrick's door and have him get the wrong idea about Tino's intentions. He would be patient, and hopefully, Henrick would come to him.

Chapter Six

HENRICK SETTLED INTO a routine in the days following his run-in with Valentino—call me Tino—Alessi. He woke early, ate breakfast, packed himself a small lunch, and went to the beach. On the second day of his holiday, Dardan, the beach chair boy, approached him and told him he'd saved Henrick a set of chairs in the front row, and so it went that he always had the best seat, even if he was later than the other beachgoers. Henrick got in the habit of talking to Dardan when the guy passed by, so when Dardan approached him on the third day, after he'd waded out of the sea in search of a drink and some warming rays, he smiled a genuine smile for the nervous-looking young man.

"Mr. Henrick." Dardan always called him mister even though Henrick had told him time and again. "I have something for you."

He continued to smile even though, up close, Dardan looked more distressed than he did nervous. "I told you, Dar, it's just Henrick. What have you got there?" He noticed Dardan was holding an envelope in his outstretched hand.

"It's for you. Signor Alessi gave it to me and asked me to pass it on to you." Henrick knew the near panic surfacing on his face at the mere mention of the man's name was uncalled for and felt bad when Dardan hastily added, "I'm sorry I couldn't just tell him no. It is my job after all."

Henrick made himself smile again as he took the small package from Dardan's hand. It was thick with whatever

Valentino had decided to give him. "It's fine, Dar. To tell you the truth I'd rather you give it to me than him." He added a flirty wink because he liked how it always affected Dardan.

Dardan's cheeks pinked a little, but the shy smile betrayed how much he liked being the object of Henrick's flirtation. "I sort of figured that, Mr. Henrick. That's another reason why I didn't tell him no."

He touched Dardan's muscular bare chest with the lightest of touches. "I appreciate that, Dar. Thank you again for being so good to me." The oily sun-warmed skin under his fingertips broke out in gooseflesh, which made Henrick's smile even brighter.

"It's not hard to be good to you," Dar said and then blushed in earnest at his own words.

Laughing, he slapped Dardan lightly with the hand he had already resting on his chest. "You better get back to work before you get in trouble." He was curious about what he was holding, but he didn't want to open it in front of anyone in case it upset him.

Dardan beamed at him. "You're right, Mr. Henrick. I may end up in trouble if I stay around you too much longer." Then he surprised Henrick by adding a wink of his own before jogging away.

Henrick plopped down on his chair. It was getting harder and harder to convince himself that a little holiday fling with the cute young native, who was obviously interested, was a bad idea. Sighing, he stared at the envelope like maybe he'd be granted X-ray vision and not have to open it, but when that didn't happen, he decided there was no time like the present. He tore the flap open and peered cautiously inside, then giggled because he felt a little ridiculous when there was only what looked like paper inside. What had he expected? A snake to pop out at him?

He pulled the paper out and unfolded it to find a pile of lek. Henrick couldn't figure out why Tino would be giving him money, and thankfully there was writing on the paper that explained it to him. Tino's handwriting was short and blocky but totally readable.

Henrick, you left this the other night at the restaurant to cover the tab. I'm sure you didn't realize how much you'd left—more than enough to cover the meal many times over. I'm sorry it took me so long to return it to you, but you know how holidays go—you seem to lose track of time, and before you know it days have passed you by. Thank you again for your company that night. I enjoyed the time spent with you, and if you ever want to do it again just ask at the front desk of the hotel for me. Codeword: Pavarotti. Hope you are having a lovely holiday. Yours, Tino.

Henrick read the little note over and over. He remembered leaving the money, but he hadn't bothered to do the conversion to figure out how much he'd actually thrown down in his hurry to escape. He counted out the lek and quickly did the math—crap, there was over three hundred euros there. That would teach him to get drunk and run. It could have been a costly mistake if Valentino hadn't been an honest man. Of course, it wasn't like Valentino needed the money, but still it was nice that he'd returned it.

Henrick studiously ignored the invitation to repeat the experience because as much as he had to admit the man was attractive, he just couldn't get past Valentino's history. At best, he would end up being just another notch in the other man's belt, and at worst—Henrick shuddered before he cut that thought short. There was going to be no best or worst in this situation because he was going to take pains to give Valentino freaking Alessi a wide berth.

HIS PLAN WORKED perfectly for a couple more days, but on his fifth day of lying on the beach, things took a turn in an unexpected direction. Having just woken from his afternoon doze, Henrick's vision was a bit blurry, but he swore he saw a god rising from the sea. Henrick reached up and rubbed his eyes, but the vision was still there. The sun was directly overhead and so bright that it cast a white haze around everything as Henrick grabbed his sunglasses and slipped them on while the vision walked toward him.

With the shade from his lenses taking the sting out of the sun, Henrick recognized the man standing in front of him. Valentino smiled down at Henrick, making his heart thud against his ribs. Henrick closed his eyes to break the spell the sun and the beautiful man were trying to weave over him, but when he reopened them, he spotted something else that set his pulse racing even faster. Why hadn't he noticed the tattoo just peeking out of the other man's tiny speedos the other day at the pool? *What was hiding under there?*

"Mind if I sit here for a moment?" Valentino asked as he continued to drip in front of Henrick.

"Um..." Henrick dragged his eyes off the perfect V of the other man's abdomen. "I guess so. I mean, yeah, yes you can."

"Thank you." Valentino sat on the chair facing Henrick. He seemed to be searching Henrick's face for something because Henrick could almost feel those eyes caressing him as they roved over his skin.

"What?" Henrick finally broke down and asked when he could no longer stand the scrutiny.

Valentino shook his head slightly. "Nothing...just... I was wondering, did you get the package I left with Dardan?"

Henrick's face heated because he should have thanked Valentino for returning the money. It had been rude not to. "Yes, he gave it to me. Thank you. I didn't realize how much it was."

"The currency can be tricky when you're not used to it. I would have returned it to you sooner but—"

"Yes, I read your note and it's not a problem. To be honest, I hadn't realized it yet, but I appreciate that you returned it all the same." Henrick interrupted Valentino because he didn't want to hear whatever excuse he was going to use for not having the time to return the money. Even if Henrick wasn't interested in Valentino, it didn't mean hearing about his other conquests was something he wanted to pass the time with.

They sat there in silence for a bit until Valentino asked, "Would you consider doing something with me?"

Henrick screwed up his face and bit his tongue to stop himself from saying no before he heard the man's request. "I guess it depends on what it is."

Valentino grinned and pointed to the choppy sea. "Would you go bodysurfing with me? The waves are perfect for it, and there's hardly anyone out there. How about it?"

Henrick shook his head. "I don't know the first thing about surfing."

"Well, luckily, I grew up only a few kilometers from the beach, so you have a good teacher sitting right next to you." Valentino was sure full of himself, but before Henrick could tell him so, he made puppy dog eyes and begged a little. "Please, Henrick, I promise you'll have fun."

Henrick thought about it for another minute. He had to admit he was getting bored after spending so much time alone on the beach. It would be nice to have someone to do something with, but why did it have to be something he knew nothing about and was bound to make a fool out of himself in front of Valentino trying? He looked at Valentino's hopeful expression and gave in.

"Okay, but you have to promise not to laugh at me."

Valentino put his hand over his heart. "I promise, on the name of my father, that I will not laugh at you. Besides, I'm sure you'll get the hang of it quickly."

"Oh I don't know about that. I'm not terribly athletic," Henrick disagreed.

Valentino stood. "I don't believe that for a minute. You look incredibly athletic." He made a show of looking Henrick's body up and down, making Henrick snort as he stood. "Come on, I know where we can get a couple of boards."

Henrick followed Valentino down the beach a bit to a guy who had a bike with a type of trailer built onto it. There were all kinds of water toys hanging from various nails on the top of the frame. When Henrick looked closer, he realized the guy was selling everything a person could ever need on the beach from sunscreen to swimming trunks. If you could use it at the sea, this guy had it. Henrick stood by while Valentino spoke to the guy in Italian. They must have been haggling because it took a few minutes before Valentino produced a little pouch from the inside of his speedos—Henrick had no idea where it had been hiding in the skintight fabric—and handed over some euros in exchange for a couple of small boards.

"Here's yours." Valentino handed Henrick the bright neon-yellow board and kept the blue one for himself.

"I could have paid for it. I thought you were just renting them."

"Don't worry about it. It was my idea. I'll pay for the equipment we need."

Henrick stopped walking. "Valentino, I don't need for you to pay. I make plenty of money to pay for my own things." Not understanding why it bothered him so much to have the other man pay for something so small, Henrick couldn't help but voice his concern over it anyway.

Stopping and turning back to Henrick, Tino put the hand not holding the board on his hip. "I never said you couldn't afford to pay for it, and if it will make you feel better, I'll either take the extra board back when we're done, or you can pay me for it. Now can you stop being pissy so we can go have some fun?"

Henrick felt like an ass all of a sudden. "Okay let's go then, but please try not to get me drowned." Henrick tried to lighten the mood again, and Valentino's crooked grin proved he'd been successful.

"I'll make you a deal. If you will call me Tino like I asked you to, I'll make sure you don't drown."

Henrick rolled his eyes. "Fine, *Tino,* but now if I drown, the blame will be squarely on your shoulders. My life, as they say, is in your hands."

A strange look passed over Tino, making Henrick wish he could take his little tease back, but then a smirk appeared on his handsome face. "Oh well, then I guess I better make sure you know what you're doing when I get you on your stomach." Henrick's eyebrows hit his hairline in surprise at the obvious double entendre which made Tino chortle. "On the board, Henrick. You'll be on your stomach when you're surfing. Get your mind out of the gutter."

Tino turned and walked into the surf before Henrick could even form a comeback, let alone get it out of his suddenly too-dry mouth. He hoped he wasn't making a huge mistake as he gripped his board to his chest and followed Tino into the chilly water.

"OKAY, SO YOU just paddle out again, and this time when the wave starts to come, you turn toward the beach and stroke hard until you feel it lift you. Then you just hold on and enjoy the ride," Tino instructed Henrick once more. They'd caught maybe ten waves and each time Henrick got better, but he was still hesitating when it came to paddling with the wave to get on top of it. "The swells are breaking sooner, so we should go out a bit farther to catch them earlier."

Henrick nodded, indicating that he understood the instructions. "Okay, I think I'm starting to get it."

Tino liked that Henrick was having fun even if he wasn't getting it perfect right away. It was nice to just hang with him, but it made it even better to know that the other man knew things didn't just come easy, he had to work at it. Tino watched as Henrick lay on his board and started to head back out. He followed but stayed a good distance away to avoid a collision when the wave took them.

"Let the next one pass. It's too small and will break too soon," Tino shouted to Henrick over the sound of the waves. Henrick gave him a thumbs-up to show he'd heard, and they lay there bobbing as the small wave passed. When Tino spotted one that looked good, he signaled to Henrick that they were a go. He made sure Henrick pointed his board toward the beach and started paddling just as Tino had instructed him to do before he began his own journey toward the shore.

The thrill of the ride hit Tino as the wave pushed him up, but the feeling lasted for only a few seconds because the wave broke quickly, pulling Tino under the water and tossing him about before he figured out which way was up and was able to surface. He sputtered and wiped at the salty water and hair that was blinding him. Once he could see again, he searched the waves for Henrick, hoping he'd gotten ahead of the wave enough to spare him the wipeout Tino had just suffered.

After a quick sweep of the shallow water near the beach with no luck in spotting Henrick, Tino turned his eyes farther out with a growing sense of dread. When Tino spied Henrick's bright-yellow board bobbing in the waves, but no Henrick, the dread turned to panic. Tino had been steadily making his way to where he'd last seen Henrick, but he changed direction and started swimming full out toward the riderless board.

Tino stood in the chest-deep water next to the board and searched the water for signs of life. When he assured himself Henrick wasn't making his way to the beach, he started to walk the area in tight circles. Then he saw Henrick's blond head a few feet away from him, facedown no less, and the adrenaline surged into his bloodstream. He was there lifting Henrick's limp body out of the water faster than he could ever have imagined he'd get there and wasted no time in slinging Henrick's slight weight over his shoulder. Henrick made a retching noise when Tino's shoulder hit his midsection, and Tino felt the warm fluid being expelled from Henrick's limp form run down his back. Henrick stilled after the involuntary vomiting stopped, and Tino started running as fast as he could through the waist-deep water.

When Tino got about fifty meters from dry land, he started calling for help. There were few people on the beach since it was nearing dinnertime and most people didn't care to swim in the choppy water, so Tino set his sights on the one person he knew would be of some assistance. Dardan was there within seconds and helped get Henrick off Tino's shoulder and onto the wet sand. Tino knew what needed to be done, but he couldn't steady his hands enough to administer the first aid himself, so instead, thanked god when Dardan started doing it.

"Push number six on the speed dial," Dardan said as he dug his phone out of his pocket. "It's the hotel's doctor. Tell him we need him here and to call 1-2-7 before he comes." Tino took the phone as Dardan turned back to Henrick and slapped his face gently. "Henrick, can you hear me?"

Tino turned away and made the call to the hotel's doctor. The sounds coming from a couple of feet away as Dardan worked on Henrick made Tino's stomach turn. He couldn't watch because it was his fault Henrick was lying there lifeless on the cold, wet sand. He'd promised to keep him safe and he'd failed.

"There we go. Just lie still, you're going to be fine, but I need to make sure you're not injured anywhere." Dardan's soothing voice made Tino turn back quickly to the scene.

Tino's heart started beating frantically at the sight of Henrick's dazed eyes, not because they were a bit unfocused, but because they were open and trained on him. Tino tried to decipher the look Henrick was giving him to see if it was blame in those murky blue eyes, but then Dardan drew Henrick's attention back to him. Tino was left with an uneasy feeling in the pit of his stomach as Henrick stared up at Dardan with a mixture of gratitude and worship.

Dardan ran his fingers through Henrick's hair as he murmured to him low enough that Tino couldn't make out the words. Jealousy coiled hotly in Tino's chest as he watched the caresses. He wanted to push Dardan away and stake his claim right then and there, regardless of the fact that Henrick was injured and in need of medical attention. But then Tino reminded himself that this was real life, not a game. There was no calling the ball in real life, and besides, Henrick wasn't up for grabs.

The hotel doctor finally made his way toward them, moving as fast as a man in his sixties could over loose sand.

He had one of those old-fashioned doctor's bags in one hand and a phone pressed to his ear in the other. Tino turned back to find Dardan's hands running over Henrick's neck and then down his shoulders. Tino bit his tongue and waited for the doctor to tell Dardan to stop feeling up the patient.

To Tino's surprise, the doctor did no such thing as he got gingerly to his knees on the opposite side of Henrick. "He's got a good-sized knob on his head just above but behind his right ear, probably where the board hit him. His pulse is steady and respiration is normal. I didn't feel any other injuries around his neck or back, and he has sensation in all his limbs. You'll want to check his pupils since I don't have a penlight so I couldn't do that. I'm thinking possible concussion," Dardan said, surprising the crap out of Tino with his medical knowledge.

The doctor took out a blood pressure cuff and handed it over to Dardan before searching his bag and pulling out a penlight. The two worked together like seasoned professionals, and Tino started to wonder exactly who Dardan was. "Pupils are equal and seem reactive. What is his blood pressure?" the doctor asked after checking Henrick's eyes.

"One fifteen over seventy, a little low but not bad. He answered all the questions correctly, so I think there's little chance that it's serious enough to need a CAT scan. Maybe if he has someone watch him through the night, it would keep him from having to go to emergency." Henrick just lay there silently as the men discussed him, and Tino wondered what was going through his head.

"Yes, I would agree. Is he staying in the hotel? I am here all weekend, so if there was a problem I could always see to him if he's close by." The doctor was still examining Henrick, but it seemed both he and Dardan had already come to their conclusions.

"He can stay with me. I'm staying at the hotel and I can watch him." Tino seized the chance to be the one to take care of Henrick before Dardan could step in and take over again. He shifted when all three men looked at him; perhaps they had forgotten he was still there. "That is, if he doesn't want to go to the hospital," Tino added to make himself look less eager.

"Henrick, do you want to go get checked out? I'm pretty sure they aren't going to do much more than Dr. Dushku and I have done, but it's your decision to make," Dardan said.

Henrick's eyes flicked from Dardan to Tino and held, and Tino smiled what he hoped was a reassuring smile. "Can you help me sit up?" Henrick asked while still looking at Tino. It was Dardan who slid an arm under Henrick and gently lifted him so he was upright. Henrick's hand went to his forehead. Tino wanted to demand that he go to the hospital, but Henrick dropped his hand quickly and once again looked to Tino. "I think I feel okay. I don't want to go to emergency unless you really think I need to."

"I think you will be fine but someone needs to stay with you, and you need to stay awake for a few hours. I have some papers I can give you on the aftercare for such an injury as you have sustained," the doctor said.

"I know all about concussions and how to watch for signs of things worsening." Tino was an athlete after all, and he'd had his share of knocks to the head.

"Okay then I guess..." Henrick said but then paused and the other men waited. "I guess you're it." He finished his thought while looking at Tino.

"Dar, do you want to help me get him to my apartment?" Tino asked, taking control of the situation. Tino tore his eyes away from Henrick when Dardan didn't answer him right away. Dardan had a dark look on his face that Tino didn't really care for, but Tino matched it with one of his own until the other man broke the stare down by turning his head to look at Henrick.

"Yes," Dardan said curtly. He stood and gave the old doctor a hand before he bent and picked Henrick up into his arms. Henrick gave a small squeak at the unexpected act, but Dardan ignored it as he turned and strode up the path to the hotel, leaving Tino to follow with the doctor.

"Thank you for rushing down here to help him," Tino said.

"Oh, it's no problem. That is what I am here for, anyway. You were lucky Dardan was there. That boy has saved more lives working on this beach than he will in his first year at hospital," the doctor said.

Tino's brow furrowed at the doctor's words, and he couldn't keep from asking about them. "What do you mean by his first year in the hospital?"

"Well, once he finishes his studies he will no doubt be recruited by a fine medical facility, though his father wants him to follow in his own footsteps. Dardan has been in the top of his class since he was a small boy. His father brags endlessly about him when we go to football matches together."

"His father is a doctor?" It was a surprising fact to learn because if it was true then Dardan was an anomaly. A person from a wealthy family who was working a menial job was not something that happened often. It also meant Dardan was more of a challenger for Henrick's attention than Tino had previously thought. One could overlook a harmless flirtation with a beach worker while on vacation, but when that seasonal worker turned out to have a promising future, it changed things. Tino was suddenly seeing Dardan in a whole new light, and he wasn't liking that his competition had just gotten stiffer.

"Oh yes, he was in fact the head doctor for the Albanian national team until he retired two years ago," the doctor said as they entered the hotel.

Dardan was standing by the elevator, still holding Henrick to his chest, waiting for Tino. Tino tried not to do what his mind and body ached to do—he wasn't going to walk up to Dardan and tear Henrick out of his arms and tell him to go to hell. Tino told himself Dardan was only being helpful like he always was, but Tino's new knowledge of the man wouldn't let him see the lowly beach worker any longer. Dardan now looked like what he really was and had been all along—a worthy challenger for Henrick's affections.

Tino thanked the doctor one more time before he bid him good evening. He pushed the button for the elevator, and they all entered silently. The ride up, though short, was incredibly awkward, and Tino sighed in relief when he opened the door to his apartment to let Dardan enter with Henrick in front of him.

Dardan went straight for the couch, but Henrick protested. "Not on the couch. I'm full of sand. Just put me down, and I'll sit at the counter."

Dardan looked to Tino for help, so he rushed to the bathroom and pulled a couple of towels off the shelf. He covered the couch haphazardly but good enough that Henrick allowed Dardan to set him on it. Tino expected Dardan to leave once his duty was done, but instead, he sat next to Henrick on the couch.

"Henrick, Tino is here to take care of you, but I want to give you my phone number in case you need anything." Dardan pulled his little notepad and pen out of his pocket. He scribbled on a piece of paper before ripping it out and handing it to Henrick. "You call me anytime if you need anything, no matter how small or no matter what time, you can call me."

Henrick took the paper; then he gasped and Tino rushed to his other side, but Henrick didn't notice him there. "I left everything on the beach. My phone was in my bag," Henrick said, trying to push himself up.

Grabbing his arm, Dardan held him in place at the same time as Tino reached for his other arm. "I'll get all your things and yours, signor Alessi, and bring them up to you." Dardan let go of Henrick and stood, but Henrick grabbed his hand.

"Thank you so much for everything." Henrick wiped a tear from his eye. "Thank you for saving my life."

Tino wanted to gather Henrick into his arms and comfort him, but Dardan was standing there looking at him with the same emotion Tino supposed was on his own face. He could only watch as Dardan bent down and gently hugged Henrick. "You're very welcome, but signor Alessi was the one who pulled you out, and if he hadn't acted quickly, I'm afraid we wouldn't be sitting here. He is the hero." Tino wondered how much it galled the man to have to give Tino some of the credit for saving Henrick's life.

"I figured he did," Henrick said into Dardan's chest.

Dardan released Henrick and stood to look at Tino. "I'll get your things and bring them up as soon as I can."

Tino walked him to the door while he fished the little pouch out of his swim trunks. Dardan opened the door to leave, but Tino stopped him as he stuck out his hand which held all the money that was left after his day on the beach. "Here, take this for your services. You did much more than your job today, and you should be compensated," Tino said, speaking in Italian so Henrick wouldn't hear him insulting the man responsible for saving his life. Tino knew what he was doing by reminding Dardan of his place. It wasn't like him to be petty, and he hated himself for letting the jealousy drive him to it, but it didn't stop him.

Dardan looked at the money Tino was offering and wrinkled his nose in disgust. "There's no need to tip me for doing something I would do ten times over for free. Just remember that he doesn't like you before you try to do what you always do. Not everyone was put on this planet to please you, signor Alessi." Dardan turned and left him with his words ringing in Tino's ears.

Chapter Seven

HENRICK WASN'T SURE if it was the best idea in the world to go back to Tino's apartment to recover from almost dying, but he was too tired to care once Dardan set him down. He sat there on the couch with his head thrown back against the cushion, eyes closed, waiting to see what Tino would do once they were alone. He thought about Dardan and let a little smile tickle his lips at the thought of Dardan's arms around him. It was so the wrong time to be thinking the thoughts he was thinking, but Henrick had really liked being pressed against that firm chest as he'd been carried from the beach. Even the indignity of being treated like a damsel in distress hadn't stopped the uptick in his pulse at the closeness of another hard male body. The cushion dipped on his right side as Tino sat next to him, but Henrick didn't open his eyes to acknowledge him.

"Hey, you can't sleep for a few hours yet," Tino said softly.

"I know. I'm not sleeping, just resting my eyes. The light hurts a little."

"Oh, hold on a minute then." The cushion shifted again, and he heard Tino moving around the room before his weight was back, making Henrick shift with its new closeness. "There try opening them now."

Henrick slowly cracked one eye open, and when he didn't get that stabbing pain the light had caused earlier, he opened them both fully. Tino had pulled the blinds and turned on a small lamp in the far corner of the room so there was only a soft glow illuminating the apartment. "That's better, thanks."

"I'm sorry. I should have thought about that. Had enough near misses myself that this should be automatic by now." Tino's eyes roamed over every inch of Henrick's face, making him want to squirm under the scrutiny. "Is there anything I can get you to make you more comfortable?"

Henrick sighed because the only thing he wanted, besides to lie down and sleep, was a shower to get all the drying sand off his body. He was beginning to itch and was pretty sure there was sand in his ass crack that was trying to invade his body, but he really didn't want Tino to help him shower. He was afraid if he asked for a shower that was exactly what was going to happen. "Not that I can think of right now."

Tino's eyes narrowed. "How about a shower? You look like you need one." Tino sounded like he'd read Henrick's mind.

Henrick stared at the man next to him before answering. "Fine, I really want a shower but..." Henrick hesitated to tell Tino why he hadn't said he did.

Tino's snort turned into a laugh. "Oh man, I'm not going to take advantage of you in the shower, Henrick. In fact, I'll make you a deal, if you can get up and walk to the bathroom, I'll let you shower on your own as long as you leave the door open so I can hear you if you call or fall."

"That sounds reasonable, but can you help me stand up or is that a deal breaker?" He tried to look pitiful enough that Tino would help him up but still let him shower alone.

"Nope, I will get you on your feet, but it's up to you to stay there." Tino stood and held out both hands. Henrick grabbed them and let Tino pull him to his feet where he swayed a little with the dizziness, but Tino's hands were right there to steady him. Henrick closed his eyes for a second, and the sensation of spinning stopped.

"Okay, you can let go now." He opened his eyes. The concern in Tino's amber gaze was so intense that he almost closed his eyes again, but the thought of Tino denying him a private shower kept them open. Tino released him slowly.

"Just take it slow; there's no hurry. We have all night."

Henrick shuddered a little at the way those words sounded coming out of Tino's mouth. They would have held so much promise if the situation had been different. He slowly put one foot in front of the other, building confidence in his steps with the knowledge Tino was only one step behind him, ready to catch him if he fell. He made it to the bathroom, and Tino made sure he had what he needed before he left Henrick alone, but with the door standing wide open.

Grabbing the sink for support as he struggled out of his still-damp trunks, he let them and the sand they contained pool at his feet. He stepped gingerly across the gritty tiles to the shower. The warm water felt so good on his chilled skin. He hadn't realized just how cold he was until he started to shiver almost violently under the warm stream. He rubbed his arms and tried to hold it together long enough to get clean. The thought of having to call Tino to help him spurred him into action. Pumping some of the hotel's shampoo onto his hand, he washed his hair quickly and then his body, making sure to get the sand from between his cheeks. The shakes set in as he rinsed himself, but he managed to shut the water off, step out, and pull a towel around him before calling for help.

"Tino!"

Henrick's knees started to buckle, but strong arms were there to catch him before he took a header into the bidet. Tino lifted Henrick's quaking form into his arms and carried him back to the couch, where he lay him down gently and then pulled a down comforter up around him, tucking it tightly around Henrick's body as he shivered uncontrollably.

"Th-th-th-anks. S-s-s-s-soo c-cc-c-old-d." Henrick's teeth chattered, making for an interesting combination of sounds as he tried to talk.

Sitting next to him on the edge of the couch, Tino rubbed his hands up and down Henrick's blanket-covered arms. "It's probably partially due to shock. Your mind is finally catching up to the fact that you almost died." He continued to rub, not just Henrick's arms, but his torso and then his legs and back up. Henrick's shivering started to abate enough that he wasn't vibrating like a plucked guitar string, but then the emotion hit him, and he started crying with no warning.

"Shh, it's okay, *tesoro*. You're okay. I'm going to keep you safe now." Tino stopped his rubbing and leaned down to wrap his arms around Henrick, lifting him up to press him tightly to his chest.

"I'm sorry," Henrick sobbed. All of a sudden, he couldn't stop the heaving body-rocking sobs that were coming out of him. He pulled his arms free from the confining blanket and clutched Tino's body to hold him closer—so close he could feel the other man's heartbeat against his own, assuring himself they were both alive.

"No, *bello*, there's nothing to be sorry for. It was my fault. I failed to keep you safe like I promised. I should have been keeping closer watch on you, instead of enjoying myself. I knew that you didn't know what you were doing and I messed up, I—"

"Tino..." Henrick needed to stop him. He could feel the self-loathing coming off Tino for his perceived failure. He didn't blame Tino for his accident, and he didn't want Tino to blame himself either. Henrick looked up into Tino's eyes and leaned forward, but the knock on the door stopped Henrick from doing something completely stupid just to make Tino feel better. At least, that's what he told himself was the reason he was just about to kiss Valentino freaking Alessi.

Tino untangled himself from Henrick and pushed him back into a prone position before pulling the blanket back over him. "I'll go see who it is."

Tino answered the door to Dardan. Neither of the two men looked all that happy to see the other, but Tino let Dardan into the apartment. He handed Tino his things from the beach. "I left the boards down by the pool. Jak said he'd keep them behind the bar for you." He stepped past Tino, sights set on Henrick.

"He's resting fine," Tino said somewhat tersely, making Henrick's eyes shift from the man coming toward him to the other, who was still standing by the open door.

"I'm sure he is, but I'd like to see for myself how Mr. Henrick is."

Henrick detected a chilliness between the two men that hadn't been present before and wondered what had happened to put it there. Dardan sat in the same spot Tino had occupied only moments before, and his eyes took in Henrick's face before he frowned.

"Are you feeling okay?" Dardan reached under the blanket to find Henrick's wrist, which he held, his eyes trained on his watch.

"I'm fine, just a little emotional. It's been a long day." He pulled his wrist out of Dardan's grasp when he realized the man was taking his pulse.

"I'm going to go take a quick shower and change, if you'll keep an eye on Henrick for me," Tino said from across the room, finally closing the door.

Henrick thought Tino looked pissed off as he made his way to the hallway. Maybe it was just the sand in his butt crack that was irritating him. He almost giggled at the thought but then stopped himself because he wondered if his brain may have been scrambled because his thoughts were all over the place.

Dardan also watched Tino walk across the room with almost a matching look of irritation on his face. He waited until Tino was out of earshot before he said, "I'm sorry you're stuck here with him. I would have volunteered to take you myself, but my parents' home is near Tirana and I didn't think you would be up for the drive. Now seeing you here, like this—" Dardan paused to wipe a stray tear off Henrick's cheek. "—makes me wish I'd have put you in my car and taken you away."

The way Dardan was looking at Henrick sort of made him wish he had, too, but the comment about his parents' house made him wonder how young Dardan really was, and again he caught his mind wandering. "It's okay, Dar. I'll be fine. Tino's being really nice. I was crying because, well, I don't really know why, probably just exhaustion."

Dardan nodded. "Okay, but I meant it about calling me if you need anything. I'll be happy to come get you if you need me to."

"How old are you?" Henrick blurted out.

"I'm twenty-two, why?" Dardan looked puzzled at the question.

He was an adult of legal age then, which prompted Henrick's mind in another direction. He'd almost died on the beach. That was an eye-opening experience, making him realize life was short and maybe he should grab an opportunity when he saw it. The man sitting on the couch with him was gorgeous, interested, and Henrick felt that there was more to Dardan than just his beach gig, more things Henrick would like to discover about his rescuer. "Oh well, I guess I was wondering if maybe you'd want to go get dinner one night after...well, you know, when I feel a bit better," Henrick asked the man out before he could talk himself out of it.

The pleased look on his face told Henrick all he needed to know about what Dardan thought about going out with him. "Yes, I'd really like that, and I know a great place in the city if you wouldn't mind me picking where we go."

"I'd love to go into the city, so that would be nice." Henrick was glad he'd taken the chance to ask Dardan out.

It was Dardan's turn to surprise Henrick. He leaned down and brushed his lips lightly across Henrick's and pulled back only an inch before he said, "Been wanting to do that since you first smiled at me."

Henrick smiled again, and this time when Dardan pressed his lips to Henrick's, he kissed back. It was just a brief meeting of the lips, but Henrick wanted to feel something like a spark or the earth moving. Unfortunately, it was just a pleasant kiss and nothing more. "Thank you again for saving my life."

Dardan sat back up, putting some space between them. "I'd do it again in a heartbeat, but I hope I never have to."

"Me too." Tino's voice startled the two of them out of their soft moment. Walking out of the hallway, wearing only a pair of gym shorts slung low, he stopped and put his hands on his hips, drawing attention to them and everything they encased.

Dardan coughed but couldn't hide the smirk on his face as he stood. "I guess I should go and let you rest. You have my number, so call me when you're feeling better, and we'll set a time for that date," Dardan said with a pointed look at Tino.

"Yeah, you should probably leave so I can get Henrick fed and into bed." Tino used his words to jab back.

Henrick watched as both men postured until he couldn't take it any longer. "If either of you are thinking of pissing on me to mark your territory, you can forget it because I'm so not into golden showers." Both men looked down at Henrick with the same startled expressions on their faces. Henrick shrugged. "It seemed to be the direction you were heading in."

Dardan shook his head but smiled again. "I think you'll be fine. I need to get going. I have things to finish up on the beach."

Tino gave Henrick a withering look as he followed Dardan to the door. "Thank you for bringing our stuff and for watching Henrick for me for a few minutes," Tino said politely, but Henrick could hear how he emphasized *our* and *for me* as if he was trying to make a point to the younger man.

"Not a problem, signor Alessi, as always I'm happy to be of service," Dardan said before walking out the door. Henrick could hear the man whistling in the hall before Tino shut the door a bit harder than necessary.

Tino walked through the room, ignoring Henrick's questioning look. He wondered what Tino was up to, but a minute later, Tino came back holding a pair of track pants and a T-shirt. He tossed them on Henrick's blanket-covered legs, reminding Henrick that he was naked, save for the towel he'd wrapped around himself.

"Figured you'd want to get dressed before I call down to order us some dinner," Tino said on his way to the phone.

"Yeah, thanks." He sat up and pulled the shirt over his head; it was big, but since he didn't want to bother Tino with running to his place to grab his own clothing, he'd have to deal with the extra fabric. At least the pants had a drawstring on them, so they would stay up. Henrick pulled them on while still lying on the couch and then fully dressed, and exhausted, he pulled the blanket back up over himself and snuggled down as his eyelids started to droop.

"No sleeping, Henrick." Tino's sharp voice cut through the light doze he'd quickly fallen into.

"Mmm not," Henrick murmured even though he knew he was.

TINO KNEW HE had no claim on Henrick, but that bastard Dardan making a date with him when he was barely functional pissed him off to no end and in Tino's apartment no less. He looked longingly at the minibar, but alcohol wasn't the answer. Besides, he needed to make sure Henrick was taken care of, and speaking of Henrick, Tino walked over to the couch where Henrick was wrapped in the comforter he'd brought from his bed. The man was sleeping, no matter what he'd said, and Tino couldn't stay mad at Henrick for accepting a date with Dardan, especially when he looked like an angel while he slept.

Tino sat on the edge of the couch, grabbing the blanket and pulling it out of Henrick's clenched fists. Henrick reached for it without opening his eyes and mumbled something in his sleep, but Tino kept pulling the blanket down Henrick's body, making him frown and mutter a curse. It made Tino smile but Henrick really did need to wake up, so he stopped teasing him and leaned over to get in his face.

"Henrick, *dolce*, you gotta wake up." He couldn't stop the endearments from crossing his lips, and since Henrick so far hadn't protested, well, he was just going to go on using them.

"Leaf me lone, Klaus, 'm sleepy." Henrick slurred his words.

"Who the hell is Klaus now?" Tino asked louder than he'd intended.

Henrick's eyes popped open, and it seemed to take him a minute to focus. "Where's Klaus?" Henrick asked as he looked around with wide eyes.

Tino cupped his cheek to bring Henrick's focus back to him. "Hey, were you dreaming? There's no one named Klaus here, just me. You remember me, right?" Tino was suddenly worried Henrick was showing signs of a concussion rather than just being discombobulated from sleep.

Henrick relaxed at Tino's words, and his eyes cleared even more. "Of course, I remember you. Who could forget? Did I fall asleep? Because I remember the doctor saying I shouldn't sleep."

So Henrick remembered the doctor's words; that was good, and Tino was relieved. "Yeah, he did say you shouldn't sleep, but you dozed off the minute I turned my back on you. I ordered some food. You need to eat, and then you can sleep a bit. I'll have to wake you every couple of hours to make sure you still know who you are though."

Henrick squinted at Tino. "How many concussions have you had?"

Tino chuckled. "I've had my share of them but even more near misses. You wouldn't think football is such a rough sport, but we get banged up more than most people know. Are you hungry?"

Henrick pushed himself up against the arm of the couch into an almost sitting position. "I could eat. Can I have a bottle of water?"

"Sure, hold on. I'll get it. Do you want to eat at the table, or would you rather stay on the couch?" He handed over a bottle of water.

Henrick sat up straighter before opening the bottle. "I could sit at the table, I think. I'm feeling better." His actions betrayed his words as his hand went to his head and rubbed.

Tino watched him closely as he drank half the water and recapped the bottle. Henrick shifted so he could swing his legs over the side of the couch and sit up properly. Tino's track pants completely covered Henrick's feet, and the way it made him seem almost childlike made Tino smile. "Okay?" Tino asked when Henrick was fully upright. Henrick nodded but then grimaced at the movement. Tino wanted to tell him to lie back down, but he didn't want to push because he knew how it felt when someone hovered and made a fuss when you were hurt and not in the mood.

"I'll be fine. Just let me sit still for a minute until the food gets here." Henrick rested his head on the back of the couch, once again closing his eyes.

Tino patted Henrick's knee before he got up. "I have to check my messages quick. You rest but no sleeping," Tino instructed as he grabbed his cell phone and checked it. Every day he hoped there'd be something from Bernardo, but every time he checked, there was nothing from his agent. This time there was, however, a message from his *girlfriend*, Rijeka Andersson. Tino pressed the sequence of numbers that let him hear her heavily accented voice as it said, "Val, dearest, I heard about the latest scandalous news. I'm sorry I cannot be at your side right now. My shoot in Brazil has run long. I will be back in Europe next week. Let's get together then. Call me soon."

Tino shut the phone down after deleting the message. At first he'd hated the way the press had taken the photo of him and the beautiful Norwegian supermodel and run with it. Of course, his agent had been overjoyed, but Tino felt cheap betraying his friendship with Rijeka that way. It surprised and hurt Tino when Rijeka had gone along with it, having her people send out a statement about respecting their privacy while they embarked on this newest stage in their relationship. Rijeka had hitched her star to Tino's, and her stock had risen overnight. She'd gone from a simple runway model in Milan to an international cover model in a matter of weeks, and while Tino didn't begrudge his friend her success, he had felt a bit used. Now they were over a year into their fake relationship, and before Tino had been accused of liking underage girls, the press had been speculating about an upcoming proposal. One day soon Tino would have to talk to Rijeka about ending their *relationship,* but for the moment, he was sure she'd come into play when Bernardo figured out how to handle the mess Tino was in.

The food arrived, pulling Tino from his morose thoughts. He helped the man roll the trolley into the kitchen, tipped him, and sent him on his way. Henrick was still sitting with his head thrown back and eyes closed, but his uneven breathing told Tino he hadn't fallen asleep again. Tino decided making Henrick sit at the table would be cruel, so he picked up his plate and carried it to the coffee table.

Henrick's eyes popped open. "What are you doing?" He looked at the plate on the table in front of him and back at Tino. "I thought we were eating at the table."

"You didn't look up to it, so I thought you could just stay there where you're more comfortable." Tino pulled the cover off the meal he'd ordered for Henrick and watched his eyes light up. "I figured you'd like this. Each one is the perfect little bite."

The corner of Henrick's mouth twitched. "You just didn't want to watch me fiddle with my food," Henrick said as the twitch turned into a grin.

"Maybe, or maybe I just remembered how much you like the perfect bite and wanted to make it easy for you." Tino went to retrieve his own meal and then sat next to Henrick on the couch.

Henrick picked up one of the little tomatoes filled with mozzarella and herbs and put it in his mouth. He hummed as he chewed with his eyes closed. Tino couldn't stop watching him. Henrick swallowed. "That was just right; so good." He picked up a tiny sandwich that resembled a cheeseburger and repeated the process. "That wasn't hamburger. Maybe lamb?" He didn't wait for Tino's answer before he took another that looked like a mini pizza on a biscotti. Henrick was obviously still able to enjoy his food even with a headache.

"Can I ask you something?" Tino queried over the crunching sound of hard bread coming from Henrick's end of the couch and Henrick nodded. "Why do you close your eyes when you eat?"

It took Henrick a minute to finish his bite and take a drink to wash it down. "It helps me concentrate on the taste. It's not like I do it all the time, only with food that I have to appreciate. Not like I sit around with my eyes closed while eating a fast food burger."

"How do you know if it's food you have to appreciate?"

"Well, if it's something I haven't had before, I want to see if it's worthy of appreciation, and then if it's not, I don't have to concentrate when I eat it again, but there are those foods that no matter how often I eat them deserve to be worshipped."

"Like what?"

"Well, like *pilzconsomme mit kipferl*; no matter how many times I eat that dish, it deserves to be savored." Henrick picked up his next bite but paused before putting it in his mouth. "Oh, and any type of cheesecake, of course."

Tino snorted out a laugh at the look of pure happiness on Henrick's face at the thought of cheesecake. "It's a wonder you're not a blimp." Tino took a bite of his cheeseburger and decided, although it was good, it didn't deserve to be worshipped.

"I've a good metabolism, but I also know when to quit." He popped another of the little tomato things into his mouth.

They ate in silence for a few minutes, each lost in their own thoughts. Tino's thoughts were all about Henrick and all the things he wanted to learn about him, but he didn't know how to go about it without seeming like he was being nosy. Henrick was the one to break the silence.

"What's it like?"

"Hmm?" Tino bought himself a little time because his mouth was full. "What's what like?"

Henrick glanced down at his lap. "Being famous, having everyone know who you are and know everything about you?"

Tino bit his lip. It was a common question when he met new people, and he had a stock answer, but for some reason he couldn't just tell Henrick that it was interesting and fun but trying at times too. "It's weird and crazy, and I hate it more than I enjoy it. I know everyone always hates when celebrities complain about how hard it is to be rich and famous, but it's true to some degree. Sometimes I wonder if it's all worth it. I think probably if I didn't love playing the game so much, I'd say to hell with it and go live in the mountains like a hermit." Tino let it all spill out before he could think. "More often than not, I wish I could just be a regular guy so I could live my life the way I want without any consequences."

When Henrick didn't respond right away, Tino felt that maybe he'd overshared or he was one of those who hated whiny celebrities.

"It sounds like it's not as fun as it looks from the outside," Henrick said quietly. "I guess I thought having anything you want pretty much whenever you want it would outweigh the unpleasant aspects of fame."

Tino shook his head. "I can't get whatever I want whenever I want." Tino looked directly into Henrick's eyes to make his point clear, and Henrick flushed before he turned away. "I guess being rich and famous is no match for a guy who gets to wear swim trunks to work on the beach all day." Tino had meant for the comment to come out light and teasing but realized after the fact that it sounded a bit snide.

"Dardan's a nice guy." Henrick shifted on the couch, broadcasting his unease.

"Oh yeah, he's a really nice guy, and he's really young."

"He's twenty-two. That's not that young, and besides the younger the better, right?" Tino took Henrick's flippant comment as a jab at his current situation with underaged girls, and his mood soured immediately. He was sure it showed on his face when Henrick's mouth went from a smile to a small oh of surprise. "I didn't mean it that way. I wasn't referring to your problem at all, Tino; please, I'm sorry if you thought I was. I honestly wouldn't joke about something like that."

Tino put his plate on the table and got up. He couldn't say anything to Henrick because he had a feeling that whatever came out of his mouth would be something he'd regret. He went to the minibar and grabbed the bottle of scotch he'd brought with him from his father's private stock. He slammed a glass on the counter, poured a healthy shot, and downed the entire glass before pouring another. He didn't drink it but instead picked it up and took it with him, grabbing his cell phone on the way past.

"Just leave your plate on the table when you're finished. I need to make a few calls. I'll be out to check on you in a little while." He walked to his bedroom and shut his door just as Henrick started to speak. He didn't want to listen to Henrick's sad attempt at trying to placate him. Henrick didn't want Tino's attention; he'd made it clear a couple of times, even going so far as to tell Tino flat-out that he wasn't interested. Maybe it was time Tino took the man at his word and quit trying to change his mind. He couldn't make Henrick see what the man behind the image was really like, and he was getting sick of trying. Nobody could ever accuse Tino of not taking a hint...eventually.

Chapter Eight

TINO STALKED OFF to his room, the slamming door cutting off the second apology Henrick was about to issue. He hadn't intended to offend Tino. He was having a good time talking while they ate, getting to know the man instead of the celebrity was sort of interesting and fun too. Why Tino had to take a jab at Henrick making a date with Dardan was beyond him. Dardan's age really shouldn't have been an issue. Yes, he was only twenty-two, but a four-year age difference wasn't that unheard of.

Henrick's appetite disappeared with his dining companion, so he got unsteadily to his feet and picked up both plates to carry them to the trolley. His head was pounding by the time he got back to the couch. He lay down and pulled the comforter over his head.

Henrick was dreaming about the sea. The waves were calm, and he was floating on his back while the sun beat down on his face. The difference in temperature between his front and back left him with an odd sensation of being caught between two worlds. He was content to stay there floating along until the familiar and unwelcome swell started to push his body up. His breath caught in his chest as panic started to set in. Henrick tried to roll over so he could swim to safety, but he was unable to move against the pressure of the wave. He began to struggle with the effort until he went under. Just when he thought he'd have to go through the unpleasant experience of feeling water fill his lungs again, a pair of arms pulled him back from the abyss.

Henrick startled awake as Tino lifted him from the couch. "You're okay. I'm just taking you to bed." Tino's breath was fragrant with the alcohol he'd imbibed, but his voice was clear and steady.

"I could just stay on the couch." Henrick made a halfhearted attempt at protesting.

"No, you'll be more comfortable in the bed," Tino said as he carried Henrick, still wrapped in the blanket, down the hall.

"But it's your bed." The image of Tino lying naked in the same bed came unbidden to his mind.

Tino pushed a door open and walked into a small bedroom. "I have a spare room. You won't be kicking me out of mine." He placed Henrick on the bed, where the covers had already been turned down.

Henrick crawled between the sheets, and Tino pulled the blankets over him. "Tino, I—"

"Do you know what day it is?" Tino cut him off.

"Wednesday, if it's still the same day," Henrick answered. "Tino—"

"Who is the prime minister of Austria?" Tino asked, once again interrupting Henrick.

"Werner Faymann. Tino, I'm fine, but could you please listen—"

Tino leaned over the bed, putting one hand on each side of Henrick's head as he lay there on the pillows. "No, you listen to me. Someday I will find a man who will love me for who I am, and you know what? He'll be one lucky son of a bitch because when I find that guy I'm going to make him feel like he's the most important man on earth. I will love him and cherish him and give him the world. I *will* find someone who will be worthy of all I have to offer because I believe I deserve that. I deserve to be happy, and no matter what the world thinks, I deserve to be able to find love and to be loved. You mark my words, Henrick, one day you'll read about that love and you'll remember you had a chance to maybe be that guy, but you couldn't look past the end of your nose to see what was standing in front of you." Tino stared into Henrick's face for a moment before he straightened up. "I'll be back to check on you in a couple of hours." Tino left Henrick lying there staring after him, wondering what the hell had just happened.

Since he'd left the door open, he could hear Tino moving around. The clink of glass against glass, the liquid flowing, and then the sound of Tino's harsh hiss told the entire story of what was happening in the other room. Henrick tossed for a bit, letting Tino's words run on a loop through his mind. Tino was right—he did deserve happiness and love; everyone did. Had Henrick been so blinded because Tino was who he was that he hadn't seen how the man craved the same basic human connections everybody else did? Henrick tried to see things from Tino's point of view, but it was hard since they led very different lives. Before he could figure anything out, his tiredness got the better of him and sleep pulled him under once again.

"Henrick." Tino said his name in an almost whisper as he shook Henrick's shoulder to wake him. "Henrick, wake up."

"Time is it?" Henrick muttered as he surfaced, thinking his mother was waking him for school.

"Doesn't matter; wake up so I can ask you something."

Henrick sat up as awareness of his surroundings came back to him. He wasn't at home in his childhood room, and the man standing there looking down at him, backlit by the hall light, was most definitely not his mother. A small light on the side table came on, blinding Henrick for a moment and causing him to squeeze his eyes shut to block it out.

"Sorry, but I need to be able to see you to make sure you're okay." Tino's voice was surprisingly clear. Henrick had been expecting Tino to be pretty drunk by then.

"I'm fine. I know what day it is and everything. You don't have to do the question thing." Henrick opened his eyes fully so Tino could see he was fine.

"That wasn't what I was going to ask you." Tino took a shaky breath before he asked, "Henrick, do you hate me?" The question took Henrick totally by surprise and threw him for a loop, causing him to pause before telling Tino that, of course, he didn't *hate* him. In fact, he was starting to kind of like the guy a little before he'd put his foot in his mouth, and after Tino's earlier outburst, Henrick was starting to see him in a whole new light. "That's what I thought, so I was just going to tell you that you don't have to worry about me after you're okay to be alone. I'll stay away because I shouldn't—"

"I don't hate you, Tino." Henrick got up on his knees so he was face-to-face with Tino. "I'm sorry about earlier. I didn't mean to make you feel bad. I didn't know how you felt about being stuck playing to an audience all the time, how hard it is for you." Tino's eyes were shiny. Henrick didn't know if it was from the alcohol or if the man was trying to hold back tears, but the sadness in those amber depths was real. Henrick felt terrible for being the one who hurt a guy like Tino, a guy who remembered he liked to have the perfect bite and then went out of his way to give him just that. He realized Tino was probably right—the guy who won Tino's heart would indeed be the luckiest guy on the planet.

"You already told me how you felt. You don't have to lie to make me feel better just because I'm throwing myself a pity party."

Henrick took a chance and put his hands on the sides of Tino's face. Tino's eyes widened as Henrick leaned in and kissed him. It started soft and sweet and tender as Tino gently kissed him back. It was simply lips brushing and then tongues slowly exploring. Tino's hands mirrored Henrick's hold as the kiss deepened and turned into something more demanding. The harsh bursts of breath from Tino's nose tickled Henrick's cheek as the man took control and plunged his tongue deep into Henrick's mouth. The world shifted and sparks danced behind his eyelids for just a moment before the pain hit, and he jerked his head back, causing another stab of agony to shoot through his brain, adding to the initial shock of having Tino accidentally press his fingers on the goose egg above his right ear.

"Oh shit, Henrick, are you okay? I'm so sorry."

Henrick lay back on the pillows, breathing hard more from the pain than the pleasure of the kiss, but he knew he needed to say something to keep Tino from feeling even guiltier about his injury. "I'm okay. My head just hurts a little. Could I maybe have a headache tablet or something?"

"I think you can. I'll go see what I have." Tino's expression was still full of concern as he stood over Henrick.

"Could you please? I think it would help." He hoped giving Tino a task would stop him from thinking about having hurt him.

"I'll be back in a second."

"I'll be here," Henrick joked. He waited until Tino was out of the room to run his fingers lightly over his tender head. He guessed he should have been happy something had stopped that kiss—that earth-moving, spark-inducing kiss. Henrick sighed because he knew Tino wasn't the man for him. There was no way he could hide in the closet with another man, and no matter what Tino said, Henrick was sure Tino's people wouldn't let him ruin the last few years of his career for some twink he met on holiday.

"Here, I found something you can take." Tino's entrance broke Henrick from his self-depreciating thoughts. Tino handed him the pills and a glass of juice and then watched closely while Henrick swallowed the tablets. Tino reached out and tipped the glass to make sure Henrick drained it. "You probably need the sugar," he said to excuse almost drowning Henrick for the second time in less than twenty-four hours.

"Thanks for the pills and juice and for taking care of me and also for saving my life. I don't know if I told you thanks or not for that last one," Henrick said, suddenly feeling like he needed to express how much he appreciated everything Tino was doing for him.

Tino sat on the edge of the bed and took Henrick's hand. He kept himself from jerking it away as Tino sat there for a minute, staring at their joined hands. "I was so scared when I couldn't find you in the water, and it got worse when I finally saw you floating facedown." Tino looked up but not at Henrick. His eyes were sort of unfocused as he stared at a spot above Henrick's head. "I prayed, and I haven't believed in God in a very long time, but I prayed to Mary and Jesus and every saint I could remember from my childhood that you would be okay. It was my fault you got hurt, and no matter what you say, I will always feel that guilt. If Dardan hadn't been there..." Tino's breath hitched. "If Dardan hadn't been there, I don't know if I'd have been able to step up and do what needed to be done, because I was frozen in fear that you were gone before I got to know you."

"I'm sure you would have done whatever was needed."

Tino's eyes finally cleared, and they swept Henrick's face, lingering on his kiss-swollen lips before locking with his. "Henrick, you have to know that I like you, and I wish things were different, and you'd give me a chance to—"

Henrick squeezed Tino's hand to stop him. "You're not at all what I thought you were going to be like, but despite the fact that you are quite possibly one of the nicest men I've ever met, I still have to stand by my earlier statement. I'm not interested in a relationship with you beyond maybe...friendship." He couldn't let Tino think that amazing kiss had meant more than it did, just one friend comforting another.

Tino still held Henrick's hand as he said, "I understand. No matter what you think about me always getting what I want, this here, where a guy tells me no because of who I am, happens far more often than not. I get that it's too much to ask another person to take on. I respect your decision, but if you really are extending an invitation to be friends, I'd like that because I have very few friends who want me without all the star trappings."

Henrick sat up beside Tino so he could put his arm around Tino's back. "I'd like to be your friend, and I don't want anything from you but your friendship. Hell, who couldn't use another friend?"

Tino finally smiled and placed his arm around Henrick's shoulders. "Friends then," he said, and Henrick nodded slightly, keeping in mind his brain didn't like to be shaken at the moment. "So then what are you doing tomorrow? Up for a little sailing?"

Henrick pushed Tino away. "No way. I'm staying out of the sea for a day or two." Tino raised a questioning eyebrow at him. "Hey, it tried to kill me today. I think I'll give it some time to cool off before I tempt it again."

Tino laughed. "Oh my god, it didn't try to kill you but fine, we'll find something else to do then." Tino stood. "Now it's late, go to sleep." He walked to the door but stopped before crossing the threshold. "Thanks, Henrick." He slipped out of the room without a backward glance.

Henrick wondered what Tino was thanking him for but didn't have the strength to have any more emotional discussions. Lying back against the pillows, he replayed his strange day from beginning to end. He was sure he'd made the right decision when it came to Tino. Yeah, he'd just keep telling himself that until he believed it.

TINO WATCHED HENRICK from the upper deck of his small yacht. Henrick was stretched out on a towel, soaking up the sun. Probably sleeping again, Tino thought. The man could doze away the day like a cat and not feel one bit ashamed of it. It was just another of the little nuances to Henrick's personality Tino found himself drawn to. Tino himself was too antsy to just lie around. After twenty minutes of fidgeting next to Henrick, he'd had to get up and move around.

Tino smiled as he thought of how hard Henrick had fought against spending three days out on the water with him. The excuses he came up with still made Tino chuckle, but in the end he'd won, and Henrick had packed a bag and let Tino drive him to the port. Now only four hours into their trip to Vlore, Henrick was more relaxed than Tino had seen him since his near drowning just two days before.

"Signore, lunch will be ready soon. Would you prefer to take it above deck or in the salon?" Angelo, the chief steward, asked.

"Above deck, please, and leave it to me to alert my guest, thank you." The man nodded, smiled, and went about his job. Tino had arranged with the chef for very specific meals to be served, with Henrick in mind, and he couldn't wait to watch the smaller man eat every delicious morsel.

Tino made his way down the stairs to the lower deck. The small table and chairs were shaded by the upper deck while the four-person hot tub and Henrick were in the early afternoon sun. Tino settled on the chaise next to the one Henrick was on and put his hand on Henrick's back, feeling the heat seeping from Henrick's lightly tanned, sun-warmed skin into his. Henrick rubbed his face on his forearm and turned it toward Tino before cracking one eyelid. Although Tino had agreed to back off, he couldn't keep from touching Henrick when the other man allowed it, so he rubbed a light circle on the small of Henrick's oiled back.

"Mmm, that feels nice," Henrick purred.

Tino smiled. Henrick was always malleable when he first woke—another of the things Tino had learned. "Lunch is about to be served, so unless you want to eat while all oily, you should probably get up and go get ready."

Henrick groaned. "But if I do, you'll stop giving me a back rub, and that's not fair."

Tino bit back the offer to go with him and continue rubbing whatever part of Henrick's body he wanted. "I promise I'll give you a proper massage this evening if you really want one."

"Oh, well then, I guess I'll get up and take a quick shower. I hate being covered in sunscreen. How do you not get burned?" Henrick pushed himself up onto his hands and knees and arched his back in a stretch before he stood.

Tino watched the entire process, memorizing how Henrick's body looked in that position would help Tino's nightly fantasies along nicely. "I have naturally darker skin, so I tan but never burn."

"Just another reason to hate you." Henrick tempered his harsh words with a grin.

"Go shower before I throw you overboard."

Henrick wiggled his butt in Tino's face, and Tino couldn't resist giving it a light smack that made Henrick yelp and giggle before he skittered away. Tino tried to keep his cool, but it seemed Henrick's definition of "just friends" included a lot of flirting and touching—things Tino could never imagine doing with any of his other friends.

Tino was sitting at the table when Henrick got back from his shower. He was dressed in a pair of cutoff jean shorts that showed off his slender but toned thighs and a tight tank top under an unbuttoned linen shirt. He looked the picture of a relaxed man on holiday as he took his seat next to Tino.

"The coast is really rugged and beautiful. I can't believe there aren't more cities. It's like we're the only people left on earth."

"I know. It's actually refreshing after spending my childhood on the busy crowded beaches in Italy. I've grown to hate the crowds. I'd much rather spend time on my own or with a few people I like."

"So you like me?" The teasing lilt in Henrick's voice was something Tino had grown accustomed to, but he still found it adorable that he'd asked as if he were unsure of how Tino felt about him.

Tino nodded. "You know I do," he said softly.

Henrick's face took on a serious expression. "You know what? I sort of like you too. I'm glad you talked me into coming with you. Now what's for lunch?"

Tino smiled because he was hoping Henrick would appreciate what he had in store for him. "We'll have to wait and see what the chef has prepared."

Henrick pouted, but the steward showing up with the appetizers made his face brighten. "Oh what's that?" Henrick asked as the plate was set in front of him.

"Sir, this is marinated San Remo shrimps with caviar and scallops. Bon appétit, gentlemen," the steward said as he set Tino's plate in front of him.

Tino held out a bottle of wine, and Henrick nodded. Tino filled their glasses as Henrick took the first bite of his appetizer. Tino had fallen in love with watching Henrick enjoy something he'd put in his mouth, and it had nothing to do with the thing Tino wanted to put in there. It had more to do with just watching the joy the right food brought to Henrick's face that Tino couldn't get enough of.

"So good," Henrick said, but then he studied his plate for a minute instead of eating. Tino was about to ask him what was wrong. "Are you always going to feed me bite-sized food? Because you know I can eat regular food like a grown-up, right?"

Tino laughed. "I am not treating you like a child. The next course isn't bite-sized. Appetizers are almost always small. The menu for this trip wasn't planned by me. I just told the chef to make his best for you."

Henrick looked pleased. "Thanks, but really you don't have to try to impress me. I like you whether we're eating this amazing food or a gyro on the street. You know that, right?"

Tino didn't know what to say. He hadn't been trying to impress Henrick. He'd only been trying to make him happy, because he liked the feeling he got when something he did pleased the man. It was so easy to provide food that made

Henrick moan with pleasure that he hadn't even thought Henrick would see it as Tino showing off to impress him.

"That was not my intention. I just like to watch you eat," Tino said before he could think over the implication of his words.

A wicked grin spread across Henrick's lips as he leaned closer to Tino. "You know, if all you were after is a little erotic mouth viewing, all you had to do was buy me an ice cream. I'd lick that baby so good you'd come just from watching." He sat back and made a show of putting the last of his food into his mouth and slowly licking his fingers clean.

The heat rose on Tino's cheeks, and the flesh in his shorts firmed up. "Shit, you can't say things like that to me if you expect me not to throw you down and have my way with you," Tino growled. Henrick giggled so hard he snorted, which made him giggle even harder, resulting in more snorts. Tino shook his head and was happy for the interruption when Angelo came out with the main course.

"Your main course today is monkfish with prosciutto and artichokes," Angelo said as he once again placed plates in front of each man, after clearing the used ones and then disappearing.

Henrick wiped his eyes and seemed to find his control once again. He sneaked a look at Tino and let out a short giggle, but then took a minute to gather a bite onto his fork. He put it in his mouth and did the whole process while Tino watched and waited for his verdict on the dish.

"Is your chef married?" Henrick asked when he opened his eyes.

"I don't think so, why?"

"Do you think he'll marry me?"

It was Tino's turn to have a laughing fit. "He's in his fifties and weighs at least a hundred and twenty kilos." Tino explained why he found the idea so funny before Henrick could ask.

Henrick took a few more bites. "A man who cooks like this could be any age, weight, color, or be missing limbs. I don't care. I'd fall at his feet and worship them, even if they were hairy and smelly, as long as he made me this kind of food."

"I'll be sure to pass that on to Jean Claude."

"Oh, you didn't say he was French." Henrick looked disappointed.

"What, you don't like Frenchmen?" Tino delighted at another new discovery.

Henrick put his chin in his hand and looked out at the sea. "Nah, it's more like Frenchmen don't like me."

"I find that hard to believe. How many Frenchmen have you been with that didn't like you?"

"Just one, but he was a nasty man when it came down to it and ruined Frenchmen for me. He thought I should drop everything and be at his beck and call. I was young, and I thought that was the way relationships worked, but even when I did everything I could to please him, he always found me lacking. It was the worst year I ever had, but eventually, I wised up and left him when my term at the university was over. I went back to Vienna and tried to forget him and how he made me feel." Henrick shook his head and ate more, though with less enthusiasm.

"How did he make you feel?" Tino was curious to know more but pissed off at the same time.

Henrick turned so he could look at Tino. "Like I wasn't good enough. He was always comparing me to others, and I never measured up in any way to any of the people I was pitted against."

Tino wanted to kill the French bastard who'd hurt Henrick. Then he wanted to take Henrick into his arms and tell him he was perfect just the way he was, but he knew Henrick had issues he was working through, and they had nothing to do with him. He wouldn't be able to take Tino's comfort without turning it into a come-on and then into a joke. Instead, Tino took Henrick's hand and squeezed it. "I think you're great, and that guy was obviously an idiot." His words made Henrick smile, and they ate the rest of their main course in a comfortable silence.

The dessert was cheesecake, because Tino hadn't been able to resist using the information for his own gain. Henrick fell on the minicakes like a seagull on a bucket of chum. He barely finished one before he had another poised to push into his mouth. Tino ate one and let the other man polish off the rest. The noises Henrick made were just this side of obscene, and poor Angelo blushed when he came to collect the used place settings.

Henrick sat back in his chair and groaned. "Oh my god, I think I may burst at the seams."

Tino chuckled because he looked like he may do just that. "You did eat my portion of the dessert too."

Henrick's eyes grew wide. "Why would you let me eat all of that? Do you want me to get fat? Do you know how unattractive I'd be with a paunch?" Henrick rubbed his flat belly as if trying to imagine what it would be like bloated with an extra ten kilos.

"You said yourself that you have a high metabolism and also that you knew when to stop, but that was sort of a lie, I think. I'm sure you'll work it off."

"How? Do you know how much I've lain about on this holiday? It's like Albania has made me a sloth. I barely move other than to find more food."

"We can have the captain stop and we could go for a swim off the back deck," Tino suggested, but Henrick bit his lip nervously instead of agreeing. "You're not afraid of getting in the sea are you? Are you still having those nightmares?"

Henrick shifted in his chair so he was out of Tino's reach. "I guess, but they're not as bad as the first night, and I'm not afraid of the sea but maybe jumping off a boat in the middle of it isn't the best idea right now."

"You should have said something. I'd have never suggested we come out if I'd have known. I'm sorry. I screwed things up again." Tino felt like an ass for pushing him so hard to accept his invitation.

"Don't do that. You didn't do anything wrong. I'm glad I came, but maybe we could just sit in the hot tub for a bit after I've taken a nap because I don't want to doze off and drown in that tiny tub." Henrick gestured to the little four-person hot tub.

"I wouldn't let you suffer the indignity of drowning in that thing."

"That's good to know. Now, I think a nap in the cool of my stateroom would be best." He pushed back from the table but didn't stand.

"Sure, I could maybe doze for a bit too." Tino stood and helped Henrick by pulling on his arm to drag him out of his chair.

They made their way below deck and stood outside the doors to their separate rooms. Tino was just about to tell him to sleep tight when Henrick wrapped his arms around Tino's waist and rested his cheek against his chest. "I don't care what anyone says about you. You're a good guy, Valentino. Thank you for bringing me out here."

Tino hugged Henrick tightly to him while he buried his nose in his hair. Henrick felt right in Tino's arms, and no one had ever made him feel like he did with just a few simple words. The lump in Tino's throat prevented him from saying anything that would ruin the moment. Releasing him, Henrick turned without looking at Tino's face and went into his room. Tino stood there trying desperately to figure out how he could win Henrick's heart and make the other man see they could have something special if only Henrick would give it a chance.

Chapter Nine

HENRICK COULDN'T BELIEVE how beautiful the sunset was out on the open water—the yellows, oranges, and reds turned into shades of pinks and purples surrounding a small yellow ball as Henrick tipped his head to try to hear the sizzle as the sun hit the sea. The second day of their little trip had been spent exploring Vlore before boarding the yacht for the journey back. They'd eaten the most delectable meal at a restaurant, where Tino had been treated like the celebrity he was, and Henrick tried not to draw too much attention to himself. He shuddered at the thought of how many people now had a picture on their phone of him and Tino together, strangers who could at that very moment be showing his face to god knew how many other strangers. He didn't know how Tino could stand the lack of anonymity and privacy.

Hearing what he knew were Tino's footsteps as he crossed the deck to join him made Henrick tear his eyes from the gorgeous sight of the almost fully set sun to take in the equally beautiful sight of his host. Tino was wearing a pair of loose, white linen pants and a button-up silk shirt—unbelievably the same color as Henrick's eyes—that he'd unbuttoned the minute they'd gotten back where there were no prying eyes. Tino looked truly relaxed again. Not the fake relaxed—with a stiffness that only someone who knew him would recognize—that he'd been when surrounded by his adoring fans.

He held a bottle of champagne and two crystal flutes as he approached Henrick. "I thought we could celebrate a little tonight," Tino said as he sat on the padded bench next to Henrick. Henrick took the flutes while Tino popped open the bottle of what was likely a very expensive bottle of champagne. Tino laughed at Henrick as he tried to catch the bubbly liquid escaping the neck of the bottle before it spilled all over the deck. Tino filled the glasses and set the bottle next to his feet. He raised his glass to Henrick.

"What are we celebrating?" Henrick raised his own glass, mirroring Tino.

"Life," Tino said simply before he clinked the lips of their flutes together.

Henrick grinned and added to the toast. "To life and friends who let you be you and don't run away screaming."

Tino laughed as he sipped his drink. "Most definitely to those that don't turn tail when things get weird. Thank you for today. I know that the scene at the restaurant wasn't something you were prepared for, but you handled it like you'd been doing it all your life. I appreciate you not bolting out of there like I sort of expected you to do."

Henrick sipped the champagne slowly, thinking over the afternoon once again. He hadn't thought about leaving Tino to fend for himself, though he had to admit he hadn't even known it was an option or he may well have done it. "I wouldn't run out on you for something you can't control. It makes me appreciate being a nobody."

"You're not a nobody."

Henrick shook his head and tried not to hear the meaning behind Tino's words. The man had made a promise to back off, and he hadn't broken that promise per se, but Henrick wasn't stupid, and he could read between the lines. Tino still wanted more than just the friendship Henrick offered him, and every time Tino said something nice in that soft, gentle voice, Henrick ordered himself not to melt into a puddle of goo and let something more happen between them.

"I am a nobody, and I'm happy for that because I'm pretty sure I wouldn't be able to handle things like strangers coming up to me and wanting to talk or take pictures of me."

Tino refilled Henrick's already empty glass before Henrick even had time to wonder how it had gotten empty that quickly. "You'd do fine, but yeah, it's nice to be left alone. That's actually one of the reasons I like the hotel in Durres. They're all so used to seeing me there that I'm more of a fixture to them now. They don't treat me any different than they do a regular guest. Most of the restaurants I frequent are the same way. I've found the more I go to one place, the less they see Valentino Alessi, the star footballer, and the more they see Tino, the guy who knows everyone's name, you know?"

Henrick chuckled through a mouthful of the amber liquid. "Is that why you seem to know everyone's name? It's a ploy to get them to treat you like a regular guy?" Henrick was impressed and amused at the lengths Tino went to get people to treat him like a normal person.

Tino winked. "It works most of the time. There are a few people who, no matter how often I'm around them, only see the bright and twinklies, but there's no help for the likes of them so I usually just grin and bear it."

Music came out of nowhere and startled Henrick into looking around for the string quartet. "What the heck?"

"Ah, took Angelo long enough." Tino finished his glass and put it on the little table in front of him. Standing, he took Henrick's glass and set it next to his before holding out his hand. "Will you dance with me in the moonlight?"

Henrick hesitated for a moment. Then the deck darkened and only the small lights strung around the deck illuminated the two of them, making for a scene right out of one of the romantic comedies Henrick liked to watch, and he couldn't resist. He took Tino's hand as he stood and let the other man lead him out into the center of the deck. Henrick tried to keep some space between their bodies as they swayed gently to the soft music, but soon he was leaning in, and before he knew it, they were pressed tightly together. Henrick could feel every ridge and plane of Tino's hard body against his.

He rested his head on Tino's bare chest and let the gentle swaying, the soft music and lighting, the scent of the sea air, and the smell of the man in his arms lull him into a state of pliability he normally guarded against around Tino. He blamed everything that happened next on his inability to stop his brain from misinterpreting his body's signals as to where the events of the night were leading.

Henrick lifted his head so he could look into Tino's eyes. The fact that his lips parted in a way he knew would be mistaken as an invitation for a kiss could only be blamed on the romantic setting because Henrick hadn't had enough champagne to claim drunkenness. Tino's eyes held his, and when Henrick saw the question in them, he almost took the out the right answer would have provided, but it was like he was hypnotized by the swaying of their bodies. Henrick tilted his head just the perfect amount at the same time as Tino swooped in for the kiss.

Again, there was the feeling of the earth shifting under Henrick's feet when Tino's lips touched his. Tino was hesitant at first, his lips tentatively brushing Henrick's as if testing the waters and expecting the worst. Henrick moved his hands to Tino's neck and could feel his pulse pounding much faster than it should have been. His mind swirled with doubt. He wasn't ready to give in to that inner voice screaming at him that the man in his arms was worth a little hardship because in the long run he may be the one. He was much more attuned to the one whispering that he was going to end up crying on his couch when Tino turned out to be just a trumped-up version of Klaus.

Tino pulled back from the kiss, a frown marring his perfect features. "You're a million miles away."

Sighing, Henrick tried to take a step away from Tino, but the arms around him tightened. "Tino—"

"I just wanted to dance with you. It doesn't have to be anything other than that, a simple dance."

Henrick shook his head. "I can't go through this again." This time he pushed at Tino's chest in his quest to get free.

Tino dropped his arms to his sides in defeat. "Go through what, Henrick? You never tell me anything about what's going on inside that pretty little head of yours, so how should I know what it is you're so afraid of?"

Henrick crossed his arms over his chest. "You really want to know what I'm afraid of?"

"Yes, I really want to know. I want to know everything about you because you're the first man who's ever really looked at me and seen me."

"That's not true. You said you were in love with Paulo, so he must have—"

"No, he started off the same as all the others, wanting me because of what I am instead of who I am. When you paid for dinner tonight..." Tino trailed off and took a few deep breaths before continuing. "Do you know Paulo never once offered to pay for anything? He didn't even buy me a birthday present because, and these are his exact words, 'You didn't give me any money to buy you a present, so I figured you didn't want anything.' What you did when you pulled out your wallet tonight was the one thing that told me you weren't just here because of what you could get from me. You're here because you like me, and that means the world to me. Now tell me what you're so afraid of."

Henrick wanted to hug Tino because he could see Tino led a very lonely life, but he stood his ground. "I'm afraid of you, because I've already been with a guy who made me keep our relationship a secret, and I didn't like how it made me feel. I can't go through that again."

Tino bit his lip and worried it between his teeth until Henrick wondered if he'd make it bleed and was about to go to him to make him stop, just in case. When his resolve to stay aloof was about shattered, Tino let go of his lip with a hiss. "Well, I guess that's a valid reason then." Witnessing the deflated tone of his voice and the slumped posture hurt Henrick.

"I'm sorry, Tino." He really was, but more than that, he was relieved Tino was willing to admit it wouldn't work between them because Henrick was as unwilling to hide in the closet as Tino was to step out of it.

"I think I should go to bed." Tino turned away.

"Please, can we just go back to the way it was before?"

Tino stopped but didn't turn around. "The way it was before... Henrick, the way it was before was the same as it is now. I wanted you and I still want you. Knowing I can't have you but that you have a valid reason for not wanting me doesn't make it any easier for me. It actually makes it harder. Before I thought you just needed to get to know me, to start to trust me. Then you'd see you were making a mistake, and eventually, you'd give me a chance, but now I know you will never give it a chance because you know I'm stuck when it comes to certain things. I can't give you what you want no matter how much I wish I could. We can go back to the way it was before, but you see, Henrick, my before wasn't so much different from my after, except in my before, I still had a reason to hope."

Henrick's heart felt like it dropped to somewhere around his knees. He wished he was back home on his couch wrapped in his blanket with a bucket of ice cream because for some reason the words Tino just said to him felt worse than Klaus announcing his engagement had by a long shot. Henrick could only watch as Tino disappeared down the stairs without another word.

TINO WATCHED HENRICK from across the table while he tried to come up with a safe topic of conversation. They were still three hours from port, and there was only so much silence and avoidance Tino could take before he was likely to explode from the pressure to make things right between them again. Henrick looked like he hadn't slept, and Tino wondered which of the things he was dealing with had kept him up. He hoped it wasn't the nightmares, but then at least if it had been due to them, it wouldn't have been because of Tino's stupid attempt to push things to another level. His grand romantic gesture had blown up in his face, assuring it would be the last time he'd take getting-a-man advice from a movie.

Henrick looked up before Tino had a chance to stop staring at him. Their eyes met for a brief moment until Henrick jerked his head to look out to sea. "Henrick, stop it." Tino had finally had enough. "We're a couple of grown men. There's no need to act like children about this."

Henrick turned back slowly as if he expected to get hit or something. "I thought maybe you would rather not speak to me after..." Henrick let the sentence die, but Tino knew the ending anyway.

"Listen, I had a lot of time to think about this last night, and I realized I was being stupid, I mean like giant, dumb-ass stupid," Tino said, which brought a small smile to the lips of the man across from him.

Henrick fiddled with his coffee cup, still avoiding eye contact. "Yeah, you were sort of being an asshat with that stunt."

Tino snorted. "Can we just forget it ever happened and go back to the way you wanted and just be friends?" After waiting for a response and not getting one straight away, Tino added, "I promise to not ever put you in the position to have to tell me no again. I understand a relationship with someone you have to lie to everyone about is not an ideal situation for anyone, and if you've already been through it and had it end badly, well, it would just be bad form for me to ask that of you again."

Henrick let out a weighted sigh. "We can be friends because I sort of feel like you don't have many real friends. Maybe it's time for you to have someone around who tells you how it is, instead of what you need to hear to stroke that out-of-control ego of yours."

"I love how you think you have me pinned down after knowing me for all of—" Tino looked at his watch. "—oh, let's be generous and say ten days minus four hours give or take a few minutes." Tino cocked his head at Henrick.

"You know the exact time we met?" Henrick looked skeptical.

"Of course I do. Why, is that weird?"

"Really weird but you have to subtract like four days or so because I didn't see you until the day you decided I should try to kill myself."

Tino let the jab about his involvement in getting Henrick injured pass without comment. He knew Henrick held no ill will toward him on that front. It was just Henrick's strange sense of humor, and Tino was starting to catch the way Henrick's lip twitched ever so slightly when he was teasing, making it easier to let some of his more offhand remarks slide without Tino letting them rattle him.

"Fine, that makes it even worse for you to pass judgment on me since it's less than a week."

"Ah, whatever. You love it when I tell it like it is."

Tino relaxed because the light, easy banter of the past two days was back, and he had a feeling they'd gotten over a major hump in the road to true friendship. Tino had to admit that he still felt the pull toward the other man, but if the only way he could keep Henrick in his life was by tamping down those burgeoning feelings, then that was what he'd do. Maybe he could convince himself it was just lust and leave it at that.

"Yeah, I guess it will be refreshing to have someone around to tell me when I'm being, what was it you called me, an asshat?"

"Yeah a major asshat." Henrick finished his coffee and stood.

Tino watched, without trying to seem like he was being creepy about it, as Henrick stripped off his shirt and then started to shimmy out of his tight shorts. Tino held his breath as he waited to see what Henrick had under them. He was happy, yet disappointed, to see that Henrick had his little speedos on.

"Think I'm going to go catch a couple hours of sun before we get into the port. You want to join me?"

"Sure, but you know I know that is just your way of saying you're going to take a nap, right?" Tino joked as he got up to follow Henrick out into the sun.

"Yep, I know, but the fact that you don't complain about it makes you my new best friend." Henrick winked as he got out his sunscreen and started rubbing himself with it.

"Need a hand?"

Henrick didn't even hesitate in handing the bottle over to Tino before he lay on his stomach. Tino squirted the lotion on his hands first to make sure it wasn't too cold before he started rubbing it on Henrick's shoulders and then down his back. Tino took his time, but didn't linger too long; he didn't want to make Henrick uncomfortable with his touch. When he finished, he let his hands rest on the small of Henrick's slim back, not wanting to lose contact so soon.

"Want to get the backs of my legs, too, please?" The please was said in such a way that Tino almost said no because flirty Henrick was back. Tino wasn't sure he could handle him so soon after making a promise to not push things. "Tino?" Henrick's voice snapped Tino out of his thoughts and back to the deck of the ship.

"Yeah, sure. I'll do them for you," he heard himself say. He got more lotion and started at Henrick's ankles. His shorts got tighter with every inch of flesh he covered in the slick fluid. He almost stopped when he was just above the knees. Henrick giggled and squirmed a little, but as Tino's hands stilled, so did he.

"Sorry, I'm a little ticklish on the backs of my thighs, should have warned you to rub harder there." Henrick sounded a little more breathless than a man just lying on a chaise lounge should.

Tino reached down to adjust himself before he went back to, he hoped, quickly finish applying the sunscreen. Tino pressed down harder on the almost hairless flesh of Henrick's upper thighs, moving up until his fingertips brushed the elastic on Henrick's speedos. He shifted at just that moment, and Tino's hand slipped between his legs. Tino tried to jerk his hand away, but Henrick clasped his thighs together, trapping it there, pressed against the underside of Henrick's balls.

"Are you trying to feel me up?" Henrick asked. This time, Tino was sure the other man's breathy speech was from his own growing arousal.

"Do you want me to feel you up?" Tino asked because he was really confused. Henrick's jokes and flirting were sending Tino some seriously fucked-up mixed messages. Tino wasn't sure exactly what Henrick wanted from him. He pushed Tino away, but then at times like this it seemed that he was trying to get a rise, figuratively and literally, out of Tino. Tino was starting to wonder if Henrick even knew what it was that he wanted anymore.

Henrick's thighs opened, and Tino pulled his hand away. Henrick flipped over to look up at Tino, but Tino couldn't make eye contact because he was too busy staring at Henrick's crotch. There had been a major development in that area. The glistening pink head of Henrick's cock peeking out of the waistband of his speedos had Tino's complete, undivided attention.

Henrick made a noise of exasperation. "Well, don't just stare at it like you've never seen one before. It's your fault it's like this, so at least have the decency to look away."

"My fault?" Tino questioned as he tried to unscramble his thoughts.

Henrick leaned forward and pushed at Tino's shoulder. "Stop it. I mean it. Don't look at my dick like that."

"Like what?" Tino wasn't really thinking of anything but what it would taste like if he were to just lean over and lap up that little drop of clear fluid that was just crying out for his attention.

"Like you want to—"

Tino did it. He bent over and licked the head of Henrick's cock. He sat back up, and in a crude imitation of how Henrick savored his food, he closed his eyes. Tino let the flavor of the other man sit on his tongue before swallowing and letting out a little moan of appreciation. He opened his eyes to a stunned Henrick who was holding his hand protectively over his groin. Tino knew he was completely out of his mind. "Oops, I licked it."

"What... How... Why...why would you do that?"

Tino couldn't tell him the truth because Henrick didn't want to hear it, so Tino decided the best defense was a good offense. He knew that was backward, but hell, only about a quarter of his brain was firing at full power. He got up and loomed over Henrick, letting his own hard cock fill Henrick's vision for a second before he put his hands on the back of the chaise, caging Henrick in with his arms.

"If you're going to tease me," Tino said as he straddled Henrick's thighs, "then you're going to have to accept the consequences"—Tino pressed his cock against the hand Henrick still had covering his own rigid length—"of getting me riled up with no outlet for it." Tino finished with a rough grind of his hips. The stunned expression on Henrick's face made it hard for Tino to keep a straight face through his ruse.

"Tino, you promised," Henrick whined as he pushed at Tino's chest with his one free hand. Tino rocked his hips, and Henrick groaned. "You have to stop." Henrick struggled to pull his other hand out from between them, so Tino pulled back enough to let him but pressed back in as the hand joined its twin on Tino's chest. "Oh fuck, stop it before you make me come, and I have to hate you for it," Henrick hissed. Tino gave one more thrust against the man he had trapped under him and then stilled.

"You would be the type of guy who would get pissed at someone for making you come." Tino grinned as he bent down and kissed Henrick's cute little button nose.

Henrick slapped Tino's chest. "You're a shit, you know that?"

"You're a brat, you know that?" Henrick stuck his lip out in a sultry pout when Tino didn't get off him. "See, you're only proving my point by sulking like a spoiled child who got called out for his bad behavior." Tino settled back on Henrick's thighs, breaking the contact between their throbbing flesh.

"I'm sorry?" Henrick's pout turned into a smirk.

Tino rolled his eyes. "If we're going to be friends, I think we need some ground rules, because I don't know about your other friends, but I can't tell where it is you draw the line for me. I'm afraid I'll cross it accidentally and hurt you, so tell me, Henrick, how much of this is too much?"

Henrick's eyes went to Tino's crotch and then back up to his face. "This is definitely too much."

Tino huffed out a laugh. "No, really? You think?"

Henrick started giggling, which set Tino off too. He slid off Henrick's lap, and Henrick shifted to make room for him. They lay on their sides, face-to-face, as Henrick said, "I really am sorry. I get carried away sometimes, and I forget that some people have boundaries that I don't seem to have."

"I don't mind the flirting. I actually like that side of you, but sometimes I'm not sure if you're actually coming on to me or if it's just part of your game." Tino explained where his confusion came from. Henrick looked like he was thinking pretty hard about what Tino said. "We could always do the friends-with-benefits thing if you wanted." Henrick stiffened next to him and then shook his head. "Or maybe not."

"Really not. It's not that you're not incredibly hot and every boy's fantasy and all." Henrick paused to give him a wry grin before adding, "But I have enough of those guys around. I really don't need to add another into the mix."

"Oh that's nice, I don't even rate high enough to get on the list." Tino joked, but Henrick's face remained serious.

"It's because I want to be real friends with you, and if we fuck, then that would be ruined, so no more unexpected cock licks, okay?"

Tino nodded but just couldn't help himself. "You taste good though so yo— Hey, ouch, no pinching!" Tino yelped as Henrick pinched his nipple. He wrapped his arms around the smaller man to trap his hands. "Be nice or I'll sit on you again."

Henrick stopped struggling, but instead of pushing Tino away when he loosened his arms, he snuggled in and wrapped one of his arms around Tino's waist. Tino lay there, not knowing if he should stop the cuddling, but soon he realized Henrick was sleeping. He gently kissed Henrick's forehead. "What am I going to do with you, huh?" he asked the gently snoring man. Tino relaxed into a light doze and tried to forget how good it felt to hold Henrick against him while he slept.

Chapter Ten

TINO WAS QUIET on the drive from the port back to Mali Robit, but Henrick couldn't tell if it was a heavy silence or a comfortable one. After waking in each other's arms, they had acted like it was no big deal. Just friends sharing a lounge chair and nothing more, but after everything Tino had said, Henrick wasn't sure if friendship was such a good idea anymore. He had no reason to believe that once the holiday was over and they went their separate ways they'd stay in touch, so what would it hurt to maybe have a little fun? He flip-flopped on the issue so much he wasn't sure if he was coming or going anymore. On one hand, he was incredibly attracted to Tino, and if they were never going to see each other again... But no, on the other hand, he had promised himself he wouldn't be just another guy Valentino freaking Alessi could say he'd nailed.

Tino pulled into the parking lot of his hotel and shut off the engine. "Want to grab dinner later?"

Henrick thought after spending three days together nonstop Tino would be ready for some alone time. Henrick knew he surely was. "Can I take a raincheck? I need to decompress a bit." It may have been Henrick's imagination, but he thought Tino looked a bit relieved; maybe he'd only asked to be nice?

"Okay, well, we'll do something tomorrow then?"

"Yeah, I think I can squeeze you into my busy schedule." Henrick popped open his door.

Tino got Henrick's bag out of the trunk and handed it to him. "Thank you for coming with me. I had a lot of fun."

Henrick stepped in and hugged Tino. "Thanks for taking me. I never thought I'd end up on a yacht. That was probably right up there with 'things I want to do but will probably never get to,' so thanks for letting me go." Henrick tried to convey his gratitude but felt he wasn't all that successful with his rambling.

Tino chuckled. "Again, you're a pretty weird guy, but you're welcome. Okay, go, decompress, and call me if you get bored." He sent Henrick on his way with a little push in the direction of his building.

Henrick walked up the path between the buildings and wasn't surprised to see Dardan standing on the beach looking out at the water. He smiled to himself as he watched Dardan turn toward him as if he could feel Henrick's eyes on his back. Dardan waved at Henrick, but his lips turned down as his eyes took in the bag Henrick was carrying and he jogged over.

"You're not leaving already, are you?"

"What? Oh, no. I'm actually just getting back from a short excursion. Sorry I forgot to call you and tell you I was going, but it sort of happened fast." He'd remembered to send out an email to everyone who would get nervous if he didn't answer his phone for three days, but Dardan, being only an acquaintance, had slipped his memory.

Dardan's posture relaxed, and his smile returned. "Good, I thought maybe you'd decided to cut your holiday short after your accident. How was your little holiday from your holiday?"

"It was good, unexpected but good." Henrick was hesitant to tell Dardan he'd been off with Tino on his yacht. Since neither man held a position of significance in his life, he wasn't sure why he needed to hide anything, but for some reason it felt wrong to tell him. "I'm going to go relax a little and check some emails, but maybe I'll call you later and we can set up that dinner date?"

"That would be excellent. Have a good evening, Henrick."

"You, too, Dar." Henrick was relieved to finally make his way up the stairs to his apartment.

After putting his bag in his room, he grabbed his laptop, started the coffeepot, and went out onto the balcony so he could enjoy the sun while he reconnected with the world. There were emails from all the usual suspects, his family, Oskar, and Gage. His two best girlfriends, Hedy and Gerta, had both sent him multiple emails, mostly of cute kitties because they knew how perturbed he got at them. Then of course, there was a string of emails from Klaus. The man had never been much of a communicator before their breakup, but all of a sudden, he was desperate to get in touch. Henrick didn't delete Klaus's emails, but he didn't read them either.

He poured a cup of coffee and sat back down. He tried to talk himself out of what he knew was a bad idea, but in the end his fingers typed "Valentino Alessi" into the Google search bar. Henrick bypassed all the articles, hitting the images link, and there he was. There were so many pictures of the man he'd just spent the last three days alone on a boat with, but not one of them, and Henrick must have clicked through hundreds of them, captured the man he was starting to get to know. There were none of Tino's zest for life or the twinkle he got in his eye when he was teasing, and not one of them showed the deep loneliness or sadness Henrick had seen lurking in the amber depths of Tino's eyes.

Shutting the laptop, Henrick leaned back in his chair with a sigh. He wished the whole thing with Tino was simpler than what it was because it hurt his heart when he thought about that sadness. The fact that he wanted to be the one to take it away and replace it with joy and love made him twitchy as hell.

THE RESTAURANT DARDAN picked for them was on the other side of Durres, so Henrick got to see most of the city as Dardan drove them through it. He was happy he hadn't decided to rent a car because it would have just sat at the beach gathering dust, because he realized he was lost after only five minutes of the thirty minute drive.

Dardan opened his car door, but though Dardan didn't touch him on their short walk to the hotel where the restaurant was located, he did walk close enough that Henrick could feel his body heat. Dardan also held the door of the hotel open for him before following him through. They had a reservation, and looking around the dining area, he realized that was probably a good thing. The hostess seated them out on the deck overlooking the sea. It was late evening, and the sun hung low enough in the sky that it wasn't blindingly bright but held the promise of a spectacular sunset as a bank of clouds encroached on its position.

"This is great. Look at that view," Henrick said, after they were seated and had given the hostess their drink orders.

"I love this place. My dad knows the guy who owns it, and he brought me here when Mr. Collins had his grand opening. Tons of celebrities turned out, and I was so in awe that I don't think I remembered to eat."

"Who owns it?" Henrick was interested in finding out a little more about Dardan and his family.

"Nigel Collins. I'm sure you've heard of him."

"Yeah, he played with Beckham for a bit. They were so good together, but he retired, right?" Henrick didn't know a lot about football, but some names you never forgot.

"That's him. He moved here right after he retired and opened this place."

"How does your dad know him?"

"He was the team doctor for the Albanian national team for fifteen years, so he got around," Dardan said casually like it was no big deal.

"Wow, so that means you probably got to meet a lot of footballers then, huh?"

Dardan nodded. "Yeah, I guess, though when I was young I didn't really realize that it wasn't normal to be on first-name basis with star athletes."

"So did you want to play football when you were a kid?"

"No, I wanted to do what my dad did, and that's why I'm in medical school." Dardan grinned at Henrick's shocked expression.

"No way, you're in medical school?" He was surprised at the news, but then after he thought about it, he said, "That explains how you were so good on the beach. I should have guessed you had some training, but a doctor? That's impressive."

Dardan chortled. "Well thanks, I still have two years left and then, of course, all the clinical training, but so far I really like it."

"It's good to like what you do. My job is sort of boring, but for me it's interesting to figure out problems and then implement the solution to fix them. Plus, I get to travel quite a bit too."

They discussed what to order, and when the food came, Henrick was in awe of the beautiful presentation, and the wonderful aroma went straight to his stomach, making it rumble in anticipation. He did his utmost to not look like a complete idiot while he savored his first few bites. After watching Tino mock him the other day, he didn't want Dardan to do the same.

Dardan was just getting ready to speak when his eyes flicked up to something over Henrick's shoulder, and his dark eyes turned stormy in the waning light. "Well look who's here, and with his *girlfriend,* no less," Dardan growled.

Henrick was taken aback by Dardan's reaction to—he turned around to look—Tino. Henrick paled when he realized that it was Tino who Dardan was glaring at. He caught a glimpse of the tall blonde woman Tino was holding out a chair for and snapped his head back around. Tino was there with the supermodel girlfriend, which wasn't the most pleasant surprise Henrick could have hoped for, but then again, what had he expected after he turned the man down, not once, but multiple times?

"Are you okay?"

Henrick nodded and took a sip of water to try to calm his nerves.

"I'm sorry, but what did you expect from him?" Dardan's question mirrored Henrick's own thoughts.

"I didn't expect anything. Valentino Alessi and I are just friends."

Dardan reached across the table and took Henrick's hand in his. "I wanted to warn you about him, but I don't like to get in the middle when it's not my business."

He let Dardan hold his hand, but he didn't like the implications in the man's words. "I'm very capable of taking care of myself, so even with your warning, things would have turned out the same way. There's no need for you to feel responsible for my choices."

Dardan laughed out loud at that. "I'm sure you're capable of taking care of yourself and much more. I wasn't implying you weren't. Just that I wished I could have spared you from whatever happened to put that look on your face when you saw him with her."

Henrick shook his head to deny what Dardan was implying had happened between Tino and himself. "I told you we're just friends, and he's free to take whomever he wants out to dinner. Now, let's not let his presence here affect our time together." He pasted on his best fake smile for his dinner companion.

"That is the best idea you've had all night." Dardan raised his glass, but Henrick noticed he wasn't looking at him, but instead, he was staring over Henrick's shoulder to the spot where Tino was sitting. Henrick wondered if Tino was staring back or if he was engaged in conversation with his fake girlfriend, but he'd be damned if he'd turn to see. Instead, he raised his glass and clinked the rim against Dardan's.

"I have all kinds of ideas for the night, and I'm sure at least a couple of them will top that," Henrick said with a flirty wink that left no question of where they would be heading after dinner.

Dardan gulped his wine and tucked into his meal with gusto. Henrick smiled at the younger man's eagerness to get on with their new plans, but that left Henrick with the task of finishing his meal while trying to ignore the man at his back. Dardan insisted on paying, then stood and helped Henrick out of his seat, this time offering his arm. He slid his hand in the crook of Dardan's elbow and let him walk them past Tino's table.

Henrick tried to look the other way, but in the end, he found Tino's eyes with his own. Tino's face was blank with no hint of recognition when he allowed the brief meeting before he blinked and looked away. The easy dismissal hurt Henrick far more than seeing him at dinner with someone who was rumored to be his girlfriend. Henrick stood up straighter and left the restaurant, knowing a night with Dardan wasn't going to help anything, but helpless to stop himself from wanting the comfort, regardless of that fact.

TINO LET RIJEKA into his apartment and then threw his keys on the counter when he entered after her. She had shown up unexpectedly and was waiting on his couch when he'd gotten back from his yacht trip with Henrick, and it wasn't like he could just tell her to leave, so he called Nigel and got a table for dinner. Henrick and Dardan a table away had been an unpleasant surprise, and Tino was itching to go to Henrick's apartment and beat down the door, but it wasn't his place so instead he paced.

"Tino, sweetie, you are so tense. Tell me what's wrong," Rijeka said as she slipped out of her high heels and sat with her legs tucked under her on the couch. "Get us a bottle of wine, come, and let's talk like we used to."

Tino selected a bottle of wine, uncorked it, and poured two glasses. He handed one to Rijeka and then sat on the other end of the couch. "We haven't gossiped like a couple of old women for ages. Why now?"

"Something's bothering you." She waved her hand when Tino opened his mouth. "And I don't mean this nasty business with the Friedberg girls. Tonight at dinner, you seemed to change right in front of my eyes. You were happy and then poof. So what put you in such a mood?"

"I met someone." Tino's confession had the intended effect on Rijeka whose eyes widened as her lips turned up in a cover-model-worthy smile, but Tino interrupted her happiness. "He's not interested and he was with another man at the restaurant tonight, which is why I'm upset."

"Who is he?"

"He's nobody. Well, he's Henrick, but he's no one you'd know. He's not famous or anything."

"And he's not interested, why? I mean really what is he into, like...what do they call them big, hairy gay mans?"

"Bears, and no I think he's plenty attracted to me physically, and I think he even likes me, but he doesn't want me because of who I am." Tino wasn't going to lie about why Henrick wouldn't give him a chance; what was the point?

Rijeka snorted in an unladylike manner. "That is just stupid. Who wouldn't want a rich, handsome, famous man with a body like yours?" She made it clear she thought anyone who wouldn't was surely insane.

"Henrick, that's who."

"How long have you known him because you made no mention of him before?"

"I met him about ten days ago." Tino smiled softly at the memory of his and Henrick's earlier conversation where he'd accidentally revealed that he knew exactly to the minute how long Henrick had been in his life.

"Pfft, well then, he's not even worth thinking about. You're probably only fixated on him because he's the only one who's ever said no to you."

Tino didn't think that was the case, but explaining how attracted he was to Henrick, not just physically, wasn't going to be easy. The unexplained jealousy at the thought of having another man even look at Henrick, let alone what was probably happening at this very minute in the apartment across the path, took Tino's breath away at times. It was stupid and Tino knew it. He needed to get over it and fast, but he didn't know how.

"We've agreed to be just friends anyway so..." Tino trailed off and was spared from having to explain anything more when his phone rang. He picked it up, and when his agent's picture showed on his screen, he nearly dropped the damn thing. "I have to take this." Tino answered the phone with a shaky swipe of his finger. "Hallo."

"Tino, I've got good news for you!" Bernardo's voice boomed at him over the speaker. "How soon can you get to Rome?"

TINO HATED THE way they had to cover his face in pancake makeup when he did anything in front of the camera. On this particular late morning it was more than necessary since he'd shown up with dark circles under his eyes, looking like he'd just taken the red-eye, which was in fact what he'd done. A quick meeting with Bernardo in his office was all it took for Tino's life to get rolling again. Tino and Herr Friedberg were scheduled to appear together on one of the talk shows that aired at 11:00 a.m. to clear the air about what really happened in that now-infamous hotel room.

"There, you look fresh as a daisy," the makeup girl said after she finished and pulled the little paper napkin from the neck of Tino's shirt. "Someone will be back to get you in a few minutes; try not to smudge yourself." She gathered her things and left.

Tino sat there wishing the interview was over. He hated sweating under the bright lights, answering questions nobody should have to answer about their personal lives. It was just another price he paid to do what he loved. A light tapping on the door made him turn to face it. He figured it was showtime, but when the door didn't open right after the knocking, as it would if the stage manager was coming to get him, Tino called, "Come in."

The door swung open, and there stood Herr Friedberg in a three-piece suit looking like he'd just returned from the spa. Upon closer inspection, Tino could see the lines around the man's eyes were deeper than when he'd last seen him, and his ice-blue eyes had a sort of melancholy look to them that made Tino remember why he'd gone away and been unreachable in the first place.

Tino stood and offered his hand. "Herr Friedberg, I'm so sorry you have to go through this after suffering what I can only imagine is a tremendous loss. I hope you'll accept my condolences on the passing of your son."

"Thank you. Your words are greatly appreciated. Though, as you can imagine my heart is very heavy, I felt it necessary to set the record straight on this matter since you made my son smile on one of his last days on this earth," Herr Friedberg said quietly as he shook Tino's hand. "I know he would not have wanted you to suffer because of the act of kindness you showed him."

"That's very good of you, sir, and I appreciate your help in this matter," Tino said as the backstage hand knocked on the doorframe.

"Well, I guess it's time then, shall we?" Herr Friedberg asked.

Tino followed the other men down the hall and out onto the soundstage. The live audience cheered as the two men were introduced, and the hosts of the show had smiles so wide and fake on their faces they made Tino cringe. He knew this exclusive interview was a huge score for their show, but did they have to be so damn happy when their guests were a soon-to-be, yet not-quite-exonerated, accused pedophile and a man who had just buried his child?

They took their seats and listened to the hosts as they read the introduction to the segment from the teleprompters. Then the manic duo trained their sights on their guests. After welcoming them and extending their own condolences to Herr Friedberg, they turned to Tino.

"Valentino Alessi, why don't you tell us what happened that night in the hotel so we have the whole story," the female co-anchor asked with a fake look of concern on her face. Tino remembered the morning after the news had broken. Her adamant statements of how out-of-control celebrities getting off with just a slap on the wrist should end with Tino, who should have the maximum sentence handed down if found guilty to teach a lesson that one can't get away with these things no matter how famous, still rattled around in Tino's brain.

Tino walked them all through his version of events, the same one Bernardo had released to the press. The hosts nodded along and smiled indulgently as Tino explained that he always liked to meet his fans, so when he'd heard Pieter was terminally ill, he'd agreed to go back to the room with the girls.

"So then that's where you come in, Herr Friedberg. Care to tell us what happened when a famous footballer showed up at your door? I bet you were a bit surprised, weren't you?" the male host asked with a good-humored chuckle that got the audience laughing along.

Herr Friedberg cleared his throat and pasted on a smile, which looked even more forced than those of the hosts, before he said, "Oh yes, it was a bit shocking to have Mr. Alessi standing there with the girls. He introduced himself and asked if he could visit with Pieter for a bit. You can't imagine the joy he brought to my son with his visit. It was all he could talk about afterwards. My wife and I had been discussing sending a thank-you note to Tino for his kindness only to come back from our vacation, where we had no communication with the outside world, to see he had been slandered in the media for that very act. You can't imagine how upset we were that this has caused Tino so much trouble, and we'd been able to do nothing about it before now."

The hosts nodded along with every word until Herr Friedberg added, "I believe this fine young man is owed many apologies by many people and media outlets, but let me be the first to offer one in public." Herr Friedberg turned to Tino and put his hand on his shoulder. "I'm so very sorry this has caused you so much trouble. I know words will not make it better, but please know that I am now, and will always be, in your debt for the time you took out of your busy life to sit with a sick boy for an hour to make him happy. You are a true role model. I only ask that you continue to do these small kindnesses, even though the world has not shown you the gratitude you deserve."

Tino's heart pounded hard because if Herr Friedberg knew just what a fraud Tino really was... Tino bit his tongue to stop the words that wanted to pass his lips to clear the air and really step up and be a true role model. "Thank you, Herr Friedberg, and just so you know, even knowing the results of my actions, I would still choose to do the same thing I did that night."

The applause thundered through the studio, and Tino tuned out the rest of the segment since he wasn't called upon to answer anything else. Just when he was thinking the whole ordeal was over and he could get back to his life and put the incident behind him, the male host turned to him right before they were scheduled to leave the stage during a commercial break.

"Mr. Alessi, on another front, there have been rumors that you and a certain runway model are getting ready to make things official. Care to make any announcements since you have the nation's attention?" he asked with another of those fake-as-hell smiles that made Tino want to puke.

Tino knew he had to say something, but he sat there like a deer in the headlights as the audience quieted enough for Tino to hear his own heartbeat. The female host giggled and snapped Tino out of his stupor. "Um, no, not at this time, at least." But Tino's grin would leave them all thinking the rumor was true.

THERE WAS A lot of backslapping and welcome backs when Tino returned to Munich for his first practice after his suspension. His meetings with the management had gone well; they'd all but bent down and kissed his ass, but Tino wouldn't soon forget how no one had batted an eye when the ruling from the IGF had been handed down. They'd all thought he was guilty. The rumblings about Tino's agent looking for a new team for his star striker when free agency came up had already started. Tino endured the sideways glances from his teammates without a word of explanation to them, because in the end, no one had wanted to get their reputations ruined by associating with him while he'd been in exile. Not one phone call to see how he was doing was something Tino took as a personal affront even though he knew most of them had probably been advised by their own agents to keep their distance.

"Alessi, I see you've gotten away with it again. At least this time it was little girls instead of little boys; guess it makes it marginally better," Stigler, the middle back, said as Tino walked into the locker room after practice. The man didn't even have time to turn to his snickering buddies before Tino raised his fist, and before he knew it, he was back in the office defending himself once again.

Chapter Eleven

HENRICK WENT TO the hotel next to his apartment building to have breakfast the morning after his date with Dardan. He told himself he wasn't hoping to run into Tino, wasn't even thinking about him as he sat on the veranda and ordered a light meal. He'd just been served when the supermodel walked in, sat at the table right next to him, and ordered a coffee without taking her eyes off her phone. Henrick tried not to stare, but his eyes kept flicking to the beautiful blonde woman as he wondered where Tino was. Henrick ate distractedly while listening to the woman make several phone calls before she finished her coffee and left.

Henrick finished his own meal and went back to the apartment to get ready for the beach. When his phone rang, seeing it was another call from Klaus, he ignored it. He'd lost count of how many times his former fuck buddy had tried to call him, but the number was getting up there, to be sure.

The beach was much more crowded now that the season had officially begun, but his chairs were empty thanks to Dardan. Henrick spread out his towel and lay down. The expanded crowd made for better people watching, at least. Henrick watched naked toddlers standing at the edge of the sea and then bending down to play in the wet sand. He laughed softly when a surprise swell rose up to hit one of them in the bare butt, making them squeal from the chill of the water against sun-warmed skin. It wasn't long before Dardan showed up and sat on the end of his lounge chair, blocking his view of the frolicking children.

"Hey there, how are you this morning?" Dardan asked. Henrick could hear the smile in his voice before he looked up and saw it.

"I'm good. Back to my regularly scheduled holiday."

Dardan sat there looking at Henrick for a moment, and Henrick could see something in the other man's eyes even before Dardan took a deep breath and said, "Valentino Alessi left last night."

Henrick sat up. "What do you mean he left?"

"The night desk clerk said he checked out, but his girlfriend is staying on through the weekend. Apparently he was on the phone the entire time arranging for someone to get his car since he was flying back. He must have been in some hurry because I remember him saying one time how much he loved that car."

The news hit Henrick hard, and tears pricked at the back of his eyes, making him glad he was wearing his sunglasses to hide his emotion. "He must have gotten that call he was waiting for." He wondered if Tino's troubles were finally over, and he'd be able to get back to his life—the one that didn't include him.

"I'm sure it will hit the news soon if that's the case." Dardan waited as if he thought Henrick would respond, but he couldn't think of anything to say. "Well, I have to get back to work, but can we get together when I'm done tonight?"

Henrick wanted so badly to say no, but the hopeful look in the young man's eyes made him nod. He couldn't trust his voice yet, but as soon as he could, he'd tell Dardan he wasn't feeling up to doing anything.

"Great, well, have fun today, but don't wear yourself out." Dardan winked as he got up and then ambled off down the beach.

Henrick had a hard time sitting still because his mind was racing. Even though he'd seen Tino with his supposed girlfriend the night before, he guessed he must have still held out some hope that he'd talk to Tino again before either of them departed. Now he was left with another week of holiday on a beach that only held memories of a man he'd been too chicken—no he'd been too smart, he amended—to get involved with.

Henrick got off his chair and waded into the water. He'd been having nightmares—only while asleep in Tino's arms for that brief nap had he not dreamed of suffocating pressure—about drowning, and now it was time to face his fear. Henrick took a deep breath and dived under the water, letting the pent-up tears escape to join with their salty brethren of the sea.

HENRICK KNEW HE shouldn't do it. He paced the apartment after watching the newsclips of Tino's morning show appearance, and that last line still galled the hell out of him. Why would Tino let everyone believe he was going to marry that life-sized dress-up doll? Henrick let his mind slander the woman at the same time as he tried to tell himself it was unfair to judge her without knowing her. She was probably a lovely person. For all he knew, she could spend her spare time saving puppies or orphans or something else cute and cuddly. But he hated her because she had what he kept telling himself he didn't want but was pretty sure he actually kind of did, with his whole heart.

Henrick picked up his phone and dialed the number. Almost hanging up each time he heard the ring come over the line, but as soon as he was sure it was going to voice mail a familiar voice answered, and Henrick's heart skipped a beat.

"Henrick." Klaus said his name like it was an answer to a prayer.

Henrick's chest tightened. "Klaus, I saw that I missed your call." Henrick lied about why he was calling.

Klaus's chuckle came down the line. "Which one of the hundred did you see that you missed?"

Sucking in a surprised breath, he'd expected anger, not this chortling, joking man he was talking to. "I guess all of them. I'm sorry. I just wasn't ready to talk to you." Understatement of the year.

"I figured that, but I really needed to talk to you. I miss you and was wondering when you're coming home."

As soon as Klaus asked when he was returning, he realized entertaining thoughts about going back to Klaus was monumentally stupid. He couldn't carry on with a married man even if that marriage was a sham. His thoughts turned to Tino and the fact that both men were about to make the same decision. Henrick couldn't help wondering what it was that made a fake marriage seem like a better idea than a real relationship with him.

"I have another week here, and then I'll be back."

Another lonely week trying to avoid Dardan and thinking about Valentino freaking Alessi, he thought but didn't say out loud.

"That's good. I have some news for you when you get back. I can't wait to see you again. I meant it when I said I miss you. I never realized what I had until you packed up and left." Klaus sounded miserable over their breakup in a way Henrick never thought he'd hear. Klaus was really laying it on thick, but Henrick couldn't help the little flash of warmth the words made him feel. It was nice to feel wanted, even if it was just for his body.

"Well, maybe we can have coffee or something when I get back. I can call you."

"Or you could tell me when your flight gets in, and I could pick you up at the airport and take you home," Klaus offered.

Henrick bit his lip. Having Klaus offer to pick him up was new, but it also meant Klaus would probably expect to walk him up to his apartment, and then he'd want to be asked in, and one thing would lead to another and...

"Earth to Henrick. Are you there, Henrick? Come back, over."

"Oh, sorry, got lost in my thoughts."

"Yeah, sort of figured that, though I don't know what's so tough about giving me your flight information."

"I have to go. I'm getting another call that I have to take. I'll talk to you later. Bye, Klaus." He broke the connection before Klaus could say another word and then stood there staring at his phone, wondering if he'd just gone insane.

THE PHONE—IT was the phone, Henrick thought as he pulled himself out of his dream. Rolling over, he felt around on the nightstand for his phone that had stopped ringing before his unconscious mind had put two and two together and realized the ringing was coming from outside his own head.

He finally had to sit up and turn on the lamp when his groping didn't turn up the now-beeping-with-a-message device. Henrick squinted into the brightness and found his phone on the edge of the table, where it must have vibrated. Peering at the screen, the first thing he noticed was that it was almost three in the morning. Panic tried to take hold because in Henrick's experience nothing good ever came from a phone call in the middle of the night.

He swiped the screen, praying it wasn't anyone in his family calling with an emergency at three o'clock in the fricking morning. He wanted to be relieved when it wasn't his parents' or sister's number on the screen, but the fact that it was Tino's number pushed that feeling away. Henrick quickly retrieved the message and pressed the phone tightly to his ear.

"Henrick, it's Tino. I'm sorry—*heavy sigh*—I had to leave because I'm sure you know by now that my get-out-of-jail-free card finally showed up. I'm sorry I waited so long to call you, but I wasn't sure what to do. Are we still friends, Henrick? I really hope we are because I could really use a real friend right now—*heavy sigh*—Okay, I realize it's either really late or insanely early, but I just needed—*long pause*—I don't know what I needed besides hearing your voice. Okay, well, I'm going to stop talking now and leave the ball in your court. You have my number, and if you want to, you can use it. So...yeah...well...goodbye, Henrick."

Henrick listened to the message again, and then again, until the sun was peeking over the horizon. He laughed and cried and was so confused because he had no idea what to do about Tino. He wanted to call him and hear his voice, too, but he didn't want to make it seem like he'd been sitting around waiting for Tino's call. Of course, Tino had called in the middle of the night, almost ensuring Henrick would be near his phone to answer, but he hadn't, so he couldn't look too eager to talk to the other man now. He couldn't be sure if it was a calculated move on Tino's part, but it was something he wouldn't put past him.

Henrick decided to let it sit for a little bit. He wouldn't call right away and look too eager, but he wouldn't wait so long that it made him seem like an asshat either. A little thrill raced through his body, Tino had been the one to call him, which had to mean something, right? Henrick flopped back on his pillows. Why did he want it to mean something when he knew that even if it did he couldn't do anything about it?

TINO CLUTCHED HIS phone, resisting the urge to call Henrick again. It was the middle of the night, and there was no reason Henrick shouldn't have answered the phone... unless. *No, don't even imagine him in the arms of Dardan because it will just drive you crazy.* He put the phone on the nightstand and shut off the lamp. Henrick couldn't be so pissed at him that he'd ignore Tino's plea for a friendly voice, or at least he didn't think the other man had a reason to be that upset.

Rolling over, he wished he'd at least called Henrick to tell him he had to leave in a rush, but if he was being totally honest, he'd been more than a little pissed off to find Henrick at the restaurant with Dardan, and it had colored his decisions that night.

Not able to get Henrick off his mind long enough to fall asleep, Tino grabbed his phone once again and went to his picture album. He'd taken many pictures of Henrick while they'd spent time together. There were pictures where Henrick was mugging for the camera, the familiar flirty smile on his lips, but Tino's favorite pictures were the one's he'd taken without Henrick knowing he was being photographed. He had pictures of Henrick lazing about on the deck of the boat and of him leaning over to look at the waves rushing about them, but there were two Tino kept going back to. The first was Henrick laughing as Angelo said something Henrick found funny, and the next was that moment when Henrick turned to Tino, the smile still on his face, eyes sparkling with good humor, a moment of pure joy caught forever for Tino to savor.

Why couldn't Henrick just give him a chance? Tino knew he was interested, but Henrick couldn't look beyond his past hurt at the hands of another man to see that Tino was willing to be whatever Henrick needed him to be—well, other than out of the closet. He stared at the picture as the night's events ran through his mind.

Tino should have known something was up when Rijeka called him and announced she was in Munich right after Tino set up a meeting with Bernardo, who had also shown up in town unexpectedly. He'd chalked Bernardo's visit up to the big endorsement deal Herr Friedberg's company suddenly offered him. They needed to hammer out the contract, but Bernardo knew Tino needed to get back into the routine with the team and couldn't afford an absence so soon after returning.

When Tino walked into the restaurant and found not just Bernardo but also Rijeka and her agent sitting at the table, he should have turned and ran, but he hadn't, and now he was in shit so deep he could barely breathe. A strong sense of déjà vu overcame Tino, and he forced himself to shake hands and take a seat at the table alongside Rijeka. It threw him back to the night he and Rijeka had been pushed together in Milan. Their agents had both seen opportunities in getting their clients into a fake relationship after the press elevated a simple dinner between friends into something romantic. Rijeka needed exposure to kick her career to the next level, and Tino needed someone to show off to the world as his girlfriend to calm the rumors swelling after the Paulo fiasco. It had been a deal that would benefit them both and harm neither, so Tino had taken it.

Herr Friedberg's company was big on family values. He should have expected that Bernardo would have already come up with a solution to Tino's not so wholesome image problem. Together with the other agent, Bernardo hatched a scheme that Rijeka agreed to before anyone even consulted Tino on the subject. The short conversation still rang in Tino's ears, no matter how hard he'd tried to forget it.

"Nice to see you again, Tino," Orri Jaggerson, Rijeka's agent, greeted Tino as he walked up to the table.

Tino bit back the snarky response on the tip of his tongue about it never being a good thing to see Orri and opted for politeness instead. "And you, Orri. What brings you to Munich?" Tino asked, already presuming he knew the answer.

"Business as usual."

Leaning in, he kissed Rijeka on the cheek and added a murmured hello. She smiled and grabbed his hand.

"So, Tino, we've been discussing your current situation, and I believe now is the time to take your future a bit more seriously. The deal with Herr Friedberg stands to be immensely lucrative, but there are a few things I think we need to hammer out before we go ahead with the campaign." Skipping the pleasantries, Bernardo launched straight into the business at hand.

"I thought the contract Kandis offered had everything in line for me to sign. You said so yourself after the lawyers looked it over." Tino played dumb because part of him knew what was coming and dreaded it.

A stern look settled on Bernardo's face, reminding Tino his agent didn't like to be played with. "You're a smart boy, Tino. I believe you know exactly what I'm getting at here."

Tino glanced at the other two people sitting at the table who watched the back and forth with interest. "You know what he's proposing right, Rijeka? And you're willing to go along with this?" Tino was unable to keep the disbelief out of his voice.

Rijeka shrugged her slim, elegantly dressed shoulders. "I have no better options on the horizon, Tino. I can't see what this will hurt...to just pretend for the cameras like we have been doing all along."

"But I don't want a fake marriage—"

"Hold on," Orri interrupted. "No one said anything about actually getting married. We are only talking an engagement, a long engagement if necessary. You know couples don't announce their intentions to wed and then the next week do it. You could drag this out for years, until the end of your career if need be."

"This will do a lot for your image, Tino. It will show the world you are not a playboy out partying; instead, you are a grown man who has decided to make a commitment to one woman," Bernardo said.

"I don't understand why we need to take this to the next level. Why can't our dating be enough?" Tino still didn't understand the media's fascination with who was in his bed. He simply couldn't wrap his head around it to have this all make sense.

"You have time to think this over, but I would strongly encourage you to think about what's best for the remainder of your career. You're not a doctor or lawyer; you're a professional football player. You have a shelf life, and the clock is ticking down faster than ever now." Bernardo reminded Tino of how short his playing time was.

"Sweetheart, it's not the end of the world. Nothing will really change, other than the ring I will wear that tells the world I'm yours," Rijeka said with a small reassuring smile on her lovely face.

Tino met each set of eyes in turn, seeing nothing but greed staring back at him. He wanted to get up and tell them all where they could go but knew that's not how these things worked. "Fine. I'll think it over, but I'm leaving now because I've suddenly lost my appetite." Tino stood abruptly and left, hearing the clamoring he left behind, but in the end, Bernardo told them to let him be, let him think on it on his own. They did because Tino made it to his car unimpeded. He was fuming by the time he got home, and the only thing he wanted was to talk to someone who would maybe talk him out of doing what was expected of him for once.

The phone in his hand hadn't rung. The little clock on it told him enough time had passed that if Henrick had awoken with the ringing, he would have either answered or have seen the missed call and returned it by now. He most likely wasn't going to get to talk to Henrick before he went to sleep.

He put the phone on the nightstand and lay back, but falling asleep had become increasingly difficult for Tino since his holiday ended. He couldn't get his mind to settle down and rest with so many unresolved issues hanging over his life. Eventually, he fell into an uneasy doze that ended shortly after it began when his alarm rang at seven, telling him it was time to start his day.

"YOU DON'T HAVE the proper equipment to cook anything, bambino." Tino's mama was searching through his kitchen cupboards with a frown on her face. "If you are serious about this learning to cook thing, then we need to go shopping."

"Okay, Mama, how about I call a car service, and you can take Papa and get whatever you think I need while I'm at practice. We can start the lessons tonight," Tino said, coming up with a solution to two problems at once. Getting what he needed to cook and keeping his parents occupied for the few hours he had to be at the stadium for practice would make his life easier.

His parents had flown in so Tino could tell them in person that he was going to announce his engagement to Rijeka. He didn't need the phone calls with questions in surprised and maybe damning voices that he knew would have come if he'd let them hear it on the news instead of telling them beforehand. He also decided that his mama was the perfect person to teach him how to make at least a simple meal, one that would please a certain picky little Austrian man. He told them about the deal, his engagement to Rijeka, and then quickly asked his mama if she could give him cooking lessons to change the subject, not giving them time to process the information by distracting them with something else entirely.

His mother latched on to the cooking as his father looked at him shrewdly but kept whatever he was thinking hidden behind those intelligent eyes for the time being. Tino was thankful for that, at least. There would be plenty of time for a serious conversation...later.

After calling the car service, he made sure his parents had everything they needed before instructing the driver to take them to the shopping district and to keep an eye on them. The driver nodded as he took the large tip from Tino's hand. He waved his parents off before going to his own car.

Tino was lost in his thoughts when the ringing of his phone blared through the little car. He hit the button on the wheel, allowing him hands-free access to his phone.

"Hello."

"Tino, it's Henrick." Henrick's voice came over the speaker so clearly that it sounded like he was sitting in the seat next to Tino, instead of kilometers away, probably still on the beach. If Tino's calculations were right, Henrick still had another day before he headed home. "Tino, are you there?"

"Hey, yeah, sorry, I'm driving right now," Tino said, making an excuse for his lack of response.

"I'll let you go then. You can call me when you get the chance." Tino detected a hint of disappointment in Henrick's voice.

"No, no, I have Bluetooth, so it's not a problem." He didn't want Henrick to hang up after only a couple of words.

"I just wanted to call you back. Sorry it took me so long, I was—"

"It's fine." Tino interrupted before Henrick could tell him that he'd been too busy with Dardan to call him back. "It's good to hear from you. I sort of thought maybe you wouldn't want to talk to me after I left without calling you to let you know when I needed to rush back to Rome."

"I saw the news, Tino. I'm able to put two and two together. You don't need to feel like you had to call me. I'm sure you had a lot on your mind that night."

Was that bit of snark in Henrick's last remark? "I did. I mean, first Rijeka showed up without warning and then the call from my agent. It's a wonder I remembered my name that night." He left out the part about Henrick blowing him off when he'd asked about getting dinner, and then he'd gone out with Dardan instead.

"Yeah, I figured as much. I just... I'm sorry for not calling sooner. I guess I didn't know where we stood either after you left and didn't call me for days." Henrick finally got to the heart of the issue instead of skirting it.

Tino sighed. "We're friends. Nothing's going to change that, short of you telling me to buzz off."

Henrick laughed, making Tino smile in response. "Okay, well then, why don't you call me when you're not operating heavy machinery, and we'll catch up on all that's going on in your life that doesn't make the news."

"Sounds really good to me. I'll call you later tonight, okay?"

"Sure, I'll be here. Nice talking to you, Tino, bye."

"You too, ciao."

His spirits lifted at the prospect of talking to him again that night, but then he remembered he needed to tell Henrick about his upcoming engagement. He had a feeling the news wasn't going to go over all that well, and all of a sudden, his happiness turned to apprehension. Damn his fucking life. Why couldn't anything ever be easy?

Chapter Twelve

SLIDING HIS SUNGLASSES on, Henrick stepped into the bright sunshine outside the airport. He looked around and finally saw the familiar Golf parked at the curb. The occupants of the car didn't even notice him approaching; so embroiled in their conversation were they, he had to rap on the window to get their attention. They both startled and turned with surprised expressions that turned to wide smiles when they realized they recognized the knocker. Both the front doors popped open, and his friends squealed as they converged on him in a group hug.

"Oh man, it's so good to have you back, finally. I need you to settle an argument for me," Gerta said.

"Not now. He just got here. We have to look at boring holiday photos and hear about how many gorgeous men he bedded before you can ask him to take sides." Hedy gave him one last squeeze before releasing him.

"Well if it's about politics, you're both wrong, and if it's anything else, most likely you're both still wrong." Henrick was happy to again be with people he knew well enough not to have to question how they'd take his joke. He received a light slap from Gerta and a hip bump from Hedy before both women hugged him again.

"We're glad you're home. Now maybe you can tell us why you ran away in the first place." Hedy grabbed one of his bags and helped him load them in the back of the little car.

"Oh my god, she's been so nuts with the conspiracy theories that you have to tell her already before she has you joining the French Foreign Legion as an undercover gay honey trap." Gerta scowled at her girlfriend.

Henrick snorted. "I can't wait to hear her other theories. If she's already worked her way up to the FFL, then the others must be pretty good." He climbed into the back seat while the women got in the front.

"No way, buddy. You are going to spill your guts before you get to hear even one of my—they could really happen—scenarios. We bought wine and snacks, and we're not leaving your apartment until you've told us every one of your deepest darkest secrets." Hedy punctuated her speech with eye contact in the rearview mirror.

Slumping in his seat, Henrick rubbed his forehead. All of his deepest, darkest secrets would mean telling other people's secrets. He could trust his two friends, but did he really want them to know everything? He had the whole car ride to decide and was no closer to figuring it out when they followed him up the stairs to his apartment. They made themselves at home after he unlocked the door to let them into his apartment, putting stuff in the fridge and getting snacks out in bowls while he stowed his suitcase in the bedroom and freshened up before going out again to face them.

When he returned to the living room, they were both sitting on the couch. Hedy had her arm thrown casually around Gerta's shoulders as they whispered to each other. Henrick sat in the chair with his legs pulled up under him.

"Okay, so we figure that you were seeing someone. Maybe someone new since you didn't tell us about him, and the whole thing went south, so you bolted instead of staying here and dealing with it," Gerta said, acting as the speaker for the two.

Henrick sighed because he was sick of holding everything in, and except for Oskar, he hadn't told anyone that his relationship, such as it was, with Klaus had ended. He deserved to have the support of his friends while he grieved, didn't he? "I was seeing someone but it was longer term and we did break up."

"I knew it!" Gerta shrieked, startling both Henrick and Hedy.

"Why didn't you tell us if it was someone who had been around for longer than a few weeks?" Hedy's eyes narrowed, but then enlightenment dawned on her face. "Oh my god, he was a closet case, wasn't he? Was he married?"

Henrick nodded, then shook his head. "No, he wasn't married, but now you guys have to swear you will not tell another living soul a single word I'm about to tell you." He'd made up his mind that he needed a shoulder, or four, to cry on.

They both drew an X over their hearts, and Gerta said, "We swear, now dish."

"Well, you know Klaus Fuchs from my department, right?" Hedy's eyes widened. Of course she knew him—she worked in accounting with his new fiancée.

"Oh no, you didn't?" She turned to Gerta. "You remember I was telling you about that jerk Lydia was dating?"

"No, Henrick, tell me you weren't fucking around with someone else's boyfriend." Gerta's eyes held the disappointment Henrick knew he deserved.

"Actually, I was fucking him before he started dating Lydia, so technically, he was cheating on me with her." Henrick tried to dig himself out of the hole they were putting him in. "And the minute he told me he was going to ask her to marry him, I ended it. That's why I went away."

"But you knew about her, and she didn't know about you so that's just as wrong," Hedy said. "Have you talked to Klaus since you went away?"

"Yes, but only because he kept calling. He said he needed to talk to me when I got back, but I've decided I'm not going to entertain any thoughts of him beyond someone I work with. Maybe now that he's engaged, he'll get a promotion and move out of my department."

Gerta and Hedy exchanged looks. One of those silent conversations long-term couples seem to be able to have with only their eyes must have taken place because Gerta nodded and Hedy rolled her eyes. "Fine. I'll tell him, but for the record, I'm doing it under duress." After making her feelings known to her partner, Hedy turned to Henrick. "Lydia said no when Klaus asked her to marry him, and they broke up. She told me she thought he was cheating on her with Kathy in research and development. Imagine her surprise if she knew it was you Klaus had been seeing and not some big-chested redhead."

Grabbing the wine bottle off the table, he filled a glass, drained it, and refilled it. Klaus wasn't engaged, which made his demeanor on the phone, when Henrick had finally broken down and called, make so much more sense. He was going to tell Henrick he was still a free man. Henrick would bet his last euro that Klaus thought he would run straight back into his arms when he heard the news. He wasn't so sure Klaus wasn't right. The news that he could, in good conscience, go back to Klaus—back to the relationship he thought he'd wanted—hit him like a ton of bricks. But then the memory of sad amber eyes set in the most handsome face he'd ever beheld jolted him back to reality and the realization that no matter what Klaus offered it would be too little too late when weighted against all the things Tino had said he'd do for the man he loved. Even if being with Tino was a pipe dream, Henrick didn't think he should settle for anything less than someone who completely adored him—and whom he adored in return with equal ferocity.

"Henrick, sweetie." Gerta's soft voice broke into Henrick's thoughts. "You can't go back to him and have him shove you in the closet. I can't believe you kept seeing him after he started dating Lydia, though I do understand maybe why you did, but he's not going to change. Don't make the mistake of thinking he can or will."

"I have more to tell you," Henrick said in a soft voice while staring at his lap. He was about to reveal a much bigger secret and for some reason one that hurt him more to share.

"Oh, now what? I don't think we could hear anything more shocking than you doing Klaus in—"

"I think I may be in love with Valentino Alessi," Henrick blurted, interrupting her. It was the first time he'd admitted it, even to himself, but once the words left his mouth, he knew they were true. It was too soon for such a strong feeling to have manifested itself, but there was no other word he could use to describe how he felt when he thought about Tino. "But he's about to announce his engagement to a supermodel." The whispered words were like a starting pistol for the tears he'd been holding since Tino called him back and broke the news. The silence from the couch lasted longer than Henrick would ever have thought it could with his two friends obviously left speechless by his confession.

"Are you crazy? Because unless you've all of a sudden taken up with a famous footballer, you don't even know the man. There's no way you could be in love with him," Hedy said.

"I met him in Albania. I told him I just wanted to be friends when he told me he wanted more. I screwed up because Klaus fucked my head up, and I was afraid Tino would do the same thing. I'd end up alone but not just alone, I'd end up the butt of the jokes on late night TV if he denied knowing me when it eventually got out because you know it would have; things like these always do, and it never has a happy ending like in the movies—"

"Henrick, stop. You're babbling and not making any sense. Now go back to the beginning, because are you really saying you met *the* Valentino Alessi, and he wanted you, but you turned him down?" The disbelief was clear in Gerta's voice.

Henrick pulled his phone out of the pocket of his shorts and scrolled through to his holiday photos—most of which included one Valentino Alessi in the flesh. He handed it to the two women on the couch and listened as they gasped and oh'd and ah'd over the mostly naked man in many of the photos. Henrick knew when they hit the first one of him and Tino together on the yacht because Gerta gasped, and Hedy muttered, "What the hell—on a yacht, even?"

He waited until they both looked up at him. "I think I blew it."

"I don't get it. A guy this hot wants you and you say 'thanks but no thanks'? What were you thinking?" Gerta asked.

"I told you what I was thinking and it's happened. He told me he's getting engaged because that snack food company, Kandis, offered him an endorsement deal. They have some sort of new energy bar he's doing an ad campaign for. His agent thought he needed to prove to the owner that he was a good match for his wholesome company. What better way to do it than to get engaged to be married?"

"When are the fucking heteros going to get it through their skulls that being in a committed relationship with a same-sex partner is no different than being married to someone of the opposite sex?" Hedy looked disgusted by the unfairness of life.

"I thought we were past this kind of crap. Aren't there other footballers who have come out?" Gerta asked.

Henrick shrugged. There were, but everyone knew there were benefits to staying in the closet—Tino's big endorsement deal being one of them. "But he's not going to. He made that much clear, and I can't do it again no matter how much I wish I could."

Gerta got off the couch first and perched on the arm of the chair so she could wrap her arms around his neck. "I'm so sorry, honey. You know if there was anything I could do, I would do it. Both Hedy and I want to see you happy."

Hedy perched on the opposite arm. "It's true. We sit up at night thinking of ways to introduce you to the perfect man so you can settle down. Too bad there's no such thing as a perfect *man*."

He let the two women cuddle him for a bit longer because it felt good to be held. "Thank you, guys, it's nice to be loved—even if it is by a couple of dykes," Henrick joked, paying Hedy back for her earlier jab at men.

Hedy play punched his arm as she stood. "Now we're going to order dinner, and you are going to dish about Valentino Alessi because seriously, how often does one get to hobnob with a celebrity on his yacht?"

"Never," Gerta said with a pout.

"Oh, honey, maybe you'll get your chance to meet Ellen one day, but until then, we'll have to live vicariously through our friends." Hedy kissed Gerta on her still pouting mouth.

"Fine, but you do remember Ellen is on my list, so if I meet her and she wants to jump my bones, you can't get mad." Gerta gave Hedy a sharp slap to the behind.

"Yes, dear, but you have to remember I get Portia so we'd be even." Hedy gave her girlfriend a smirk before she went to the kitchen to grab the takeout menus from the drawer.

Their comfortable banter made Henrick feel a bit better about his situation. At least he had good friends he could lean on—too bad he hadn't realized it sooner. He still didn't know what he was going to do about Klaus, but he'd figure it out. There wasn't anything to think about when it came to Tino because that ship had sailed. There was only friendship on the horizon in that direction, so he may as well come to grips with that fact and get on with his life—a life that wouldn't include having Valentino freaking Alessi in his bed.

TINO WAS SWEATING as he sat once again in front of an audience with bright lights surrounding him. Rijeka sat next to him on the stage of the first of many talk shows the two would be doing as the news of their engagement hit the press. Rijeka sat on his right, looking as beautiful as ever, not even glistening under the pressure and heat. They waited for the host to finish his touch-up with hair and makeup so they could get on with their segment. Tino wondered how much this program had paid to be the first to get the scoop. He hoped it was as much as it was costing him to make the announcement.

Rijeka took Tino's hand as the host, Rob or Bob or something, turned to them with a fake smile on his face. "Ready to do this, *dear*?" she asked.

"Ready as I'm ever going to be, *honey*." He and Rijeka had some words when they'd finally gotten a moment alone, and they hadn't been nice words to say the least. Their friendship suffered a blow with her easy acceptance of the offer to be engaged to one of Europe's most eligible bachelors, making it harder for Tino to pretend he liked her, much less loved her.

The host took in their little exchange without comment, but the way his jaw tightened showed his doubts about how well the upcoming interview was going to go. However, the guy totally underestimated Rijeka's acting ability. The minute the cameras started rolling, her demeanor changed, and she looked like the blushing soon-to-be bride she was playacting.

Tino made the announcement as planned, to the thunderous applause of the live audience. He answered the questions Bob or Rob asked as follow-up but then let Rijeka take over. She told the story of how they met and then fell in love. The made-up proposal was something they'd had to do, so there would be pictures to prove it actually took place just as they said it had. Tino shuddered when Rijeka presented the twelve-carat engagement ring to the camera, but his smile remained steady. He'd paid for the monstrosity, but they signed a contract that both insured the ring in his name and ensured the return of it when their ruse was up.

Tino tried to look beyond the lights to the audience. He suddenly wanted to see his parents' familiar faces so he could remind himself he still had something real in his life when everything else seemed to be a lie. He couldn't see them, but he imagined he could and relaxed enough to get through the rest of the show without screaming like a lunatic or throwing up all over the host's shiny black shoes. He and Rijeka walked off the stage arm in arm, but the minute they were out of sight behind the stage, Tino dropped the act.

"You did well, Tino," Bernardo said, "But next time, try not to look like you're going to be ill at the mention of a romantic honeymoon."

"Tino!" Tino turned to see his mama and papa walking down the hall toward them. The rush of cool relief flooded Tino's body, and he hurried into his mother's warm embrace. "My bambino, you looked so handsome up there on the stage."

"Grazie, Mama," Tino murmured as he let her crush him to her.

Releasing him, she turned to Rijeka. "You looked bellisimo, my dear. Will you be joining us for dinner tonight?"

Rijeka looked at Tino, who gave her a little shake of his head to tell her that no, she wouldn't be joining them. "No, I'm sorry, mama Alessi, but I have a business dinner to attend. Maybe another time when things calm down a bit."

"Oh, well then, yes another time." His mama frowned, probably at the woman she knew wasn't really going to be a part of the family using the too familiar term of address on her.

"Let's go. It's been a long day, and tomorrow will be even worse for me after I drop you off at the airport. I think I need some downtime with you before you leave for home." Tino addressed his parents before shaking Bernardo's hand and then leading his parents out of the building.

"YOU HAVE TO make your own pasta because if you don't it will not come out right. You have no idea what they put in the stuff you buy at the store," Tino's mama said as she prepared the dough. She measured things out just for Tino's benefit because, as she admitted to him days before, she just knew how much to use and therefore usually dumped things in.

"But what if I'm looking for something to fix quickly if I don't have time to make the pasta?" he asked, renewing the first cooking argument they'd had during the first lesson.

"Then you make a sandwich."

Tino chuckled. "Fine, homemade pasta it is, then. Here, let me mix it so I know what it should feel like for the next time when you're not here to tell me when to stop." She moved aside and let him take over the mixing of the dough with his hands.

She stood back and watched him with a thoughtful look on her face before she asked, "I don't understand why you do it, Tino. Why do you hide who you are from the world—from us?" Tino heard the hurt behind her question but kept silently mixing the dough. "I mean you are such a wonderful man. Who cares who you choose to love, as long as you love them the way you should?"

Tino wondered the same thing. His end goal seemed to get fuzzier and fuzzier the farther down the rabbit hole he fell. "It started off as a good business decision. There have been players who have come out, and I've talked to them and learned their options are limited. They don't get offered the same opportunities as all the other players get. I'd be limited financially if I came out. Bernardo did the salary comparison for me back when I first told him. He advised me against telling the truth for as long as I could so that's what I've done." It was the only explanation he had for his duplicity.

"But that doesn't explain why you didn't tell us. Your family should have known the real you, bambino." This time the hurt was dripping from her words.

"What I wonder—" Tino looked up from his dough making at the sound of his father's voice to see the man standing in the doorway of the kitchen. "—is how much money do you need to make you happy? When is enough, enough?"

The question knocked Tino off-balance because he'd not really been thinking about it that way. He looked at it more as his chance to play the game with the best players in the world, or at least, that was how it started. Tino wasn't sure when it had begun to be more about the money than the game. If he was happy just playing now that he had more than enough money to last him many lifetimes over, then why did he have to keep up the charade?

"Gives you something to think about, doesn't it?" he asked while searching Tino's face when he got no answer.

Tino finished with the dough and washed his hands. The whole while he was trying to think of an answer that would justify what he'd allowed himself to become. His phone made a rude noise that made his parents look at him as if he'd done it. He fished his phone out of his pocket and showed it to them as it made the burping sound again with another incoming text message. Tino couldn't help smiling at the picture of Henrick on his screen, alerting him to just who was interrupting the uncomfortable conversation he'd been having.

Henrick: *Just saw the show. You looked great. Congrats on your engagement.* ;)

Henrick: *Oh I forgot, tell Rijeka she looked good too, and the congrats are for her also.* :P

Tino had hated hearing the disappointment in Henrick's voice when he'd told him he was going to announce the engagement. He'd wondered if their friendship could weather the storm to come. Henrick must obviously believe Tino was doing gays everywhere a great injustice by not coming out and being a role model for young gay people. He would have loved to surprise Henrick by being the man Henrick wanted him to be, but instead, he'd once again taken the coward's way out. With his text, Henrick was letting him know he was okay after watching

Tino tell the world he was marrying Rijeka. His jokes told the whole story—Henrick accepted that Tino was what he was, and they were still friends despite it.

Thanks. I will tell her when I decide to start talking to her again. Tino typed back.

Henrick: *Uh oh, that doesn't sound good. Call me if you want to talk.*

Tino couldn't stop smiling at the thought of unburdening all his troubles into Henrick's ear.

Will call later after the parents go to bed.

Tino put his phone back in his pocket, but the grin stayed firmly plastered across his face.

"That is how a man should look after he talks to the one person he loves most," Tino's mama said. Looking up, he'd momentarily forgotten he wasn't alone. His father was nodding to agree with his mother.

"It was just a friend congratulating me on the engagement. He's funny, and he makes me laugh."

"That smile was not from any joke, bambino. That is a smile of love, so don't you lie to me. Tell us about him while you help me feed this dough through the pasta cutter."

That's just what Tino did. He told his parents the whole story of Tino and Henrick and why it would never be anything more than friendship between the two of them. Tino ended his story just as the water for the pasta started to boil. He added the noodles while his mama stirred the sauce.

"Well, seems to me that you've already found what you're looking for," his papa said. "Now you just need to decide what you'll do to get it and make it yours."

Tino realized at that moment that his father had always been a man of few words—unusual for an Italian man—but the ones he did say were always meaningful. "I know, Papa, and maybe in a few years—"

"You don't have a few years. I'm sure if this man is all you say he is, he will find someone who will be what he needs if you don't step up to be that man," his mama said. "Get the chicken from the oven, Tino. It's done."

Tino pulled the pan of chicken breasts out of the oven and placed them on the hot pad. "I can't be that man yet. I have to finish what I started, and then I'll do what needs to be done." His declaration sounded convincing enough to his own ears but not enough to make his parents believe it if the expressions on their faces were any indication.

His mother's eyes took on a look of sadness. "We only want you to be happy; that's all. Now drain the pasta."

Tino drained the pasta and helped his mama make up three plates. They sat at the island in the kitchen and ate. The food was simple but delicious, with the added benefit of his parents having their mouths full, which meant Tino didn't have to listen to them tell him things he already knew but felt powerless to change.

TINO DIALED HENRICK'S number after he made sure his parents were settled in the guest room and he'd lain in his own bed. He felt both anticipation and nervousness as he waited for Henrick to answer.

"Hello?"

"Hey there, were you sleeping?" Tino checked the time. It was only a little after ten, but one could never be sure when it came to other people's bedtimes.

"Uh, no. I was actually just watching some television in my bed, wondering if you were going to call."

The thought of Henrick in bed made Tino perk up in more ways than one. "So here we are in bed together. What do you want to do now?"

"You were going to tell me why you aren't talking to your fiancée, but I guess if you want, we could change those plans."

The suggestive note in Henrick's voice made Tino shiver, but then he laughed. Henrick would tease him mercilessly if he opted for the second option implied in his offer. "Rijeka doesn't seem to be at all bothered by our arrangement. In fact, I think she's enjoying it."

"And that makes you what? Mad? Sad? Why is it bothering you that it doesn't bother her?" Henrick toned back the flirting and stayed on task.

Tino shifted in his bed but didn't answer. He didn't want to tell Henrick that it bothered him because she had just accepted the deal for what it was, and he just couldn't do that anymore. It was getting harder and harder to accept that he was living a lie. He needed to reassess and maybe start taking steps to take back control of his life before he ended up married and announcing a child on the way. His silence spoke volumes.

Chapter Thirteen

"ARE YOU STILL there?" He could hear the other man breathing, so he knew Tino hadn't hung up, but he still felt the need to ask when Tino was silent for over a minute.

"I'm sorry. I was just thinking about things."

"Want to tell me what things you were thinking about?"

"Not really," Tino said with a heavy sigh.

"Why not?"

"Because it's my problem, and no amount of talking about it is going to make it better because...shit." Tino sounded frustrated.

Henrick wished he could see the other man because he wasn't sure what Tino was thinking. Being able to see Tino's eyes always helped him decipher the meaning behind his words. Tino was upset about the engagement, which he knew, but he wasn't sure what about it provoked that emotion. Was it being forced to lie to the world about his sexual orientation, or was there something else bugging him about it? He was mad at Rijeka for going along with the ruse when Henrick figured Tino should be grateful to the woman for helping him out. He had no frame of reference in which to offer Tino advice if he wouldn't tell him exactly what the problem was.

"Okay, then I guess we can talk about something else if you want?" Henrick felt useless on the advice-giving front so may as well change the subject.

"Yeah, sure, um, let's see… Oh, have you gone back to work yet?" Tino hit on the one subject Henrick would prefer not to talk about, probably figuring it was a safe topic for discussion.

"Yes, I worked today, but nothing interesting happened." He wasn't about to tell Tino that the man who had broken his heart worked in his office and was once again available. There was also no way in hell he was going to tell Tino that he'd had the cold sweats when he returned to work only to find Klaus was out of the office for the day. Or that Klaus would be back in the morning, and Henrick would have to face him then. Those were all things Tino didn't need to know about his work life.

"Well, that effectively kills that line of conversation."

"Sorry. I'm sure you don't want to hear about the virus that took down Simtech's IT department." Henrick forced a chuckle.

Tino snorted a short laugh. "Yeah, probably not. So anything else happening in your life that's more interesting than viruses?"

Henrick racked his brain, trying to think of something—anything he could talk about to keep Tino on the phone with him—but the only thought that kept popping up was *I'm pretty sure I realized I'm in love with you*, and that was not something he was prepared to say, not now—probably not ever.

"Nothing. I guess I lead a boring life compared to you, huh?"

"No, not boring, just sane and normal." Tino's voice was wistful in a way that made Henrick's chest hurt in sympathy.

Henrick decided to change tactics and throw caution to the wind for one night and one night only; at least that's what he vowed to himself. "Hey, Tino, I bet you can't guess what I'm wearing." Henrick intentionally made his voice breathy. He told himself that what he was about to do was just a little harmless fun, not like he hadn't had meaningless sex with loads of guys. He could do this to lift Tino's spirits, and it would mean nothing more than that—just one friend cheering up another.

"What?"

"I said I bet you can't guess what I'm wearing." He repeated his words, hoping the man would get the hint.

"I don't know what you're getting at here, Henrick—"

"Nothing. I'm not wearing a thing, completely naked—"

"Henrick." Tino's tone was a warning Henrick didn't heed.

"Oh, keep talking like that. Makes me hard when you get all growly," Henrick said, pushing his agenda.

"I'm going to hang up if you don't stop."

"No, don't hang up! Talk to me. Say something in that sexy Italian accent of yours. Tell me something you like to do to a guy when you get them in your bed." Just the thought of Tino talking about sex got Henrick hard. He pushed his sleep pants down, exposing his bobbing length.

"You don't want to do this."

Henrick was sure the breathiness in Tino's voice wasn't in his head. He had Valentino *freaking hot as hell* Alessi turned on, and he was going to make him happy for at least a little while if it killed him. "Tino, let me be the one to decide what I want. Now, are you going to talk dirty to me or not?"

He could almost hear Tino thinking it over before he said, "Tell you what. If you send me a picture of you, the way you look right now, then I'll talk dirty to you for as long as you want."

Henrick didn't even think twice as he hung up the call and hit the button to start a video chat. It took Tino more rings than it should have for him to accept the invitation, giving Henrick enough time to wiggle all the way out of his sleep pants while he wondered if Tino was going to ignore him.

"Henrick, what are you doing?" Tino stared angrily out of Henrick's phone at him.

"I thought this may be better than just a picture and a voice." Henrick put on his best flirty expression and pulled the phone away so Tino could see his naked chest as he leaned back against the headboard of his bed. Tino sucked in a breath before slowly blowing it back out as Henrick moved the phone lower. He stopped when the top of his pubic hair showed in the little camera box that showed him what the other man could see.

"Henrick..." Tino said in a shaky voice.

"Do you want me to continue?" Tino nodded. "Then you have to tell me something. Say something that will make me want to show you."

Tino groaned. "I'm not any good at this, Henrick, but looking at you laid out like that makes me so hard. I wish I was there with you so I could touch you. Just thinking about the way your skin feels under my hands makes me want to touch every inch with my hands, my mouth..." Tino let the words die on his tongue as Henrick moved the phone down to capture his groin. "Oh fuck...touch it for me...please?"

"Tell me how you'd suck my cock if you were here." Henrick reached to take himself in hand. He tried not to feel self-conscious about the words he was saying or the intimate act he was about to perform in front of a friend. If Tino had been his boyfriend—hell, if he'd been even a fuck buddy—Henrick would have had no problem being even raunchier, but Tino was neither. It felt weird, but how could he stop when he'd been the one to start it? He wanted to make Tino feel better, and sex was the only way he knew how to do that.

"I'd start by kissing every inch of your velvety soft skin. Then I'd lick it to get it nice and slick before I took the head... Yeah, just like that, fuck, that's so sexy. Don't stop." Tino's breath began coming in faster pants that really turned Henrick's crank.

Henrick ran his hand over the head of his dick, gathering the moisture beginning to accumulate to slick his way down his shaft. He forgot about making Tino talk dirty, in favor of concentrating on his own pleasure. He was sure Tino was touching his own erection offscreen, and suddenly, he wanted to see what the other man's cock looked like more than anything in the world. "Show me, Tino. Let me see you." Henrick regretted the words as soon as they left his mouth. This little show was supposed to be about him doing something for Tino to make him happy, not so he could get a peek at the forbidden fruit he kept dreaming about. Before he could take the words back, Tino's engorged member filled his screen, and that tattoo...

Moaning in pleasure, he watched Tino's hand move quickly up and down his own arousal. Henrick increased the speed of his strokes to match those on the phone screen. He tried to memorize every inch of the thick veiny cock, creating a memory he'd lock away, only to be taken out when he most needed it. Who was he kidding? There was no way that image wouldn't haunt his thoughts for the foreseeable future. Henrick stroked faster and harder as he watched Tino do the same.

"Going to come. Come on...come on...now...now, baby. Come now." Tino's voice pulled the orgasm right out of Henrick's body. He almost dropped his phone as the pleasure hit him, and his toes curled as the warmth of his own release hit him on the stomach. For a moment, he let himself pretend it was Tino's seed splattered across his abs, and even though it wasn't, it was a nice thought, nonetheless. Just as he stopped coming, Tino started.

Henrick watched the thick fluid as it shot from the other man's cock, over his fist, and into the dark patch of hair below his navel. His eyes moved up the screen to find Tino's hooded amber gaze looking back at him with so much longing he turned away before he got sucked in. There was an awkward moment of silence where both sat there quietly while their come cooled on their own bodies.

"Henrick—"

"It was just a bit of fun, Tino." He lifted his phone up so only his face could be seen. "Don't read anything into it, okay?"

"Yeah, I know, and I won't." Tino repositioned his phone. "I should probably go clean up. Thanks for the distraction. I'll talk to you later, huh?"

"Tino..." Henrick started, but the look on Tino's face stopped him cold.

"I get it and it's fine. Let me go now so I don't say something stupid, all right?" Tino's shaky voice had a little pleading edge to it.

"Okay, we'll talk soon though, right?" Henrick recognized the same tone in his own question.

Tino was no longer looking into the camera as he said, "Yes. Good night, Henrick."

The screen went black before Henrick could issue his own farewell. He got up and cleaned himself off before crawling back between the sheets. His mind went to Tino's tattoo. A simple heart with a knife skewered through it. He wondered if Tino had gotten that after Paulo had hurt him.

He felt horrible for pushing Tino into doing something they both knew shouldn't have happened. He hoped he hadn't fucked things up. Why couldn't he have just left well enough alone?

HENRICK WAS IN the break room pouring himself a cup of coffee when Klaus found him. "Henrick, can I see you in my office when you get the chance?"

"Sure, I have a couple of things I have to get done, but I'll be in soon." Henrick walked back to his own cubicle and plonked down into his chair. He figured the work day wouldn't progress very far before he'd be summoned into Klaus's office, but he still wasn't ready to face him. Poking about on his computer for a bit calmed his nerves a little, but soon it would be obvious he was stalling for time if he waited any longer.

"Come in, Henrick," Klaus called when Henrick knocked on the door frame. "Close the door."

After closing the door behind him, he took a seat in one of the chairs in front of Klaus's desk. He crossed his legs and gripped the arms of the chair to brace himself for the upcoming conversation.

"How was your holiday?" Klaus rested his elbows on the desk as he leaned forward.

"It was good. Lots of sun and sand, good food and wine," Henrick said with a noncommittal shrug.

"That's good. I'm glad you had fun. You deserved the break, but I'm also glad you're back. I missed you." Klaus stood and rounded the desk to lean against the front of it.

"Klaus, I told you it was over between us, and I meant it." He could see where the conversation was heading and wanted no part of it.

"I'm not with Lydia anymore. There's no reason for us not to be together again, like we were before." Klaus sounded as if he thought that was exactly the right thing to say to get Henrick back in his bed.

Henrick stood. "I don't want things to go back the way they were before. I wasn't happy then, and it won't make me happy now. I want a real relationship with someone who will acknowledge my existence outside the bedroom." He turned to leave, but Klaus grabbed his wrist, stopping him before he could even take the first step toward the door.

"I'm willing to make some changes to our agreement. I want you, Henrick. Do you really think I'd give Lydia up if I wasn't willing to try to make it work with you?"

Henrick clenched his jaw, enraged at Klaus's outright lie. "I know she dumped you when you proposed to her, Klaus. Don't make it seem like you chose me over her because I know it's not true, and the fact that you'd lie to me like that tells me just how much I can trust you. If you had at least told me the truth, maybe I could have given you another chance, but now I can tell you with all the certainty in the world that it's over between us." Henrick looked down at where Klaus was still gripping his arm. "Now, if you'll be so kind as to let me go, I'd like to go back to work."

"Can't we just talk about this? Maybe over dinner. I'll take you out somewhere."

Henrick jerked his arm out of Klaus's grasp. "No. From now on if it doesn't pertain to work, there's no reason for you to talk to me." He was fed up with Klaus's shit and wasn't going to take it any longer. His anger simmered as he walked back to his desk, but he knew he wasn't going through that again *with* any man, *for* any man. He'd proven he could say no to one man, so he'd keep telling them all no until one day... An image of Tino floated across his mind. *Oh, who am I kidding? That has a snow ball's chance in hell of ever happening.*

TINO RAN HIS finger under the collar of his Armani shirt. The bow tie around his neck felt like it was cutting off his airway as the crowded elevator made its way to the top floor. Rijeka squeezed him with the hand she had in the crook of his elbow, to get his attention. Tino looked at her, and she smiled reassuringly back at him before she leaned in.

"Is it strange that I'm actually looking forward to this?" she asked.

"Very strange, but then you've always been a bit off."

It had been four months since they'd announced their engagement, and after a drunken night spent yelling at each other, they'd finally come to an uneasy truce. Rijeka explained why she'd accepted the setup so easily. The engagement meant publicity that boosted her career while helping out someone she'd come to think of as a dear friend. How could she have said no? Tino then told her why it was so hard for him and how he had grown to hate himself for the lying. She'd comforted him when he'd broken down and told her he was sure he was in love with someone who wouldn't give him a chance. Now that they knew each other's motivations, they could work past them and actually enjoy their times out in public as friends.

They stepped off the elevator and followed the crowd to the ballroom crowded with well-known faces from many sectors of society. There were famous athletes like Tino, actors and actresses, singers, and wealthy business people. They were all mingling together over glasses of champagne and little hors d'oeuvres that made Tino think of Henrick.

Tino led Rijeka into the mass of bodies and let her be the one to join in a discussion so he could just stand there and people watch. His phone buzzed against his thigh, and he pulled it out to check the message.

Henrick: *I just ate an entire jar of Nutella with a spoon. :(*

Tino chuckled as his phone beeped with another message before he could respond. It was a picture of Henrick with a chocolate-rimmed, spoon-filled mouth and a look of horror on his face as he stared into an empty Nutella jar. Tino laughed a little louder, drawing the attention of the group Rijeka was talking to.

"Sorry, a friend is having sort of a crisis, I think." Tino pointed at his phone. "I need to deal with this. I'll be at our table." He kissed Rijeka on the cheek before walking off while typing on his phone.

You just made me look like an idiot in front of Simon Fuller. Now why would you eat that crap? Tino typed and hit send.

He found his name on one of the tables and sat down.

Henrick: *Because I did something I shouldn't have today, so I needed something sweet and I didn't have any ice cream :,(*

Tino wondered what he'd done now, but then knowing Henrick, Tino wasn't sure if asking him was wise. Of course, he did so anyway.

Oh yeah? And what did you do that you shouldn't have done?

There was no answer for a bit, and Tino was sure he wasn't going to answer because it was one of those *things* Henrick did and alluded to in their conversations but never came right out and said he'd fucked someone he probably shouldn't have.

Henrick: *I volunteered to go on a business trip with my former fuck buddy, and now he thinks we're good again.*

Why would you volunteer to go if you knew it would end up causing him to think that way?

Tino tapped the little letters on his screen so hard he thought he might end up damaging the phone. Tino was pretty sure he would punch Klaus if he ever met the guy. From what he'd gleaned about Henrick's former, closeted fuck buddy from their conversations, the prick deserved it for how he'd treated Henrick.

Henrick: *Because the trip is to Munich…*

Henrick: *And I know that a certain someone will be in town that week because he has a home game…*

Tino sucked in a breath and let it out through his teeth. Henrick was going to be in Munich, and Tino lived in Munich, and even though it was only a short drive to Salzburg, neither one of them had ever brought up visiting the other before. Tino wondered what it meant that Henrick wanted to see him in person.

When is this trip? he typed, hoping it was the next home game, which was only a week away.

Tino sat there staring at his phone for the answer, so when a hand landed on his shoulder, he jumped before turning to see Herr Friedberg and his wife standing next to him.

"Tino, so nice to see you," Herr Friedberg said as Tino stood to shake the man's hand.

"Good to see you too, sir." Tino turned to Frau Friedberg. She smiled brightly before leaning in for air kisses on each side of his face. "Frau Friedberg, you look stunning this evening."

"You look very dashing yourself, signor Alessi," She batted her eyelashes at him.

"Please call me Tino." He liked the Friedbergs. They were a lovely couple, and the few times Tino had the pleasure of meeting with them both, he'd had a reasonably good time. He had to ignore the vibrating phone in his pocket, no matter how much he wanted to find out when he'd get to see Henrick again.

"Where is that lovely woman you talked into marrying you?" Herr Friedberg asked.

"Last I saw she was engaged in a conversation about the Cannes Film Festival with a couple of up-and-coming directors."

"Oh, is she thinking of getting into the business?" Frau Friedberg asked, looking rather more interested in the topic than Tino.

"I'm not sure, but isn't that what models do these days?"

"What do models do?" Rijeka asked from behind Tino as she walked up to join their little group.

"Pursue acting careers." Frau Friedberg filled her in with a smile.

Throwing her head back, Rijeka let loose a throaty laugh, drawing more attention to them than Tino was comfortable with. "Oh dear, that is funny. I'm not a good actress, just a pretty face." She put her arm around Tino's waist and stood close.

"Oh, I don't know. I'm sure you could do it if you put your mind to it," Tino said with a wink. She caught his hidden meaning and smiled even bigger at him as she winked back.

"Aw, look at how sweet they are together. You two are just like Ulrich and I were when we first got married," Frau Friedberg cooed.

"It's nice to see a young couple so obviously in love. Reminds us old folks of what used to be," Herr Friedberg said.

"I'm sure you two are just as in love now as the day you met." Rijeka pressed into Tino hard enough that she could feel the vibrating of his phone as it shook with yet another text from Henrick. She leaned in to whisper in his ear. "If you need to go see what you-know-who wants, I can entertain the Friedbergs while you excuse yourself to use the restroom."

"It's fine. He can wait." Tino turned his attention back to the Friedbergs, the reason he and Rijeka were at the very prestigious fundraiser in the first place.

"I've heard the campaign is coming along at a good pace," Herr Friedberg said. It was the signal for the women to chat while the men talked business.

Tino had been surprised to see that he and Rijeka were seated at the same table as the Friedbergs. The conversation between the two couples went smoothly and included some of the others dining with them at times. Before Tino knew it, the whole thing was over, and he and Rijeka were getting into their chauffeured car, heading back to his apartment.

"Well, I think that went very well. Herr Friedberg is very taken with you. I wouldn't be surprised if he offered you more endorsement deals for his company." Rijeka sat back against the plush seat of the car, looking relaxed.

"I don't know if I'm willing to do much more than this one. The contract is for a year, and I think that's plenty of time to be under the scrutiny that working with a man like Herr Friedberg puts on a person."

Rijeka nodded. "So what do you plan to do?"

"What do you mean?"

"I mean, I know you want to live your life as a gay man with all that entails, but when are you going to start? Are you going to wait until you're done playing football?"

"I don't think I can wait that long," Tino answered truthfully. Looking down, he saw that he'd pulled his phone out of his pocket without even realizing it. He rubbed his thumb across the screen to bring it to life and the picture of Henrick that he used as his wallpaper reminded him of why he couldn't wait that long to tell the world he was gay.

"Do you really think you can be in love with a man you've only known in the flesh for a week?" Rijeka watched him caress the screen like it was a lover instead of a picture of someone he wished was.

"I've learned more about him in the past four months than I've ever known about another man, and yes, I think I am in love with him."

"So what did he want earlier, if you don't mind me asking?"

Tino checked the missed messages from Henrick.

Henrick: *No, it's actually not for a month, the game against Berlin.*

Henrick: *I thought we could get together. I'll be there for the whole work week and maybe I could stay the weekend?*

Henrick: *Tino? Are you there?*

Henrick: *I don't have to stay for the weekend...*

Henrick: *Maybe we could just have dinner one night?*

Henrick: *Or maybe not...*

Henrick: *Okay, I'm sorry I was being presumptuous. I still have to come to Munich for business, if you can think about it and let me know sometime in the next month.*

Henrick: *Tino? Hello?*

Henrick: *I'm running to the shops to get ice cream now!*

Henrick: *Forget this whole conversation ever took place please and text me back!*

Henrick: *Okay I'm going to bed so good night, Tino.*

"Crap." Tino quickly typed out a message to explain his lack of response to Henrick's announcement of an impending visit.

"What's wrong?" Rijeka asked.

"He's coming to Munich on a business trip in a month, and I couldn't answer him since the Friedbergs were sitting with us. Now he thinks I was ignoring him because I don't want to see him." He was a little frustrated with how quickly Henrick was to jump to conclusions. He hated that Henrick was so insecure in that respect. Tino had recognized Henrick's insecurity early on, so he tried not to give him reason to question how Tino felt about him.

"But you do want to see him, right?"

"I want to see him more than you'll ever know." Tino's phone buzzed with another incoming text from Henrick.

Henrick: *I didn't know you were at the fundraiser tonight. I thought it was next weekend. Sorry for being an asshat. ;)*

Henrick: *I'm sure you're tired, so we can talk about it another day. Good night, Tino. XOXOXO*

Tino typed his own good night while sighing in relief. "That man is going to be the death of me." His muttered words made Rijeka laugh and hug him.

"I'm glad to see you like this over someone. It's sweet how much you care about him even if he doesn't know it," she said as she rested her head on his shoulder.

"Can I tell you a secret?"

"Sure, you know it's safe with me." She snuggled closer.

"I bought a holiday house in Duress."

"That's not a huge secret. You told me you were looking for property when I was there."

"Yeah, but I didn't tell you that one night over dinner Henrick told me what he considered the perfect house."

Rijeka sat up and looked at Tino's face in the muted light of the car. "Okay, and?"

"I bought a house that almost fit the description and then had it remodeled so it has everything he mentioned, right down to the ten pillows and ten shower heads and ten tub jets." A soft smile touched his lips at the memory of one of Henrick's oddities that Tino loved.

"You really do love him, don't you?" Rijeka asked with a look of wonder on her face.

"Yeah, I think I really do."

Chapter Fourteen

HENRICK JUST COULDN'T get in the mood for a celebration; instead, he sat on the bar stool at the little table and watched as his friends danced on the packed floor. He swore he'd left his apartment feeling anticipation for a night of drunken debauchery, but somewhere along the way he'd lost his momentum. Even the cute guy who kept cruising him from the booth to the right of his table couldn't get him out of his funk. Henrick pounded back another shot just as the hottie got up and headed in his direction. The multicolored strobe lights made it hard to determine for certain the guy's hair, eye, or skin color until he was standing in the vee of Henrick's open thighs. The guy pressed a hard hip into Henrick's groin as he leaned in, bringing the scent of his cologne and the fruity drink he'd been sipping right into Henrick's face.

"Hey there. You want to dance?" His voice was low and gravelly, making Henrick figure he was probably a smoker.

"Um, not right now, thanks," Henrick said politely. He tried to shift to get the guy out from between his legs, but the man was bigger and apparently not ready to move.

"Then let me buy you another drink, and maybe you'll be ready." He waved to the barback for another round.

Henrick searched the dance floor for Hedy, Gerta, and Remy but he didn't see any of them in the press of flesh just beyond his table. "That's very nice of you, but really, I'm not much of a dancer." Henrick tried another tack to get rid of the guy who now had his hand on the back of his stool, caging him in.

"I'm sure you're one hell of a dancer once you get enough alcohol in you," stranger danger said.

"Sorry, I'm actually not much of a drinker either." He rolled his eyes in irritation; some guys just wouldn't take no for an answer.

The guy studied Henrick for a minute before huffing a smelly laugh into his face. "You like to play hard to get, huh?" He turned so they were face-to-face, hips pressed flush. "I will chase if that's what you want, but then you better be prepared when I catch you."

Henrick stiffened at the undertone of a threat in the guy's voice and the hard glint in his eyes. "I think you need to step back a bit and actually hear what I'm saying, because in my world, after a guy has said no three times, it's time to leave." Henrick raised a hand to give the guy a little push to help him along.

He let out a squeak when the guy caught his hand and leaned over him, using his bigger body to pin Henrick to the back of his stool. Turning his face away as the guy started talking with his lips just inches from Henrick's skin, his eyes frantically searched for one of his friends.

"Listen here, you little tease. You've been giving me signals all night and— Hey what the fuck?" the guy shouted as Henrick felt the guy's body jerk away.

Henrick turned to see what had made the guy suddenly move so fast. The sight of Klaus standing there in the middle of a gay-friendly bar, holding the guy, who had been bothering Henrick, by the back of the shirt as he growled at him, too low to hear over the thumping music, held Henrick in a trance he couldn't break no matter how much he wanted to get up and head for the door. Klaus finished whatever it was he was saying and let go of the guy's shirt. The guy looked at Henrick quickly, then turned and practically ran in the other direction.

"Are you okay?" Klaus asked a stunned Henrick. When Henrick didn't answer, Klaus put his hand on his shoulder. "Henrick, are you okay? Did he hurt you?" Klaus searched Henrick's face, and when he found no obvious signs of injury, the worry melted from his features. "Let me get you a glass of water."

Reaching out, he grabbed Klaus's wrist to stop him, making Klaus turn back with a questioning look on his face. "What are you doing here?" The question surprised Henrick because he'd intended to tell Klaus thank-you when he'd stopped him, not ask why he was there.

Klaus stepped closer to the table. "I came with a friend. I saw you sitting here and figured you wouldn't want to talk to me, but when that asshole wouldn't leave you alone, I couldn't just sit there and watch him scare you like that."

"I wasn't scared," Henrick said defensively, then quickly added, "But thank you for getting involved. That guy was a jerk who wouldn't take no for an answer."

"I could see that. Well, if you're okay, then I guess I'll go back to my friend."

Henrick didn't know if it was the shots he'd drunk or the time he'd had to think about how he needed to take some of the blame for the way his relationship with Klaus had played out that had something to do with him softly smiling at Klaus. "Would you and your friend like to join me?"

"Aren't your friends coming back?" Klaus looked out at the dance floor before meeting Henrick's eyes once again.

"They are, but there's room for two more."

"I'll go see if Jean-Luc would mind switching tables," Klaus said with a wide grin.

Henrick nodded and wondered just who Jean-Luc was and if that sour feeling in his stomach was actually jealousy. If it was the little green-eyed monster rearing its head, it was only because he was jealous some other guy got what he hadn't and not because he still wanted Klaus, or at least that's what he told himself.

Klaus and his friend appeared out of the crowd at the same time as Gerta and Hedy. They converged on Henrick's table, and the questioning looks from the girls came quickly on the heels of the dirty looks they both shot Klaus.

"Hedy, Gerta, this is Klaus from work and his friend, Jean-Luc, right?" Henrick made the introductions. They eyed each other warily as they shook hands and sat down. "How do you know Klaus, Jean-Luc?" Henrick was curious as to what sort of relationship the two men had.

"We met at the gym, then we realized we had some things in common and we've been hanging out a bit lately," Jean-Luc said with an obnoxious French accent. Leave it to Klaus to find a Frenchman, Henrick thought, as he realized it had been a bad idea to invite them to sit at his table. He downed another shot and then another as he listened to Hedy and Gerta pump Jean-Luc for information about Klaus—they were as subtle as a sledgehammer to the head.

Henrick had no idea how many shots he had before Klaus got him out on the dance floor, but he was now pressed tightly against the wall of familiar muscle that was Klaus. They didn't grind like the other couples; instead, they swayed gently as if listening to a totally different track than everyone else. Henrick didn't even mind when Klaus bent and pressed light kisses to the side of his neck and then his cheek.

"I've missed you so much. Can you please give me another chance to show you I really can be the guy you need me to be?" Klaus asked.

The deep loneliness of the past five months seeped out from the place in his heart where he'd tried to lock it away by telling himself that alone was better than together if it meant you were unhappy. He nodded before he could think better of it. Klaus kissed him and he let it happen. Henrick went with the flow for the rest of the night, and that's how he ended up waking with a throbbing head and Klaus snoring in his bed.

"OUR TRAIN LEAVES at seven twenty-three, so we should be there around nine," Henrick told Tino over the phone. "We're staying at The Charles on Sophienstasse." It was Monday afternoon. Henrick had his bags packed and was waiting for Klaus to pick him up. They were taking the train to Munich, instead of driving.

"Okay, do you want me to pick you up?"

"No, we have a car service set up for the week." Plus, he really didn't want Tino to meet Klaus. He and Klaus hadn't defined their relationship yet, and Henrick was fine with that, because he was in no hurry to hang the title of boyfriend on Klaus. Klaus had hinted at wanting more, but to his surprise, Henrick was the one who was reticent this time around.

"Okay...so then, when do you want to get together? We could meet at the hotel bar after you get settled if you want."

"I don't think I'll be up to it. I'll probably be tired and not very good company. Train rides tend to make me grumpy." He was making excuses and hoped Tino wouldn't pick up on it.

"Okay, so not tonight then. What about tomorrow, do you work all day?" Sounding like he was barely containing his rising frustration, Tino's words were clipped.

"It'll probably be a long day tomorrow until we figure out what exactly we're looking at, but I'm sure I'll have time to see you afterward."

Tino snorted. "Well, don't sound so enthusiastic about it."

"I'm sorry. I'm just trying to remember if I packed everything I need as far as work goes. I'm really looking forward to seeing you again. I've missed you."

"I've missed you too." Tino's voice lost the hard edge it had taken on as Henrick made his excuses. "I just can't wait to see you in the flesh again."

Tino's frank admission made Henrick's heart swell and then drop. He wasn't supposed to want Tino to want him, and it was mean to hope for that when he was unwilling to return the feeling. "Me, too, but now I have to go, my ride is here." He heard Klaus's unmistakable heavy footsteps outside his door.

"Okay, see you soon, Henrick. Have a safe trip, ciao."

"Yeah, see you, bye." Henrick answered the door after the first light rap, startling Klaus. "Hey, I thought you were going to be late again."

Klaus looked at his watch and then kissed Henrick's cheek. "Nope, right on time." He took Henrick's bigger bag and carried it down the stairs and put it into the trunk of the car. He held the door open, and Henrick climbed in before Klaus got in the other side and told the driver to take them to the train station.

"I'm glad you're the one going on this trip with me," Klaus said. "Back when it was on the board, I was sure you'd pass it up when you saw my name. I couldn't believe my eyes when I saw that you'd volunteered. That's when I knew that there was still hope for us."

Henrick wondered what Klaus would say if he told him he'd only taken the trip so he could see Tino again. He decided not to share that little tidbit with Klaus. He didn't need to know anything about Henrick's friendship with the famous footballer. "I figured it was time to bury the hatchet, and what better way than being forced to work with someone closely for a week?" Henrick lied but it satisfied Klaus enough that he got a kiss, and the rest of the ride was spent in silence.

They had seats in the last car of the train that was completely packed because of the time of day. Klaus let Henrick have the window seat. His phone buzzed with a text from Tino just as they pulled out of the station.

Tino: *Hey I forgot to ask you if you decided whether or not you're staying for the weekend. Let me know so I can make plans.*

Henrick typed a quick message back: *I'm going to stay. Just got on the train, going to try to nap the trip away. Talk to you soon.*

He was going to tell Klaus he had something personal to do in Munich that weekend and leave it at that. Henrick settled back into his seat and closed his eyes.

The screeching of metal ripped Henrick out of the light doze he'd fallen into shortly after they'd left Salzburg behind. The lights on the train flickered as the car rocked violently, and Henrick reached out to grab for Klaus as the lights went out and the emergency ones clicked on. There was a tremendous crashing sound, and the rending of metal was like a trigger for people in the car to start screaming. By the time the window in front of Henrick broke, panic had already taken hold, so the slicing of his skin by the flying shard of glass didn't hurt as much as he thought it should have.

TINO WAS PUTTERING around his kitchen, trying to figure out why Henrick was being so dodgy. The only explanation coming to mind was that Henrick was trying to hide the fact that he'd taken up with his ex fuck buddy again. The thought made the short hairs on the back of his neck stand up. He told himself he was jumping to conclusions, and of course his mind would conjure up the worst case scenario when it was much more likely Henrick was just preoccupied by his business trip.

Tino went into the living room and clicked on the TV. He would be patient even though knowing Henrick was going to be in the same city soon made Tino want to rush down to the train station to meet him. He settled back to watch some inane television comedy to take his mind off Henrick. He was halfway into the second half hour of a mind-numbing sitcom when the station interrupted the scheduled program with breaking news.

Tino sat forward as a live image came on the screen. The reporter stood on a road in front of what looked like a burning building, but before the man could start his report, Tino realized that it wasn't a building—it was a train. The flashing lights of emergency vehicles surrounded the mess as people wearing reflective vests rushed around in the chaos. Tino switched the station to one that would broadcast the news in English so he could understand what was happening without having to pick through the words he knew and put it all together. The angle of the camera was slightly different on the other channel, but it was undoubtedly the same scene Tino had seen before. Tino's heart started beating double-time as he waited to hear what had happened.

"I'm standing in front of the scene of what appears to be a derailment of one of Railjet's high-speed trains. Our

sources tell us this is the train that left Salzburg at seven twenty-five this evening: the nonstop direct to Munich commuter train. Calls started coming in around eight thirty this evening when drivers of cars on this road heard and then saw the train as it left the tracks after the conductor applied what sources are saying was the emergency brakes to avoid a collision with something on the tracks. There is no word as to what the conductor saw that provoked the action that led to the train derailing," the reporter said over the wind that blew steadily around him.

"We're getting little in the way of reports from the scene, but already we've been told there are fatalities and many injuries as all but two of the cars toppled over onto their sides. The police, fire departments, and ambulance services are working alongside railway workers to extract and transport the victims to Klinikum rechts de Isar, which has called in all available staff to help deal with the influx of emergency patients." The report continued, but Tino wasn't listening any longer.

He stood, and in a daze, put on shoes and a jacket before grabbing his keys, wallet, and phone. He was going to go find Henrick. The drive to the hospital seemed to simultaneously take forever and went by in a flash because Tino couldn't remember how he'd gotten there as he parked in the ramp. He made his way through the crowded hallways outside the emergency area, looking for someone who could tell him Henrick was okay.

He found a man with a clipboard who was talking to other frantic-looking people and stood in the line when he heard the man telling people where their loved ones were. Tino waited as patiently as he could until it was his turn.

"Name?" the man asked.

"Val...no, um, Henrick Kohler?" Tino asked, almost giving his name instead of Henrick's.

He watched as the man looked at his list and then checked looked once more before turning back to him. "There's no Henrick Kohler on my list." He looked at the man and woman behind Tino and asked, "Name?"

"But what does that mean?" Tino asked. "If he's not on the list, what does that mean?"

The man sighed. "It means he wasn't brought in, which could mean many things. Are you sure he was on that train?" Tino nodded. "Well, then either he's not been brought in yet or..." The man trailed off and looked around before adding in a very soft voice, "They're not bringing those who were DOA at the site because of the lack of transport vehicles. They're focusing on the living first."

Tino's heart leapt into his throat at the thought of Henrick lying dead on the ground at the site of the accident. "But..."

The man put his hand on Tino's shoulder. "They're still bringing people in. It may be that he was one of the few who were not seriously injured, and therefore he's not a priority." Then he turned to resume his job of telling people if their loved ones were grievously injured or not there at all.

Turning, Tino walked off in a daze. When a hand touched his arm, he jumped at the unexpected contact. It was an older lady who looked at him with kind sympathetic eyes as she said, "I've heard they started sending some of the less severely injured to Sean Munich Schwabing. You might want to check there, just in case." Tino blinked at the information as he tried to form a response to her kindness. She patted his arm. "It's okay. I understand, so much emotion until you know something for sure. You go see if you can find who you're looking for."

Tino nodded and managed a strangled "Thank you" before he took off at a fast walk until he hit the pavement at a sprint. He remembered the drive to the second hospital because he passed more and more emergency vehicles heading in the other direction. With the passing of each one he wondered if it was the one Henrick was in, maybe hanging on to life by a thread. When he arrived at the second hospital, he found it much calmer but still quite busy.

Tino watched as an ambulance pulled up, and after the driver opened the back doors six people clambered out—the walking wounded—and Tino supposed the old lady had been right. He took a deep breath and let hope grip him once again. He followed the ambulance victims and waited patiently while the staff got them situated before he approached the woman behind the window.

"Hi, I'm looking for someone who was on the train."

"Okay, do you have a name?" the woman asked with a raised eyebrow.

"Yes, Henrick Kohler."

"And are you relative of Herr Koller?"

"No, I'm a friend. He was coming to visit me."

"I'm sorry, then I can't give you any information on anyone admitted to the hospital if you are not a relative." She looked at her computer screen, and Tino tried to read her expression to see if maybe he could get anything more from that but her facial features remained blank.

"But surely you can at least tell me if he's here and if he's okay?" Tino pleaded.

The woman pursed her thin lips and gave Tino a hard glare. "No, I surely cannot give you that information. As I said, I can only give that information out to family members, and since you are not one of them, you are not someone I can freely speak to about one of our patients."

"So he is here?" Tino had caught the woman's slipup.

"I didn't say that, and I'd appreciate it if you would step away now as I have other people to attend to," she said while looking past Tino to the next person in line.

"I just want to know if my friend is alive. Is that so much to ask?"

"Sir, if you don't leave, I'll call security and they will make you go." She picked up the phone as if to prove her threat was real.

Tino was at the end of his rope, so the thought of being dragged out of the emergency room by security guards—though not high on his to-do list—didn't really bother him all that much. He put his hands on the window and pressed his forehead to the glass. "Would you please just tell me where he is?" Tino asked in a voice loud enough that everyone in the hall turned to look at him.

The woman punched numbers into her phone as she glared at him.

"I just want to know where—"

"Tino?"

Henrick's voice sent a shiver down Tino's spine, and he realized he'd already written him off for dead. The relief flooded through him as he turned to see Henrick standing there staring at him with wide blue eyes. Tears of frustration that had been pricking at the back of his eyeballs finally started rolling down his cheeks as he took in Henrick's form from top to bottom and only noticed a patch of gauze taped to the side of his neck. Tino rushed to Henrick and wrapped his arms around him.

"What are you doing here?" Henrick asked as he reached up to wipe at the tears of relief on Tino's face. "Why are you crying? Are you all right?"

"Henrick," Tino growled, and then he started kissing every inch of his shocked face. "I thought you were dead, and they wouldn't tell me anything." The words came between his kisses, and then finally, his lips found Henrick's, and he put all the emotions of the last couple hours into that kiss so Henrick would know just what he meant to Tino. Henrick kissed him back for what seemed like an eternity, but Tino was still not ready for it to end when Henrick pulled back and broke the contact between their lips.

"You didn't answer my question."

"Which one?" Tino asked, confused and high on Henrick's kiss.

"Why did you come? You could have just called. I still have my cell phone." Tino took a breath to answer, but another voice interrupted him.

"Yeah, I'd like to know the answer to that too," a deep voice asked from behind Tino. "And also an answer as to why you're kissing my boyfriend might be good."

Tino turned but didn't release his grip on Henrick. If he had his way he never would again, but the huge guy staring at the two of them looked like he had other ideas on that subject. "Your boyfriend?" Tino took his eyes off the big guy he assumed was Klaus, to look back at Henrick.

"You are not my boyfriend," Henrick said, then turning to Tino he added, "He's not my boyfriend."

"What the hell, Henrick?" Klaus asked, but then his expression changed and Tino saw the recognition dawn on his face. He looked at Henrick and then back at Tino as if trying to put two and two together, but by the look on his face, he kept coming up with one hundred and forty-three. "Henrick, want to tell me why Valentino Alessi is hugging you?"

"You don't have to answer any of his questions. Just tell me you're all right to leave the hospital, and I'll take you home with me." Tino was hoping to head off the argument he saw brewing in Klaus's eyes.

"I still have to do my job. I should go back to the hotel with Klaus."

"How badly were you hurt?" Tino asked.

"Just a few stitches. I was lucky the glass just grazed me. I'm fine, so there's no need for me to leave Klaus to do the job on his own." Henrick sounded so calm and reasonable when Tino was vibrating apart inside.

"Let's go, Henrick. You can explain to me how you know *him,* and why he came here, in the taxi on the way to the hotel," Klaus said in English and then added something else in Deutsch that Tino didn't understand but made Henrick frown.

Tino finally let go of Henrick but only so he could step into the bigger man's space. "He doesn't have to do anything you say or explain anything to you. You heard him; you are not his boyfriend, so step back and let him make his own decision about what he wants to do now."

"And what are you going to do about it if I don't step back?" Klaus took a step closer leaving only a few inches between them.

"I'll tell you what I'm going to do—"

"Okay, that's enough." Henrick pushed his way in-between the two bigger men's bodies. "I have already decided what I'm going to do, so both of you shut up and listen." Henrick glared at both men until they ended their pissing contest by breaking eye contact and looking at Henrick instead. "I'm going to get a taxi." Klaus grinned at his supposed victory. "*By myself.* I'm going to the hotel, and I'm going to stay in a room, *by myself.* I will call *you*"—he looked at Tino—"in the morning to set up a time for us to meet tomorrow night after I'm done working. I will see *you*"—he looked at Klaus—"in the morning for work. Now you two are free to stand here and stare at each other for the rest of the night for all I care, but I'm tired and emotionally drained, so I'm leaving." Once finished, Henrick extracted his body from between Tino and Klaus.

"Henrick, wait," Tino called to his retreating back. Henrick's steps faltered, slowed, and finally, as if it took him some time to decide, stopped. "Let me drive you, at least."

Henrick shook his head. "I can't, Tino; not now. I'll call you. Thanks for coming to check on me. Sorry you had to, though. Good night," he said without turning back.

Tino was going to follow, but Klaus grabbed his arm to stop him. "Leave him be. He gets like this sometimes, and it's usually best to leave him to sort it out on his own."

Tino nodded. "Just make sure he's all right, okay? Take care of him for me." He turned away, leaving a shocked look on the other man's face at his possessive words.

Thoughts swirled in his head as Tino drove home. He needed to do something soon because his mother's words kept haunting him. Henrick would find someone else. It may not be Klaus, but eventually, he'd find someone who would sweep him off his feet and take him out of Tino's life. Tino needed to think about what was more important to him—his career as it was at that point—or a life with the man he had fallen hopelessly in love with.

Chapter Fifteen

HENRICK GINGERLY LIFTED the edge of the tape holding the gauze to his skin. He needed to shower and shave, and having sopping wet gauze on his neck all day wasn't a fun prospect. Ripping the square off in one fast yank, he hissed at the stinging pain. The little jagged line of stitches looked good. There wasn't any redness around it, but he'd still rub the antibiotic ointment they'd given him on it after he was clean, to ensure it stayed that way. He finished his grooming, took care of his wound, and was just about to call the front desk to find out what room number Klaus was in when the pounding started on his door.

"I'm coming. Stop trying to knock the door down," Henrick called as he walked over to open it. Klaus was standing there, looking furious as he held out a paper. Henrick took the offered publication and turned back to his room to get his coat and bag, but Klaus's voice stopped him in his tracks.

"This is what you get when you get mixed up with someone like him," he said in a clipped tone of annoyance.

"What?"

"Look at the damn paper, and then tell me if it was a good idea to get involved with him." Klaus looked mad enough Henrick was sure had they been cartoons, there would have been steam coming out of his ears. "Just how the hell did you get yourself mixed up with *him* in the first place?"

"I'm not mixed up or involved with him. We're friends. We met on holiday and stayed in touch, and it's really none of your damn business anyway." Henrick opened the newspaper. There was an article on the train derailment taking up the entire front page that went on for almost a full five pages after that. He was about to ask Klaus to point out what had him so pissed off when he hit the sports section.

There was a series of pictures, the first was of Tino, tears streaming down his face but a look of relief evident as he walked toward a man whose face was turned away from the camera but who Henrick knew was himself. The second captured that kiss Tino had laid on him that had left him weak in the knees. The third was of Henrick still in Tino's arms, wiping the tears away and even he could see the love in his eyes as he looked up at Tino. The fourth was of Tino glaring at Klaus while he still held Henrick close, as if he didn't want to let him go, even in the face of another man's anger. The fifth had Tino in Klaus's face, and the final picture was of Henrick standing between the two men, a hand on each of their chests, holding them apart.

His eyes took in the large headline which simply said, "Gay Love Triangle?" The text below read like something out of a tabloid. *Has Valentino Alessi gotten himself embroiled in a gay love triangle? It seems to be the case as many witnesses watched the scene unfold in the emergency ward of Sean Munich Schwabing right after the Railjet train derailment. The famous footballer was seen kissing what was reported to be another man's boyfriend. When the boyfriend walked in on the scene...* Henrick stopped reading and his first thought was of Tino. He really needed to talk to Tino to see how badly this was going to affect him.

"Klaus, I need to take the day off," Henrick said, already mentally changing his plans for the day.

"No, you need to work and stay away from Valentino Alessi. He'll drag your name through the mud to save his own ass, and you know that's what will happen." Making a stand, Klaus set his jaw and crossed his arms over his chest.

"I'll call into the office and tell them I've decided to take some time off, after all." Henrick was referring to his boss's offer for time off because of the train accident, which left Klaus with no say in the matter.

"You can't go to him. You realize they'll be hunting him after this, and if you go, you'll only make matters worse for both of you. It's better if you just ignore it."

"What, and hope it goes away?" Henrick's phone rang, and as if Tino had known they were discussing him, his smiling face greeted Henrick. He'd bet the live version of the man wasn't smiling, and the thought made him hesitant to answer. "I have to take this," he said more to himself than to Klaus.

Klaus snorted. "I'll be at the job." He slammed the door, leaving no doubt about how unhappy he was with Henrick's decision.

Henrick steeled himself and answered the phone, apologizing before Tino had the chance to blame him. "Tino, I'm so sorry."

"Don't. There's nothing to be sorry about. How are you this morning?" Tino's voice was full of concern that made Henrick cringe. Maybe Tino didn't know about the article yet?

"I'm fine, but you can't just brush off what's happening, and that it's all my fault." If he hadn't already heard the news, he soon would, and then Henrick's money was on Tino being raging mad.

"I'm not brushing it off, but I'm not going to blame you for something that is most definitely not your fault. I'm not sorry and you shouldn't be either."

Henrick sighed when he had confirmation that Tino knew, but then Tino's words sunk in. "What do you mean, you're not sorry?" He was confused by Tino's calm demeanor when he'd been expecting so much more anger, maybe some hurt and a lot of blame.

"Tell me which room you're in," Tino said, instead of answering his question.

"Four thirty, why? Tino, please—"

"Hang up the phone. I'll be up there in a minute." The line went dead.

Henrick stared at the dark phone in his hand as he shook his head. He dialed his office, told his boss he needed a day off after all, hung up, and then put his phone down to answer the soft knock on his door. Tino stood in the hallway looking beautifully rumpled.

"Henrick, let me in."

Henrick stepped back and did as he asked. Tino passed him and then waited until the door was closed to pull Henrick into his arms. "What are you doing here?"

"You keep asking me that question every time I show up, and I'm going to start thinking you don't want to see me." He pulled Henrick in closer so their bodies were pressed tightly together.

"What are you doing?" Henrick tried to push him away just to create a little space between them.

"Can I ask *you* a question?" Tino used his bigger, stronger body to his advantage and held Henrick prisoner against him.

"What do you want to ask?" Henrick continued to wriggle against Tino, partially because he wanted to get loose but also because he loved the feel of Tino's hard body against his own.

"Can I kiss you before I ask?"

"That was a question." Henrick pointed out but stilled as Tino's eyes darkened.

"That wasn't the one, but I think maybe if you let me kiss you first, you'll be better able to answer the one I want to ask you. Now, can I kiss you or not?"

Henrick bit his lip and considered his options. Saying no was probably the best answer, but deep down he wanted to feel the earth move and see the sparks brought on by Tino's kiss again. "Yes, you can kiss m—"

Tino's mouth cut off his words and then stole his breath away too. The way Tino kissed him showed him it wasn't just about lust; this wasn't foreplay or a simple *I want to get you into my bed* kind of kiss. No—the kiss Tino gave him was a deep soulful kiss that said things Henrick wasn't sure he wanted to hear from a man he wouldn't let himself have. Henrick melted into the kiss, and when Tino pulled away, he found himself following those lips in search of more.

"No, just one kiss and then one question and one answer," Tino said softly as he denied Henrick more of what he sought. Henrick nodded his agreement. He just hoped Tino wasn't about to ask him to step back into the closet with him because he wasn't sure he'd be strong enough to say no this time. "Do you want to be with me?"

On some level, Henrick knew that was going to be the question, and it meant if he said yes they'd make plans on how to explain the scene at the hospital, and then once the storm blew over he'd just be a good friend. He'd have to stand by and watch Tino pretend to be with Rijeka, but instead of being able to ignore it from afar, he'd have a front row seat. His stomach ached at the thought of what his life would be like without Tino, but life with him could be so much more painful.

He pushed Tino's chest hard enough that the other man took the hint and let him go free. "We've been over this before. In a perfect world, if you asked me that question I'd say yes without even having to think about it." He turned his back on the hurt he knew he'd see in Tino's eyes. "But we both know that this is not a perfect world and—"

"So the answer is yes?" Tino stepped up behind Henrick and wrapped his arms around him once more.

"You're not listening to me." Annoyed, Henrick grabbed Tino's hands to try to remove them.

"I asked if you wanted to be with me, not if you would be with me, there's a difference." Shaking his head, Henrick was about to say something about semantics when Tino turned and sat on the bed, pulling Henrick onto his lap.

"Well, it hardly makes a difference since we both know that no matter how much I want to be with you, I refuse to do it on your terms." He didn't even bother to struggle to free himself because he knew that once Tino finally understood what he was saying, he'd let him go.

Tino nuzzled his face into Henrick's neck, taking a deep breath before he asked, "What if I said my terms are in the middle of being renegotiated as we speak?"

"I'd say that I don't understand what you're saying. How can you renegotiate your terms without..." Henrick stopped short as the meaning of Tino's words started to sink in. *Well, I suppose there are just some scandals that you can't talk your way out of.* "You're coming out because of those pictures."

Tino lifted Henrick up so he was on his feet, but instead of pushing him away, Tino turned him and pulled at him. Spreading his legs obligingly, he sat on Tino's lap facing him this time. They were eye to eye in that position, so Henrick could see the dark circles under Tino's. He wondered if Tino had slept at all the previous night.

"It's not because of the pictures. I decided last night that I couldn't wait any longer to be with you. Twice now I've had to go through thinking I'd lost you, and both times, the only thoughts in my head were of how much more I wanted to know about you. How I'd never get the chance to love you the way you deserve to be loved. I can't go through what I went through last night again; my heart won't take another near miss. I won't be told that I don't have the right to know if you're alive or dead, because I want that right, and I want you." Tino stopped talking long enough to lean forward and kiss Henrick softly.

He rested his forehead against Henrick's as he explained. "I called Bernardo last night and told him I was going to tell the world who Tino Alessi really is, and he had one day to get his shit in order to handle the fallout. I guess the timeline has gotten sped up just a bit by the pictures, but it's not going to change anything about how I plan to do this. I just need to know if you'll be there at my side, because I could really use some support while I do this."

Henrick couldn't believe his ears because he was pretty sure Tino had just made a huge decision based on the fact that he wanted him. Valentino Alessi was going to come out to the world because he was in love with Henrick freaking Kohler. Henrick shifted his head to get their lips only a hairsbreadth away from each other as he said, "Yes, I'll be there. I've always wanted to be right there." He kissed Tino this time and he was sure to make it count.

TINO LET HENRICK have control of the kiss long enough for him to wrap his mind around Henrick saying yes. He'd been almost certain Henrick had wanted to say yes for some time but wouldn't because of Tino's situation. Tino had changed all that with one late-night phone call to his agent, and now he was free to take what he wanted.

Plunging his tongue into Henrick's willing mouth, Tino's hands roamed the sides of Henrick's body. He'd touched most of Henrick's skin while applying the ever-present sunscreen while on holiday, but never as a lover, and he couldn't wait any longer to claim the title. As he pushed Henrick's sport coat off his shoulders, Henrick dropped his arms to allow it to slide off and onto the floor behind him. Henrick's hands worked the buttons on Tino's shirt while Tino's did the same as he wondered why there had to be so many of the tiny little things between him and his goal. Shirt's off and bare chests pressed together, he lay back, dragging Henrick with him.

"You don't know how much I've wanted to do this since the first time I laid eyes on you." Tino broke their kiss to confess against Henrick's lips.

"Me too," Henrick whispered before sealing their lips together once again.

Tino wanted their first time together to last the whole day through, but he knew he wasn't going to make it more than a few minutes if he didn't slow Henrick's hips. The man was rutting against him mercilessly. Tino felt Henrick's need pressing through all four layers of fabric still separating them. Grasping Henrick's narrow waist, Tino pulled his body tightly against him, stopping his movements. Henrick groaned into Tino's mouth but stilled long enough for Tino to ratchet back his mounting need for immediate release.

"Too many clothes." Tino managed to slip the words out around the extra tongue in his mouth. Henrick nodded but did nothing to remedy the situation. Pushing his hand down the back of Henrick's pants, he ran a finger along his crease, making Henrick moan loudly. "Can't get to all the good bits with these still on." He pulled on the waistband of Henrick's slacks, and Henrick pushed himself up so he was sitting astride Tino's groin. He flicked the button on his pants open and then did the same to Tino's before unzipping them at the same time.

"I would have just come in my pants and been done with it, but if you insist on getting all fancy about it..." Henrick glared down at Tino before standing on the bed and pushing his pants and underwear off one leg and then the other, giving them a little flick with his foot that sent them flying across the room to land on the desk. Tino watched, mesmerized by the sight of Henrick standing over him in all his naked glory. "You going to take yours off, or are my good bits the only ones that are going to get some action?" The teasing glint in his eyes made Tino want to ravish him.

When Tino didn't move to take off his jeans, Henrick huffed and got down on his knees. He grabbed Tino's pants, and when Tino lifted his ass off the bed, Henrick yanked them down his legs with a strength that surprised Tino. Henrick climbed back on top and picked up where they'd left off. This time, when Henrick's hips came down on his, their cocks rubbed together, and they both let out sounds that couldn't be mistaken for anything other than pure lust.

Henrick's lips left his to nibble down Tino's jaw, then his neck, until he found one of Tino's nipples and sucked it into his mouth. Tino grabbed his head and pressed him in hard. Henrick took that as a cue to sink his teeth into the flesh trapped between his lips, and Tino hissed as the pain and pleasure mixed. Henrick raised his eyes and cocked a brow at him. Licking his lips in encouragement, Tino pressed into the bite, but Henrick let him go so he could work his way across the light patch of hair on the center of Tino's chest to get to the other small nub. Henrick repeated the process this time without Tino's hand pressing him on. Tino squirmed under the rough assault on one of his most sensitive areas, but his moans of pleasure betrayed him.

He fought the urge to flip Henrick over and have him. He'd wanted Henrick so much for longer than he'd ever wanted anyone, but it seemed only fitting that he should lie back and let Henrick run the show—at least for a little while. Moments later, he regretted that he'd gone along with Henrick's slow torture when the blond made its way down his torso and, after dipping his tongue in his navel, moved farther south and licked the head of Tino's cock.

"Oh, Jesus." Tino sat up straight and grabbed Henrick's hair before the other man could get his lips more than a quarter of the way down his shaft and yanked him off. "I'm going to blow if you do that, and I'm not ready yet," he growled as he pulled Henrick up the bed and rolled on top of him.

Henrick huffed but couldn't hide the pleased look on his face. "You do know that they're not a one-use-only type thing. They are reusable so therefore you can come and then again and again and infinite amounts of agains," Henrick said with a lopsided grin. Tino crushed his lips against Henrick's to shut him up, but Henrick pulled away, frowning. "This isn't going to be just a one-time thing. We have time, right?"

Tino kissed the little frown line creased between his eyebrows. "Of course, we have time. I just want this to be good for you, so good you'll want to do the infinite agains."

Putting his hands on the sides of Tino's face, he then let them trail back through Tino's chin-length hair. "Anything that I do with you, I want to do infinite agains. Anything." His eyes had gone soft with emotion that went straight to Tino's heart. Henrick used his hold on Tino's hair to pull him down and kiss him thoroughly but then jerked back abruptly. "Now, if I don't come pretty soon, my balls are going to explode, so please, Tino, just fucking let go."

Tino smiled and then he let go. He took Henrick's lips again as he shifted to get their bodies lined up just right. He drilled his hips down, grinding their cocks together in an almost painful mash-up of flesh. Tino wanted to get inside Henrick in some way, but there was no way that was happening on this go-round, so he'd settle for getting as close to him as he could. Plastering his body to Henrick's, he moved his hips to create the friction they both needed to get where they were going.

The kiss turned sloppy as their moans grew louder. Henrick lifted his legs and wrapped them around Tino's waist. "Faster, Tino, faster and harder." Tino sped up his hips. He could see the finish line as his balls drew up against his body. "Tinoooooo." Henrick drew Tino's name out into a howl as he came between them. Thrusting faster, Tino finally let go, following Henrick over the edge.

Lying there on top of Henrick, Tino tried to hold on to the moment. This one perfect moment Tino had told himself would never be possible. He wanted to tell Henrick he loved him—he loved him, and he wanted nothing more than to be with him like this, stuck for the rest of their lives in that one perfect moment.

"You're a lot heavier than you look," Henrick said, breaking Tino out of his thoughts. Tino smiled because it was just like Henrick to take Tino's perfect moment and turn it into something mundane by making a joke.

"Sorry, I forget what a delicate little flower you are."

Henrick snorted. "I'll show you delicate little flower." He pulled a move right out of the ICW and flipped Tino onto his back, leaving Tino staring up at him in surprise. "See, not so delicate, right?" Henrick asked from his perch atop Tino.

"No not delicate at all." Tino chuckled. He couldn't stop looking at Henrick, letting his eyes drink in every inch of him. He was still trying to convince himself that this wasn't just another of his dreams.

"What are you thinking?"

"That I can't get enough of you. That I'm not sure if I'm just dreaming again or if you're really here." Tino admitted his thoughts even if they sounded strange.

Henrick flicked his swollen nipple, making Tino flinch in pain. "I bet you never got bruised *brustwarze* in your dreams." Henrick ran his finger through their combined fluids. "Or this much of a mess on your belly.

Tino looked down at his chest, and sure enough, he had dark-purple bruises around both of his nipples. Henrick's hand was poised to strike again, but Tino grabbed his wrist and then the other just to be safe. "Okay, I get it, you're really here."

"Yeah, I guess I am. But what happens next? What's going to happen when we leave this room?"

Tino hated the uncertainty in Henrick's voice when he asked that question, but not as much as he hated having to tell Henrick the truth about how his life was going to change when they stepped out into the real world. A flash of worry spiked through Tino. What if Henrick decided he didn't want the spotlight on him? What if Henrick realized that giving up his anonymity meant people would always know things about him—personal things—and he decided Tino wasn't worth it?

"Hey, Tino? Tino, come back to me." Tino's eyes refocused on Henrick's. "It can't be all that bad, can it?" Leaning down, he kissed Tino before sitting back up and smiling down at him. "We'll get through it together, okay?"

"You promise?" Tino asked before he could stop himself asking for reassurance.

The smile dropped from his face, which took on a serious expression. "I promise I will stand beside you whenever you need me to," Henrick vowed. "I'll be there for you, so don't worry about that."

The tightness that had felt like a steel band released from around his chest at Henrick's reassuring words. They had a tough road ahead, but now he knew Henrick was aware of it and still wanted to travel it together. Tino remembered the words he'd said to Henrick about making some man feel like he was the luckiest man on earth, and right then he knew he was holding that man in his arms. He would do everything in his power to make good on his promise—that much he knew.

Chapter Sixteen

HENRICK SAT IN the comfortable leather chair; beside him Tino sat in one matching it. They were holding hands as Bernardo sat behind his massive desk talking on the phone. Henrick's palm was sweaty, but he loathed the thought of breaking contact with Tino long enough to wipe it off. They were waiting for Rijeka and her agent to show up. It was the first of many meetings and appearances they would have to weather before they'd be free to move on with their lives.

"Thank you, Herr Friedberg," Bernardo said into the receiver. He paused and said, "That sounds like a marvelous idea. I will pass it on to Tino. Thank you again, ciao." Bernardo hung up and turned his attention to them. "Well, if that conversation was anything to go by, I do believe we shouldn't have a problem with Herr Friedberg."

"That's good news, but I'm not so worried about the endorsement deal right now. I want to get out there and set the record straight as soon as possible. The less time we give them to make up stories, the better it will be for all of us," Tino said.

"Oh, I agree with that wholeheartedly. I've already got you scheduled with an eye to get the maximum amount of exposure with the least amount of work. I've talked with Martin, and you'll still be expected to meet your obligations to the team, making your time all the more precious."

Bernardo's eyes landed on Henrick only for a few seconds at a time before flitting back to Tino. Henrick had the feeling Bernardo was hiding his dislike behind a fake smile. It made him uneasy to think that the man behind the desk would play a big part in how his future with Tino would begin.

Bernardo's phone buzzed, and he picked up the receiver. "Yes, send them in."

Tino squeezed Henrick's hand as they stood. "Whatever happens next, you have to remember they know nothing about you. Anything they say should be taken with a grain of salt because me being with you will end a very lucrative partnership for them," Tino whispered. Henrick just smiled and squeezed Tino's hand.

The man who breezed through the door in front of the woman Henrick recognized to be Tino's fake fiancée looked about as happy as a man who'd just gotten a hot-sauce enema. He glared first at Tino and Henrick but ultimately turned his sights on Bernardo.

"You said this wasn't going to happen." He pointed a finger in Bernardo's face. "You assured me Tino was going to stay firmly lodged in his little closet until you told him it was okay to come crawling out of it."

Henrick's back straightened at the implications behind those words. Bernardo had been guiding Tino's career for the past twelve years, and from the sound of it, making his decisions about his personal life too. Pulling Henrick into his side, Tino put his arm around his shoulder.

"You knew the risks when you entered into this deal, Orri. The media is unpredictable, and there was no way of knowing that this would happen," Bernardo said calmly.

"That's bullshit and you know it. Your client willingly breached an oral contract by committing a homosexual act in public." Orri's anger was making his voice harsher with every word.

"Let's sit down and discuss how we can make the best of this for all concerned." Bernardo showed more patience than Henrick would have.

Henrick listened to the men, but his eyes stayed on the pale-blonde model. She didn't look particularly upset about the circumstances; she looked more bored by it than anything else as she stared at the screen of her phone. Eventually, she looked up and caught Henrick staring at her. She smiled and wiggled her eyebrows at him, which made him instinctively smile back. She must have taken the smile as an invitation because she crossed the room as the men argued and leaned in so her head was between Henrick's and Tino's.

"Listen to those two. You'd think the end of the world was upon us, instead of a little kiss between two men being caught on camera," she whispered.

Tino stood and wrapped an arm around her waist. "It was more than a little kiss." Tino kissed her cheek. "That was a little kiss." Tino stepped back a bit so they stood face-to-face. "Rijeka, this is Henrick Kohler, the man I told you about." Tino introduced his boyfriend to his fiancée.

She looked Henrick over with a discerning eye. "It's nice to finally meet you, Henrick. I can see why he was so taken with you." She extended her hand for Henrick, and he shook it.

"It's nice to finally meet the woman who was engaged to the man I love," Henrick said, slipping the L word in there for a little added punch. It seemed to slip past Tino as his eyes and attention had wandered back to the two men who were embroiled in a heated conversation on the other side of the room.

Rijeka laughed, drawing the attention of the two agents to the three of them and finally shutting them up. "Oh, Tino, I like him. He's feisty."

"Rijeka, don't start, we're here to finish—"

"Oh, Orri, shut up will you?" Rijeka rolled her eyes. "Tino is my friend, and being associated with him has made both you and me a lot of money. Now, you two figure out how you're going to present this to the press while I take these two men out for coffee." Rijeka managed to get herself between Tino and Henrick so she could slip a hand into each of their arms. "Let's go, boys. We have so much to talk about. I want to hear how you guys finally figured out you were both being giant jackasses and ended up kissing in an emergency room."

Tino smiled at Henrick, and Henrick shrugged as he let her lead them both to the door. They ignored the protests of the two agents and went into the hallway. Once they were alone in the elevator, Tino sighed. "I really am sorry about this, Rijeka. It's not at all how I planned to come out."

"Tino dear, I think it's about damn time you do something in your life that's not planned out." She pushed the button for the lobby.

Henrick couldn't have agreed more.

IT WAS NERVE-WRACKING waiting for his parents to get into town. Tino kept trying to reassure him he was just as nervous about meeting Henrick's parents as he was about introducing Henrick to his own. The Alessis were flying in that evening in time for Tino and Henrick's first public appearance together. The day had flown by in a blur, and Henrick wondered how Tino kept sane if his whole life was one big circus all the time.

"You're sure they'll be able to find the apartment building?" Tino asked for the fifth time. He was also straightening the couch cushions that had just been put to rights not two minutes before.

"Yes, my papa is very capable of navigating the city. We used to come here all the time for day trips when I was younger. They know their way around," Henrick assured him as the buzzer by the door sounded. Tino answered the call and told the doorman to let them up, and Henrick noticed Tino looked a bit paler than usual when he turned back.

"Tell me again that your parents are okay with you having a boyfriend."

Henrick went to him and wrapped his arms around Tino's waist. "They've met a couple of men I dated when I was younger. The first was while I was still in secondary school. They have always been supportive." Henrick hoped his words would calm Tino's nerves. Tino told him he'd only come out to his family right before he met Henrick in Durres, so Henrick understood Tino's uneasiness with the whole family meet and greet. "That would be them." Henrick inclined his head toward the door when a knock sounded.

Straightening his spine, Tino released Henrick to walk to the door and open it cautiously. Tino didn't get a chance to say a word as Henrick's mama practically pushed him aside to get to Henrick, crushing him hard enough to make him short of breath.

"Du hättest nach dem Unfall nach Hause kommen sollen—"

"Mama, please, speak English. Tino doesn't understand Deutsch very well," Henrick said as his mother clung to him. "I'm fine, I told you on the phone it's just a scratch."

"Well, you still should have come home." She gave him one final squeeze before releasing him.

"Mama, Papa, I'd like you to meet Tino Alessi." Henrick led his mother over to where his father was intently studying Tino.

His papa held out a hand for Tino, which Tino shook. "It's good to meet you, Herr Kohler." Tino turned to extend his hand to Henrick's mother, but she wrapped him up in a hug that rivaled the one she'd bestowed on Henrick. "And also you, Frau Kohler," Tino squeaked.

Henrick chuckled at the panicked look on Tino's face, but he gently extradited him from his mother's grasp. "Don't crush him, Mama. He has a game on Friday."

"So this is the young man who is causing such a fuss," his papa grunted, looking not at all impressed.

"Papa, be nice. Tino's had a rough day," Henrick admonished even though he knew his father wouldn't be mean to someone he'd just met.

"Yes, so we've heard. I guess you two had better tell us the whole story before your mama goes nuts wondering how her little boy got mixed up in such a mess."

"Please, make yourselves at home." Tino ushered his guests to the living room and offered refreshments.

Henrick loved his parents, but even he had to admit they could come on a little strong at times. They passed the time by recounting some of their adventures in Durres, and before Henrick knew it, he was greeting Tino's parents in much the same manner Tino had his. Henrick blushed when Tino's father said he was a pretty little thing and gave him a hug.

They were all seated around the table eating takeout when Tino's mother said, "So this is the boy who inspired my bambino to take up cooking." She eyed Henrick over the table. "But yet he feeds his mama takeaway."

It was Tino's turn to blush. "Mama, there was no time to make the pasta, and I figured you'd be more insulted with a sandwich than good takeaway." Tino's eyes stayed glued to Henrick's shocked face as he spoke.

"You've learned to cook?" Henrick asked.

Tino shrugged. "Just a little, I can't make many things."

"Oh, don't be so modest. His tortellini is almost as good as his mama's, and don't get me started on his gnocchi," signor Alessi said proudly, making Tino blush an even deeper shade of red.

"He never showed an interest before, but all of a sudden, he was begging me to teach him and he's good," signora Alessi confirmed.

Henrick couldn't stop smiling. "You'll have to cook me something soon."

"Well, that was the whole point, was it not, bambino?" she asked Tino.

"Yes, Mama, that was the whole point. Thanks for ruining the surprise."

"DO YOU THINK this shirt makes me look pale?" Henrick asked Tino as they stood together in Tino's bedroom getting ready to leave for the television studio. "I have no idea what to wear. I've never been on TV before."

"You look amazing." Tino stopped dressing himself to take in Henrick's appearance.

"Are you sure I shouldn't be wearing a suit? Jeans and a button-up seem so informal." Henrick looked down at his outfit with a critical eye.

"You don't want to come off as stuffy, and if you're all buttoned up, you will look as stiff as a board. Besides I like those jeans—they do wonderful things to your ass."

"Maybe we could just skip all this and stay here and you can do wonderful things to my ass," Henrick offered, knowing the answer had to be no but wishing it could be otherwise.

"Tell you what. If you make it through your first interview, I'll bring you back here and blow your mind so hard you'll forget it ever happened," Tino countered.

A shiver ran up his spine at the prospect of sharing Tino's bed. "Deal. Let's go get this over with then, shall we?" Henrick was eager to get on to the after party.

Tino laughed. "We shall, my dear, but first maybe you should put on some shoes." He pointed to Henrick's bare feet.

"That idea might have some merit."

They took a hired car to the station, another following with their parents, who were getting along wonderfully. Henrick held Tino's hand in a tight grip. He was so nervous, knowing he'd most likely be torn to shreds in the morning papers. He couldn't believe he was actually going to go through with the whole horse-and-pony show, but then he looked over at Tino's profile. Tino had to be freaking out, but he seemed calm and cool as usual. If Tino could do this, then so could he. He could do anything for Tino.

BERNARDO HAD THEM booked on *Late Night with Dieter Schmidt*. Dieter was an annoying little man whose sexuality was ambiguous at best. Why Bernardo had chosen him for their first interview was obvious but still a bit aggravating to Tino. They would do three of Dieter's four segments. Tino would start off the show on his own for the longest of the three segments. He kissed Henrick, who whispered good luck, before Tino left him in the green room with Rijeka and the two agents.

Standing with the guy in headphones, Tino waited until he heard his name, and the guy gestured toward the stage. He walked out to the applause from the crowd, but he also heard a few boos as he made his way to where Dieter stood in front of a chair and a sofa. After shaking Dieter's hand, the host leaned in, grabbing Tino's face, sloppily kissing both his cheeks. Tino kept the smile plastered on his face and even managed to fake chuckle along with the audience at the host's antics, then sat on the sofa while Dieter took the chair.

"It's good to have you back again, Tino. It's okay if I call you Tino, yes?" Dieter asked.

"Only if I can call you Dieter."

"Oh, honey, you can call me anything you want," Dieter winked and the audience laughed. "So let's get straight"—another wink—"to it, shall we?"

"That's what I'm here for." Tino knew Dieter would camp up the interview, but he hoped that it wouldn't get too out of hand.

Dieter smiled brightly at Tino and then looked at the audience. "Okay, so I know we're all just dying to know if the rumor is true. Would you like to set the record straight right now and tell us all: are you gay?"

A drop of sweat made its way down Tino's spine. This was the moment of truth, and he was ready. "Yes, Dieter, I'm gay." Tino stated it simply. There were a few gasps from the audience, but then the applause started in one corner of the room and took over until most of the audience was standing and clapping.

"Wait a minute, so this whole time you've been hiding, denying, and even outright lying about your sexuality?" Dieter waited until the applause died down to ask his question. "Why would you do such a thing? There are other footballers who have come out and are even playing for big-name teams. Why would you live a lie?"

"The league has changed a lot in the twelve years since I signed my first contract. Back then, I was advised against announcing my homosexuality." He wanted to keep his answers simple and to the point but also truthful.

"But surely you could have come out any time since then but you chose to deny it even when Paulo Gianotti gave an interview in which he said he and you were dating. Were you dating him, and if you were, why not take that opportunity to go public with it?"

"I did have a relationship with Paulo. I guess at the time I was upset that he had betrayed my trust and well... You know how it is when you're going through a bad breakup, right?" Tino hadn't wanted to get into that whole mess but should have figured Dieter would bring it up. "I just didn't want to be pushed out into the spotlight like that, so I let the opportunity pass me by."

"What were you afraid of that kept you quiet, Tino? Were you afraid your teammates would treat you differently? That you'd lose fans? Or maybe it was all about the money, and you felt your endorsement deals would be in jeopardy?"

Tino bristled at the question but tried not to show how much it bothered him. "I guess I was afraid if people knew they'd treat me differently. I was okay with the way my life was going, and I thought it wasn't anyone's business who I slept with."

"But don't you feel like you did a great disservice to not only your fans by hiding the truth, but also to the gay community at large? You deprived millions of a role model they desperately need. How many gay teenagers would have loved the chance to have you to look at and say 'If Tino can make it to the highest point in football, then what's stopping me from obtaining my dreams?' Have you gotten any backlash from the gay community yet?" Dieter had dropped the act and looked like he was truly interested in Tino's answer.

The question was like a gut punch because he did feel guilty about how he'd handled everything. "I haven't really had the time to read the papers or surf the web to see, but I'm sure there will be negative stories out there. There's nothing I can do about it now. I will say that I have always been supportive of the gay community. I have volunteered at the football camp for gay youth every year since it was founded, and I also donate to my local LGBT organizations. I have contacted some of the other gay footballers about starting a foundation. Now that I'm out, I fully intend to be an involved member of the community." There was applause after that, and Dieter smiled what seemed to be an actual genuine smile.

"That's good to hear. So speaking of other footballers, have you talked to your teammates yet, and how do they feel about this new development?"

"So far, I've gotten some phone calls, and they've all been positive. I can say for certain that management will be supportive, and the team will continue to be successful."

"That's good to hear because we can't have our team losing now, can we?" Dieter asked playfully.

"That wouldn't be good. I can tell you that."

"Okay, well, we need to take a break, and when we come back, we'll be joined by Rijeka Anderson," Dieter announced, and Tino waited until the red light on the cameras went off to let his smile drop, giving his cheeks a much-needed break. The makeup girl came and gave them touch-ups.

"You're doing very well. The next segment is shorter because we want to give your new boyfriend some time in the limelight." Dieter thanked the makeup girl when she finished and looked ready to get on with the next segment.

All Tino could think about was how pleased Henrick would be with Dieter's consideration—not. Tino remained on the couch while Dieter got up to introduce Rijeka. She walked out to more applause than Tino had gotten, and he stood to hug and kiss her after she greeted Dieter.

"You've done excellent, but stop looking so damn scared," Rijeka whispered in his ear during their quick hug. They settled down on the sofa, and Tino put his arm around Rijeka's shoulder which made Dieter give him an odd look.

"So, Rijeka, darling, it seems like only yesterday you were telling me about your engagement, and now here you are caught up in the scandal of the year. Are you an innocent woman shocked by the news, or did you know all along?"

This had been one of the sticking points for Orri. He'd wanted Rijeka to act like the wronged woman, but Rijeka had rejected that idea. She told Orri he could shove it, and if he didn't like it, he knew where the door was. Rijeka gave Dieter her best impish smile. "Do you really think I'd be sitting here supporting Tino if I was the woman scorned?"

"So tell me, dear, how *were* you recruited to help in Tino's endeavors to fool the world?" The question came out as tongue-in-cheek, but Tino still felt like he was the mastermind of some nefarious plan to dupe the entire world when all he'd wanted was to live his life in peace.

Rijeka laughed. "You make it sound so sinister, but really it was people like you who started it all. I mean really, a man and a woman can't go out for dinner without being romantically involved these days. I saw an opportunity to help a friend, and I took it because I believed Tino had a right to his privacy. I don't see every heterosexual announcing they're straight, so why should Tino have to announce that he's gay? It really has no bearing on anything at all when it comes right down to it." Rijeka's speech left the men on the stage speechless, but the audience roared with cheers and applause. Tino tightened his arm around Rijeka, and she put her hand on his thigh and squeezed.

Dieter once again waited out the applause. "Well, my dear, you do have a point there, but then if being gay is supposed to be treated the same as being straight, why didn't Tino just treat it as such? Why the hiding and a fake engagement; isn't that going a bit far?"

Tino opened his mouth to answer, but Rijeka leaned forward like she was about to tell Dieter a secret. "You and I both know what everything always comes down to. It's always money driving the world. And to be fair, it's not always an easy decision to make when it's not just you depending on your career. Tino had advisors, and he followed the advice he was given. I know Tino. Like I said, we're friends, and if it had been up to him, he'd have come out a long time ago." Rijeka sat back and added, "You want to know why there was a fake engagement? Ask the people responsible for it."

Dieter looked at Rijeka for a moment as if sizing up an opponent. "Are you upset that your arrangement has ended this way?"

"No." Rijeka turned to smile at Tino. "I'm actually happy it ended this way because Tino got the man he wanted and deserves to have. How could my friend finding love upset me?"

"Well, that is a wonderful sentiment to end this segment on. But stay tuned because next up we have the man behind all this uproar. Yes, that's right, Henrick Kohler, the man who captured the world's attention, not to mention Tino's, will be right here after the break!"

Dieter stood and pulled Rijeka up off the couch and into his arms. "You were fabulous, darling, I couldn't have scripted it better myself," Dieter said as he hugged her.

"I know it was a bit off the path of what we discussed, but really, what do they expect? That I'm going to be a bitch about this? Thank you for asking the right questions, and now, be nice to Henrick. He's a sweet man; don't break him before Tino has the chance to." Turning to Tino, Rijeka winked before addressing him. "Make sure you touch him. He's so nervous I think he may throw up." Rijeka left Tino looking a little shell-shocked.

Dieter shook his head as he watched her walk off stage. "I'd ask her to marry me, if she was my type, that is. Loosen up, Tino, this is going great, and I heard your boyfriend is quite the looker so that will help, I'm sure."

"He is, but he's not used to this, and I'm a bit afraid he'll get scared off," Tino admitted truthfully before he remembered who he was talking to.

"He'll be fine. I promise not to bite...too hard." Dieter stood to make Henrick's introduction.

Tino's heart was pounding so hard it drowned out all sound, but the sight of Henrick making his way across the stage was what left him lightheaded. Henrick greeted Dieter as Tino stood, then turned to Tino who took him into his arms. He'd only intended to give Henrick a hug and a quick peck on the cheek, but Henrick turned his head a second too soon. Their lips brushed, and Tino wanted to kiss him long and deep right there in front of the world just because he could. Henrick, thankfully, had his head on straight because he pulled back after just a taste.

"Hey there," he whispered as he looked up into Tino's eyes.

"Hey there yourself, how are you holding up?"

"Good, I'm good." They sat together on the couch.

"Well, that was sweet," Dieter said, fluttering his eyelashes. Henrick blushed, and Tino wrapped his arm around his shoulders much the same as he'd sat with Rijeka. "So it's nice to finally meet you, Henrick. There's been so much speculation about the man Tino finally came out for. How does it feel knowing you're the one?"

"I wouldn't say he came out for me, but it feels pretty darn good to finally be able to be with him." Henrick's grin stretched from ear to ear.

"What do you mean finally?"

"Well we've known each other for a while now, but I was hesitant about a relationship with him."

"Is it because of your boyfriend?"

"I don't have a boyfriend." Henrick's brow furrowed, showing he was obviously confused by the question.

"But what about the other man, the one from the hospital, was he not your boyfriend?"

"No, he wasn't." Henrick left no room for argument.

"He was mistakenly under the impression that he was more than he actually was to Henrick." Tino almost growled at the thought of Klaus and Henrick together.

"So you were hesitant about the attention Tino gets and maybe how it would put stress on your budding relationship?" Dieter asked.

"No, I was actually not willing to live a lie, so there was no point in pursuing a relationship with him."

Dieter sat forward, intrigued by this turn of events. "So let me get this straight, you turned him down?"

"Yes, he did, over and over and over." Tino butted in to answer, and the audience laughed as Dieter smirked.

"So do you think that Tino would have come out if the pictures hadn't forced his hand?"

"No," Henrick answered.

"Yes," Tino said at the same time.

Dieter tapped his chin as if thinking while Tino and Henrick stared at each other. "That's very interesting. Why would you say to that, Tino? Were you thinking of coming out before the latest scandal broke?"

Tino shifted on the sofa, once again feeling like he was under a microscope. "I had been questioning my choices for some time. I actually just came out to my family recently, and my parents put some things into perspective for me over a cooking lesson. When I realized Henrick was the one, as you put it, the thought was all the more appealing. The night of the Railjet accident, I called my agent and told him I was coming out." Tino turned his attention to Henrick. "Please believe me. You can ask Bernardo. I told him I wanted to come out because I'd found someone I couldn't live without."

"Tino..." Henrick whispered, but Dieter broke in with another question.

"How did your family take the news?" Dieter had his own agenda and a sappy moment between his two guests wouldn't waylay it.

"They are supportive of me. They have always been my biggest fans."

"It's nice that you have the support of your family. But what about you, Henrick, how does it feel to suddenly have the world wanting to know everything about you? Is this going to be hard for you? Do you think you'll be able to stand by Tino as his life is turned upside down?" Dieter asked, firing questions before Henrick had the chance to answer.

"I'm not in love with being put on display, but Tino has my support, and I will stand by him because..." Henrick's words died out. Noticing a line of sweat running down

Henrick's temple, Tino realized Henrick was more nervous than he was letting on.

"Because..." Dieter baited.

Henrick turned to Tino and their eyes locked. "Because I love him."

Tino's heart did what felt like flips in his chest at hearing Henrick say he loved him for the first time. "I love you too." He leaned in, and to the thunderous sound of applause, he kissed the man he loved in front of the world. Just like that, Tino knew the interview was over and the rest of his life was just about to begin.

Epilogue

SITTING BACK IN his chair, Henrick stared at Tino, who sat across the table from him. The table was cluttered with dirty dishes and half-finished glasses of wine. He'd never get used to the fact that Tino had learned to cook because he'd off-handedly mentioned it was something he looked for in a man. He was slowly learning that Valentino—*he's my man now*—Alessi was a man of many talents and secrets.

"Are you full, baby, or can you do coffee?" Tino asked.

"Coffee with a twist?"

"Sure, anything you want." The sincerity in his tone told Henrick the words were absolutely true.

He wouldn't ever get used to Tino's wealth. Having everything he could want at his fingertips was an unusually unsettling thing for someone as middle class as Henrick. He was thankful Tino seemed to want a normal quiet life, and therefore Henrick didn't feel too out of his depth very often. He also wasn't put on display too much since Tino limited his public appearances to those he felt were important. The times when they did have to go out, Henrick actually enjoyed dressing up and hanging on the arm of—what was always to him at least—the hottest man in the room.

"Why don't you go upstairs, take a shower, and I'll meet you in the bedroom with the coffees?" Tino stood and started clearing the table.

"No, let me help clean up. You cooked. I should clean."

"Na uh, you go up, because if I wait until you've cleaned and showered, the coffee will be cold, and then you'll complain that you have nothing warm to drink." He pulled Henrick from his chair and pushed him toward the stairs.

"Fine, but I'm making breakfast in the morning then," Henrick threatened.

"No way. All you know how to make is toast with Nutella on it, and you know damn well that I can't stand that crap." Henrick stood there looking at Tino. Watching the man do domestic chores around the house was one of Henrick's biggest turn-ons, and he indulged in it until Tino looked up from his work. "Go on now, I swear, if I get up there and you're still in the shower, I'm going to flush the toilet on you."

Henrick stuck out his tongue and turned to run before Tino could decide he needed a playful spanking. He made it up the stairs without Tino giving chase and felt just a little disappointed. The master bedroom was Henrick's favorite room in the house—a house Tino had confessed he'd modeled on Henrick's drunken description of what he'd buy if money were no option. The king-sized bed had a fluffy down comforter on it, and when Henrick complained about having to remove seven of the ten pillows at bedtime, Tino laughingly reminded him that ten was his magic number, and he should shut up and deal with it.

The bathroom was fit for a king, or two, if you wanted to look at it that way. After stripping down, he climbed into the shower where ten shower spouts kept him warm as he washed himself. He wasn't overly quick about his shower, but he also didn't dally. He really did despise when Tino flushed the toilet and the water ran cold. It was just an evil way to get someone out of the bath, if you asked him. Dressed in a pair of silk pajama bottoms and a skintight tank top, he entered the bedroom to find Tino building up the fire.

"Hey, look who showered in under an hour. Must be a record." Tino looked over his shoulder when Henrick came out of the bathroom.

"Oh, hardy har har, look who thinks he's a comedian."

"You know you love it." Tino sat on the loveseat facing the fireplace. "Come sit with me, my love." Tino patted the spot next to him.

Henrick shivered at the words *my love* because he also was having a hard time wrapping his mind around the fact that Tino loved him and said it often enough that Henrick wasn't likely to forget. Grabbing the throw blanket off the back of the chair they never used, he walked over to Tino. The chairs, it turned out, had been negotiable and he had to admit the loveseat was a much better idea. He sat down, not beside Tino, but in his lap.

"Oh, so it's going to be like that now, is it?" Tino asked with a chuckle.

"Yes it is, because if I don't sit on you, you'll get antsy, and then you'll get up and do something, instead of cuddling me while I drink my coffee."

Tino sighed. "One time a guy gets up, and he's got to pay for it for the rest of his life." He tickled Henrick's sides, making him wiggle and giggle.

"Stop it. You know I hate to be tickled. I'll get off you if you stop."

Tino wrapped his arms around him. "No, you won't move an inch." Tino cocked his head at the table where the coffee was sitting. "Well, maybe you can move enough to hand me my coffee, but that's as far as I'm willing to let you go."

Henrick handed Tino his spiked coffee and then took his own off the tray. He snuggled down with a contented smile as he sipped the hot drink. What could be better than sitting on the couch with the man you loved? Henrick could think of few things that would ever top it, and he grinned because he was sure he'd do one or two of the things on that short list a bit later in the evening. After that there was the rest of his life to look forward to, and the future was looking pretty good from where he was sitting.

Acknowledgements

A huge thanks to the usual suspects: Tonna Saunders, Jamila Lindsey, Christina Quinn and BJ Toth. You all are the cat's pajamas!

About the Author

CL Mustafic is a born and bred American Midwesterner who mysteriously ended up living in a tiny Eastern European country. Left with too much time on her hands—let's be honest here, it was the lack of television channels in her native language—and too many voices in her head trying to fill the silence, she decided to give her lifelong dream of writing a novel a shot. So now between shuttling kids back and forth from various activities, risking her life on the insanely narrow, busy streets of her new hometown, she loses herself in her own made-up world where love always wins.

Email: clmustafic@gmail.com

Facebook: www.facebook.com/clmustafic.author

Twitter: @CL_Mustafic

Website: www.clmustafic.com

Other books by this author

Falling for Him
"Satin Secrets" within *Beneath the Layers*
Glory Hole to Hell
Christmas Cookies
Loving Sarajevo
Bad Moon Arising
Trouble's on the Way

Available Now from CL Mustafic

Read more about Henrick in

Loving Sarajevo

Excerpt

Gage set his drink back on the bar and looked apologetically at his drinking companion before he pulled out the phone to check it.

It was from Nikola: *I'm in your room. Where are you?*

Shit, Gage hadn't expected Nikola to show up after their fight. He looked up from his phone to his new buddy to find a smirk on the guy's face. Gage forgot to hide his reaction, and the guy picked up on the fact that whatever was in the text had surprised Gage.

"Not good news, I take it?" he asked.

"No, it's just that guy from the other night showed up unexpectedly. He's downstairs wondering where I am."

"Oh, well then, it's a good surprise I suppose." He winked.

Gage smiled in return but then was perplexed as to why the guy's expression turned first to one of surprise and then to what could only be described as fear in a second as he looked over Gage's shoulder. Gage turned to see what put the expression on his face, and Nikola's chest filled his vision, so he tilted his head back to look up at him. Nikola was obviously angry—very angry if the flared nostrils were any indication.

"What are you doing here?" Gage asked.

"I was just about to ask you the same damn question." Nikola looked over Gage's company with a sneer.

The Austrian—god, Gage realized he didn't even know the guy's name—put out his hand. "Hi, I'm Henrick." Nikola gave him a withering glare but shook his hand quickly.

"Nikola," he said curtly before he turned his attention back to Gage. "We need to talk."

Gage didn't like the tone Nikola was using or the possessive vibe he was giving off. But then he reminded himself just a few hours earlier he'd been struggling with his own bit of possessiveness and decided to cut Nikola a break. He turned, grabbed his drink, and tipped it in a go-on gesture before draining it, trying to be cool in the face of Nikola's anger.

Nikola wasn't willing to play along with the act though. He took the glass out of Gage's hand and slammed it down on the bar before grabbing Gage's arm and pulling him off the barstool. Gage stood there, a little unsteady on his feet at being yanked to standing, but not trying to get out of Nikola's tight grasp, which sent a flare of warmth through him.

"It was nice to meet you." Nikola's gruff words made it clear that it was in no way nice to meet Henrick. Nikola turned them abruptly and pulled Gage to the elevator before he could even say good night. He did hear Henrick snort and say, "Have fun, boys," at their retreating backs.

Also Available from NineStar Press

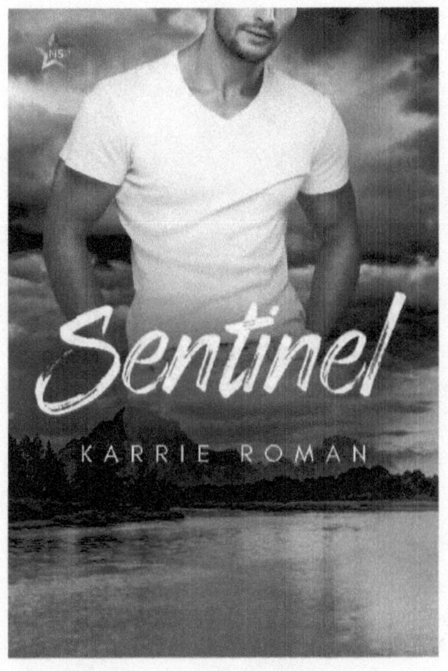

Connect with NineStar Press

Website: NineStarPress.com

Facebook: NineStarPress

Facebook Reader Group: NineStarNiche

Twitter: @ninestarpress

Tumblr: NineStarPress